Keeping You

ALEX TAYLOR

Keeping You

Destined Love Book 3

Alex Taylor

Character art by Paige Moreland

Cover Design by Kimberly at KBG Designs

Editing by Editing by Andrea

Print ISBN: 978-1-7381786-4-3

Ebook ISBN: 978-1-7381786-5-0

To those struggling and hiding behind a facade of strength.
You've got this.

Please note that some of the subject matter in this book may be
triggering for some people.
If any of the following subjects cross a line for you, please do not
continue.
Your mental health matters.

Mentions of sexual assault (not experienced by the MC's)
Discussions of miscarriage
Discussions of attempted suicide.
Sexual degradation
Explicit sex scenes

Looking for a Dicktionary? Check out the back of the book.

Playlist

This I Promise You
*NSYNC

get him back!
Olivia Rodrigo

Call It What You Want
Taylor Swift

Too Sweet
Hozier

imgonnagetyouback
Taylor Swift

Somebody to Someone (I Just Wanna Fall in Love)
Natalie Jane

Breakfast
Dove Cameron

Guilty as Sin?
Taylor Swift

Man! I Feel Like A Woman!
Shania Twain

Boot Scootin' Boogie
Brooks & Dunn

The Girl's Gone Wild
Travis Tritt

If He Wanted to He Would
Kylie Morgan

Houdini
Dua Lipa

Genius (feat. Sia, Diplo, and Labrinth
Sia, Diplo, Labrinth, LSD

SLOW DOWN
Jessica Baio

Mine (Taylor's Version)
Taylor Swift

How You Get The Girl (Taylor's Version
Taylor Swift

Heaven
Julia Michaels

I Think I'm In Love
Kat Dahlia

All of Me
John Legend

Afterglow
Taylor Swift

True Love (feat. Lily Allen)
P!nk, Lily Allen

I Think I Fell in Love Today
Kelsea Ballerini

End Game
Taylor Swift, Ed Sherran, Future

Belong Together
Mark Ambor

CHAPTER 1

Hannah

A fucking diamond ring and matching platinum band are sitting on my left hand.

What the fuck!?

I stare at the rings I don't remember buying or being gifted. Granted, I don't remember much of last night, and now I'm naked in a hotel room with what looks very much like an engagement and wedding ring sitting on my left hand.

My head is pounding and my stomach is queasy, a clear sign I drank way too much last night.

I groan and lie back on the pillow, closing my eyes and taking deep breaths as I try to push past the nausea.

The sound of the shower filters out from the washroom, and I hold the throw sheet against my chest, wrapping it around myself as I slowly slide out of bed to look for my clothes.

What is wrong with me? Getting drunk with my friends and not remembering it the next day is one thing, but I'm in a strange city with people I don't know and I went way overboard last night.

I find my clothes scattered around the room and dress quickly, freezing when the door to the washroom opens. I inhale the scent of the soap that wafts out of the open washroom door and steel myself.

When I turn around, my jaw drops and anger courses through me.

I'm staring at Grayson Maxwell, the arrogant doctor I had to come to this convention with, in nothing but a white towel wrapped around his waist as he leans against the door frame, watching me. His blond hair is completely mussed as if he just quickly rubbed a towel over it. Water droplets trail down his chiselled abs, and my eyes catch on the strip of hair leading into his towel. I can't believe what I'm seeing.

This is the man who a couple of years ago I thought was a good guy, until he showed me otherwise. It's bad enough I have to deal with him at work, but when one of my best friends started dating one of his, I was forced to spend my personal time with him, too.

I was less than pleased when I found out the two of us were selected to come to this convention, but I told myself we'd have different seminars. After all, he's an ER doctor and I'm a nurse. I told myself I'd only have to see him at the meet-and-greet mixer and that was it. Now I'm standing in his hotel room while he's half-naked and I was just fully naked in his bed.

Anger at him and myself has my stomach rolling. How could I have let this happen? I know better than to get close to Dr. Grayson Maxwell, the renowned playboy.

I finish adjusting my shirt and spot a cardholder with my room number on it on the edge of the dresser. Clutching it in my hand, I turn toward the door.

He smirks. "Running away already?"

His nonchalant tone has me clenching my hands into fists.

"I would love to get away from you as quickly as possible," I say through gritted teeth. Looking between the bed and Grayson, I ask, "We didn't sleep together, did we?"

"I woke up completely dressed this morning. I don't think so."

He reaches up and runs his left hand over his face, and the light glints off something on his finger. Moving quicker than I probably should with my pounding headache, I grab his hand and examine the platinum band on his left ring finger.

Even at five-foot-seven, I have to tilt my head back to meet his deep-blue eyes.

"What is this?" I ask.

My stomach tightens as I prepare myself for the answer I'm sure he's going to give.

"My wedding ring."

My hand goes to my stomach as I stumble back. Okay, Hannah, deep breaths.

"And where is your wife?"

Humour fills his eyes as he smirks again. "I'm looking at her."

That does it. Between the booze and this news, I feel my stomach turn a final time. I push past him into the washroom, bend over the toilet, and begin emptying my stomach. Grayson comes behind me and pulls my hair into a ponytail and gently rubs a hand over my upper back.

When I feel like I've finished, I settle on the floor beside the toilet, and Grayson crouches beside me, tucking a stray strand of hair behind my ear. I'm too tired and feel too gross to reject the comforting touch.

I take a few deep breaths as Grayson leaves the washroom. Returning a minute later, he hands me an open bottle of water.

I offer him a weak smile as I say, "Thank you."

He settles beside me on the floor, trying to ensure his towel stays closed. He plays with the wedding ring on his left hand before his head turns to me.

"You feeling better?" he asks.

Taking a small sip of the water, I nod. "Yeah. Thanks."

Silence fills the small space, and it makes me want to crawl out of my skin.

Picking at the label on the water bottle, I ask, "What happened?"

He doesn't say anything, and when I turn to look at him, he's watching me. Different emotions I can't decipher flicker across his face before he says, "I don't know. I woke up this morning not remembering last night. When I went to my bag, I saw a marriage license with our names on it." He continues to fidget with his ring.

In all the years I've known Grayson both at work and out, I've never seen him seem unsure. He's always been so full of confidence that his behaviour has me watching his every move.

His shoulders are tight despite the fact I know he took a hot shower. The mirror is still fogged over and the air in here still has a bit of a sticky feeling to it.

"Okay, so we can get it annulled," I say.

His entire body stiffens. As he opens his mouth to say something, a phone rings in the other room.

"Excuse me," he says as he pushes off the floor, leaving the washroom.

I slowly push myself up and grab a towel, cleaning off some fog from the mirror. I can't help but laugh to myself as I take in my dishevelled look. Mascara and eyeliner are smudged under my eyes, my lips still have a faint red tint to them, and my hair is a disaster.

I wet a washcloth and gently clean my face of the leftover makeup. I run my fingers through my hair before making my way to the bedroom. When I enter, Grayson is sitting on the end of the bed, tying his shoes. He looks up at me with a tentative smile.

"You could have told me I looked like shit," I say.

He shakes his head quickly. "Hannah, you never look like shit. You look beautiful."

His words surprise me, and I stand in the entryway of the room as I watch him pack his bag. Slinging it onto his shoulder, he stops and stares at me. He looks at me like he's taking in every inch of me. My skin tingles as his eyes rake over my body slowly.

He clears his throat and says, "I'm really sorry, Hannah, but the hospital called and asked if there was any way I could come in for the evening shift tonight. I guess Dr. Brighton called in sick so they're down a doctor. We can talk at home."

I nod, not sure what to say. He closes the distance between us, hesitating before kissing my cheek and leaving the hotel room, the sound of the door closing signalling his departure. My hand comes up and touches my cheek. The spot tingles, like that feeling when you put cooling gel on your muscles, but it's warm. I shake my head and drop my hand. Grayson's behaviour this morning is so different from the last two years. I'm not sure what to do with that.

I walk over to the bed and sink into it. I run my hands over my face but stop when the feeling of something cool grazes the left side of my face. I look at my hand.

Those freaking rings.

I came to Vegas for a work conference with a man I can't stand, and I'm leaving married to him. I'm not sure this could have gone any more wrong.

Grayson

I have no idea how in the world I woke up this morning married to Hannah Smith. That gorgeous, snarky woman has hated me for almost two years, and I can't blame her. I kept my mouth shut when everything went down back then, thinking it was better for both of us. Now, I have the time it takes for both of us to fly back to Vancouver to figure out what the hell I'm going to do about being married to her.

I twist the ring on my left hand as I sit in the Las Vegas airport waiting to board my flight. After the hospital called, I was able to change my flight and snag one of the last seats on the 10 a.m. flight.

I pull out my phone and text my buddy Caleb to let him know I've changed my flight, and he confirms he can still pick me up.

Locking my phone, I lean my head back against the wall. I lied to Hannah back at the hotel. I don't entirely not remember last night. It's only bits and pieces, and it's mainly a blur, but there's some there. I remember how stunning she looked as she walked down the aisle to me in a white dress with little green flowers on it. A slit came up to the middle of her thigh, and the white-and-beige wedges she wore accentuated her long legs. Some guy dressed as Elvis married us. I remember her radiant smile as we stood there. I remember promising her forever, and I'm not one to break promises.

I've spent my entire life watching my parent's marriage. I've heard them disagree and fight, but I've also watched them support each other through everything life has thrown at them. They've shown me that marriage is something you work and fight for. You don't give up. This may not be how either of us imagined getting married—hell, I didn't think I would ever get married—but we are, and I'm going to fight for it. Being married to Hannah Smith is a privilege I'm not going to let slip through my fingers easily.

I'm pulled out of my thoughts as my flight is called, and I grab my bag and start boarding. I make my way down the aisle of the plane as people load their bags in the overhead bins. I slide into my seat and pull out my headphones, opening my go-to playlist and setting it on smart shuffle. As I sit there watching the clouds, "This I Promise You" by NSYNC comes on, and I really listen to the lyrics. For some reason, this song is only solidifying my resolve to make this marriage work.

After the plane touches down in Vancouver and I drudge through customs, I find Caleb outside in his truck.

"Thanks for picking me up, man. I hope I didn't interrupt your family plans," I say, running my hand through my hair.

Caleb doesn't say anything, and when I look over at him, his eyes are homed in on my wedding ring. Fuck.

"Looks like you had some fun in Vegas," he says.

"You could say that."

We continue to sit in the pickup lane as Caleb stares at me like he's willing me to speak more. I'm not usually one to be tight-lipped, but I don't want to tell anyone what happened until I've had a chance to talk to Hannah. This impacts both of us, and the last thing I want to do is involve our friends before the two of us know what's going on.

An airport attendant finally comes up and tells Caleb he's got to get moving, so he pulls out into traffic.

"So, did she fly home with you?" he asks.

"No, she's still in Vegas."

I can hear the gears turning in Caleb's head.

"Will she be flying here?"

"Eventually."

It's the truth, Hannah will eventually be flying home. She has her place, her job, and her friends here. As much as I know she's looking for an escape plan from this marriage, I doubt she'd run away. She's too determined and strong to do that.

"Eventually, that's all you're going to say about when your wife is coming here? Or should I be asking when you're going to her?"

I grip the back of my neck, giving it a couple of squeezes. "She'll be coming here. I just don't know when yet."

Caleb side eyes me, and we make the remainder of the drive to my place in silence.

When he pulls up outside my building, I jump out as quickly as I can and say, "Thanks for the ride, man, I appreciate it. I'd also appreciate it if you didn't say anything to anyone about me getting married. I'd like to figure it out before I say anything."

He stares at me before subtly nodding. I grab my bag and make my way inside. I unlock the front door of my apartment and drop my bag on the floor, heading to the couch and grabbing my laptop and work on putting together a plan.

My alarm wakes me a few hours later. I fell asleep while working and am still on the couch. I change into my scrubs and head to the hospital. I've always enjoyed the quick pace that comes with working in the emergency room. I was eighteen when I decided I wanted to go into medicine, but it was during my residency rotation that I settled on emergency medicine. The fast pace and being the first one to step into action when a patient comes into the hospital needing help makes my adrenaline pump.

After stashing my bag and grabbing my stethoscope, I make my way onto the floor for patient handover. Dr. Kaper is at the nurses' station filling out patient charts when I join her. She fills me in about the man in bay two experiencing symptoms of a heart attack and all the tests that have been ordered, the stitches that need to be done on the kid in bay three who took a hockey stick to the mouth during a game of road hockey, and the man in bay four complaining of stomach pain who is just waiting for some test results. Once she's done, I review all the charts myself to make sure I don't miss anything and go to join the boy who needs stitches.

I pull the curtain aside and step into the little room. The mom is

sitting in the chair on her phone while the boy lies in the bed playing a game on his.

"Okay, Tucker, I'm Dr. Maxwell. Why don't you let me have a look at that cut," I say, pulling over a rolling stool to sit in front of him.

The cut isn't that big, but it does need a couple of stitches. I leave the room and grab the necessary supplies and rolling tray to set up. The kid is a trooper as I inject the numbing agent and get to work on the stitches. It only takes three to get him closed up.

"Okay, so you want to keep those as dry as possible, and then in five days you can go see your family doctor and have them removed. Try and avoid playing with them. A nurse will be in shortly to bring you your discharge papers."

"Thank you, Dr. Maxwell," the mom says, and I nod before stepping out and completing some information on the patient's chart.

Samantha, one of the nurses, leans on the counter in front of me. I feel her eyes on me as I type my final notes. Looking up, my eyes are met with her breasts as she's pulled her scrub top down and is using her arms to press her breasts together. A few years ago, that would have gotten my attention and I might have asked if she wanted to meet me in an on-call room, or maybe an unused office, during her break, but now all it does is have me shaking my head.

Leaning back in my chair, I look up and meet Samantha's wanton gaze with a flat one of my own.

"Is there something you need, Samantha?"

Grasping my hands in front of me, I watch as her eyes track the movement and widen slightly. I look down quickly and realize I'm still wearing my wedding ring. When I look back at her, her eyes are stuck there, a look of deep concentration on her face. I clear my throat, hoping to pull her out of her trance.

"I'm sorry, what?" she asks.

"Is there something you need?"

Her eyes dart around the room before they finally come back to me. "I was just going to ask you how your trip to Vegas went. I'm sure Hannah wasn't any fun. I wish I could have gone instead. I know the two of us would have had a great time." She bats her eyelashes, and it bugs me. She obviously saw my wedding ring, but also why does she think she can shit-talk Hannah to me?

Pushing up from my chair, I say, "My trip was fine. Hannah and I were there for work, we attended the convention. We didn't go to party or have fun. Now, if you don't mind, please go check on the results for the tests from bays two and four and page me when you get them."

I turn and leave the nurses' station and head towards the cafeteria. I need caffeine if I'm going to make it through tonight. Once I return with my coffee, the night moves pretty steadily. By the end of my shift, I'm dead on my feet. I do the patient handover to Dr. Friedman before grabbing my bag and heading home.

When I walk in the front door, the first thing I do after ditching my bag is pull out my phone and hunt for Hannah's number from the group chat. I've never actually saved her number, because there hasn't been a need. Until now. After saving her number, I text her.

GRAYSON

Hey, I just got home from night shift. When's your flight home?

She reads my message but doesn't respond.

GRAYSON

Can we meet and talk about this? Please just let me know when you're free and if I'm not working, I'll make it work.

SPITFIRE

I just landed. We can meet tomorrow morning.

GRAYSON

Is someone picking you up from the airport?

SPITFIRE

I'll manage.

GRAYSON

Hannah, do you have a ride from the airport?

SPITFIRE

Liv is coming. I'm fine.

Liv has a one-month-old at home, so I don't believe she'd ask her to pick her up. Knowing I'm not going to get any more out of Hannah, I decide to call Liv. After confirming my suspicions, I make my way to the airport as quickly as possible and see Hannah walking towards the SkyTrain.

I throw the car into park and hop out, calling her name. Her head whips around, and her eyes widen as she takes me in when I jog up to her.

"What are you doing here?" she asks

"I'm picking my wife up at the airport." I smirk.

Her eyes harden as she stares at me. "Don't call me that. We're getting this thing annulled as soon as possible."

Her response doesn't surprise me. I knew this wasn't going to be easy.

"We should talk," I say as I reach for her bag. "I've got this. Come on." I grab her suitcase, surprised to notice she's still wearing her rings. Reluctantly, she follows me. I open the passenger door for her, and she climbs in. As I go to reach for the seat belt, she grabs it from me.

"I can do it myself," she says and glares at me.

I put my hands up in surrender then grab her bag and put it in the back before rounding to the driver's side. Hannah has her entire body turned to face the door as she looks out the window. The air is tight with tension. We really need to have a conversation, but I want to avoid having it in this small and public space. I take the exit towards my place, and Hannah looks at me confused.

"Where are you going? This isn't the exit for my place."

"I know, it's the one for mine. We need to talk, and I figured you wouldn't want to have this conversation in public."

Her eyes narrow as she stares at me before she finally nods and returns to staring out the passenger window. Well, this is going to be fun.

CHAPTER 3

Hannah

What the hell is happening with my life? Am I stuck in some kind of nightmare? I have to be.

Over the last few days, I had to travel to a work conference with a man I can't stand and I woke up married to him, and now I'm in his car as he takes me to his place to talk about our marriage. If you had told me a week ago this is where I'd be, I'd have laughed right in your face.

Why did he even show up at the airport? I said Liv was coming to get me, which was a lie, but I didn't want to bother my friends. I'm perfectly capable of getting myself home from the airport. I've been taking care of myself for years. That kind of happens when your parents start to not care or are just too busy. I don't need help now.

I watch the city pass by as Grayson takes us to his place. I have no idea where he lives. I assume it's somewhat close to the hospital, but that's all. People bustle down the streets, enjoying the warm May sun. After the cold winter we just had and the reprieve from the usual rain we get, everyone's enjoying the change in weather. Grayson pulls up to a large building and turns into the parking garage. I open my door and hop out. Grayson meets me at the front of the car with my bag.

"You can leave that in the car. I don't need it."

"I'm just going to bring it up," he says.

I want to get upstairs and get this conversation over with so that I can pretend all of this never actually happened. I follow him into the elevator and watch as the numbers count up. It feels like forever before the number finally lands on thirty. The elevator doors open, and Grayson gestures for me to leave first. I step out and wait for him to lead the way to his apartment.

I watch the muscles of his arm move as he twists the key in the lock. I shake my head.

What the hell is wrong with me? I cannot be noticing things like this. I'm here to discuss getting an annulment, and then I'm leaving and avoiding him as much as I can.

I follow him, taking my shoes off at the front door. His apartment is surprisingly clean. Shoes are lined up neatly by the front door. His kitchen is to the left, and his counters are clear and there are no dishes sitting in the sink. There's a small table on the other side of his kitchen island set for four. His living room screams bachelor pad. A large, black sectional couch sits facing a large TV mounted on the wall that looks like it's connected to two or three different gaming consoles.

I slowly pad my way over to his couch, sitting on the edge of the seat as he watches me. The silence is killing me. It was like this in the car, too. I don't particularly have anything to say other than I want an annulment, but I've got to break this silence.

I clear my throat and say, "You said you wanted to talk."

He takes a seat next to me, resting his arms on his thighs as he taps his fingertips together. His gaze is focused on his fingers, watching them tap. I start bouncing my leg; the silence is getting to me.

"I want to make this work," he finally says.

I open my mouth and then close it. That was the last thing in the world I thought he'd say. How does he expect us to make this work? He enjoys being able to sleep with anything that walks, and he's hurt me before. He showed me two years ago that being with him wouldn't work. The last thing I want is to be married to him. I'm not sure why he thinks things have magically changed and we can make a go of it.

"This can't work," I say.

He stares at me, his eyes brushing over every inch of me. My skin prickles as he takes his time. He seems deep in thought as he watches me. I move to stand, but his arm shoots out as he grabs my wrist and I wait. His touch and the feeling of his gaze pull me back to when it was good. When I wanted his eyes on me and to feel his skin against mine. I shake my head, reminding myself not to dwell on those feelings.

"Ninety days," he rushes out. "Give me ninety days to prove we can make this work." His voice is confident yet pleading.

I stare into his eyes, trying to decipher why. "Grayson, ninety days isn't going to change anything. You're drawing out the inevitable. Let's just get the paperwork drawn up and signed. Let's get it annulled."

He opens and closes his mouth, and I stare into his eyes. They're a deep blue like the Pacific Ocean. I remember sitting across from him in a restaurant two years ago and getting lost in them. The memory has the hurt that came after bubbling back to the surface. Going from a feeling of hope to betrayal was hard. I withdraw my wrist from his grasp and clasp my hands in my lap.

"Ninety days, and if I haven't convinced you this can work, I'll sign the papers uncontested. I'll end it just like you want. But if we're going to do this, I want to do it right. I want you to move in. We go on dates. No avoiding me. We both put the effort in."

"What about my apartment?" I ask. "I'm still renting my place."

He looks at me, hope in his eyes. "I'm not asking to give it up or to help me pay the rent here. I'm just asking that you move in and give this a real shot."

If he were to fight the annulment, it could drag on for months, but uncontested, this would quickly be in the rearview mirror, and I could get on with my life. I remember how nasty my parents' divorce was. It took them years to actually get divorced and be done with one another. They haven't been in the same room since. I don't want that for myself. I've seen the persistent side of Grayson before, and even if he didn't drag it out to hurt me, he'd do it to get his way. The plus is Grayson and I don't have kids who could get caught in the middle, but fighting this out in court for years is far from what I want.

What's ninety days?

It's the summer.

I can put up with living in Grayson's nice apartment for the summer. It's not far from work or Liv's. And who knows, maybe if I give him enough reasons, he'll call it quits early.

I nod. "Fine. Ninety days and then you sign the papers."

Something in his eyes changes. It's almost as though he's hurt by my words. I shake my head and push those thoughts aside.

"I was going to make some food before I left for the airport. Are you hungry? I can make us something quickly."

Right then, my stomach decides to grumble.

He smiles softly. "That sounds like a yes."

His demeanour is throwing me off. Where is the guy who's always acted like he's the cream of the freaking crop? My stomach grumbles again, and I remember how long it's been since I've eaten real food.

"That'd be great. Thank you."

He nods as he pushes up from the couch and moves into the kitchen. The open space allows me to watch him as he grabs ingredients from the fridge. I make my way over to his entertainment centre and pick up a picture of what looks like his parents. They're both smiling, his dad's wrapped around his mom from behind as they beam at the camera.

"That's my parents the day I graduated from medical school. They're celebrating their thirty-fifth wedding anniversary this summer. They were high school sweethearts."

Looking over my shoulder, I take in his smile as he talks about his parents. I wonder what it must be like to grow up with parents who love each other as much as his obviously do. I place the picture back down and move on to the other pictures. I'm surprised he has so many. There's one of his hockey team after they won the championship a few years ago, one of all the guys at Josh and Olivia's wedding in October, one of him and his dad, and a few others scattered about.

"Lunch is ready," Grayson says as he carries two plates over to the table.

I join him and see he's made chicken breasts with rice and a salad. Slipping into the seat beside his, I say, "Thank you."

"Of course," he says as he digs in.

We eat in silence. Sitting here with Grayson is awkward. Every other encounter we've had in the last two years has been around other people who could act as buffers. I slowly pick at my food. When he finishes, he leans back in his chair, hands clasped and resting over his stomach as he watches me. He's not looking at the food, but at my face, like he's trying to figure out how to approach me.

"Do you have a shift tonight?" he finally asks.

I shake my head. "No, I work night shift tomorrow."

He nods. "I have plans tomorrow night, but I'll be home to have dinner with you before you leave."

His game. With his friends. *FUCK!* I haven't had time to process everything yet, let alone time to tell my friends, *Oh hey, by the way, you know that work trip I went on? Yeah, well, I kinda came home married to the man I can't stand.* Because that will go over so well.

"About that…" I take a deep breath and roll my shoulders back. "I'd like for you to not say anything about us being married. I want to tell the girls beforehand."

He nods and leans forward, resting his arms on his thighs. "Okay, but know I'm not keeping this a secret for ninety days. I'll give you some time to tell your friends, but I'm not treating this or you like a dirty secret, because you're not one."

The conviction behind his words has me wanting to melt, but I know I can't. I have to stay strong. I can't let myself get fooled by pretty words again. Especially not from Grayson.

"Okay."

Nodding, he reaches for my plate. "You finished?"

"Yeah. Thanks."

He grabs our plates and heads to the kitchen sink, rinsing them before putting them in the dishwasher. Drying his hands, he looks back at me.

"I'm beat after my shift. I need a shower and a nap. I'm not sure if you're tired or not. If you want, you can put whatever you want on out here or there are some game consoles. Remotes should be on the coffee table."

"I'm good."

I watch as he moves down the hall into what I assume is his bedroom. I settle back onto the couch, grabbing a blanket that's lying over the back and my Kindle from my purse. I need the escapism of a good book. Settling in, I allow myself to get sucked into the story.

I'm woken up by the smell of pizza. Stretching, I open my eyes and take in my surroundings and it all hits again.

Grayson. Ninety days.

I sit up and see him standing in the doorway, grabbing a pizza box from the delivery guy. He thanks him and turns back to me. He grins.

"Hungry, sleepyhead?"

God, that pizza smells good. My mouth is watering already.

He chuckles. "I'll take that as a yes."

He grabs a couple of plates and napkins and then joins me on the couch. He hands me the remote to find something to watch, and I open Netflix. We agree on *Brooklyn Nine-Nine,* and settle in with the pizza. We both laugh at the jokes, and I relax more as the episodes roll into one another. I feel myself crashing again despite the nap I took.

At the end of the episode, Grayson nudges my leg. "Take the bed. I'll crash on the couch."

I raise a brow.

"Hannah, go, take it."

"I'm not sleeping in some bed that's seen God knows how many women, Grayson. I'll go home."

His face turns from playful to serious as he looks at me. "First, you're too tired to be going home right now, and you agreed to move in, so you're not leaving. And second, no one but me has slept in that bed. So please, take it. You've already napped on the couch."

Why is he bombarding me with so much to process all at once? A yawn tears through me, and I know I don't have the energy to fight him on this. I get up and grab my bag, rolling it into his room. A large king bed sits in the centre of the room with a navy-blue comforter spread over it. The right nightstand is riddled with little things. His charger, a tissue box, a notepad and pen, a water bottle, and a pair of glasses.

I didn't know he needed glasses.

I move into the washroom and quickly wash my face and brush my teeth before changing into my pyjamas. I'm glad I packed some for the work trip, because I usually don't wear any. I prefer to sleep in the nude, or if I do wear something, it's definitely sexier than the shorts and tank I packed.

Slipping under the blanket on the left side, I relish in the soft feel of the sheets against my skin. I don't think I've slept on something so soft. I'll need to ask Grayson for the brand so I can buy myself some. I stare up at the ceiling, trying to process everything. I can't wrap my head around Grayson's behaviour. He's always been so laid back and go with the flow, but today, he's been rigid. Firm in his decisions. Since the hotel, he's said two very clear nice things about me.

Hannah, you never look like shit. You look beautiful.

I'm not treating this or you like a dirty secret, because you're not one.

I fall asleep with his words bouncing around in my mind.

CHAPTER 4

Grayson

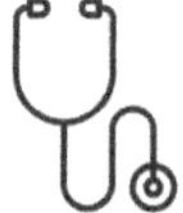

When I wake up, I decide to go on an early run. I have a plan to put into motion, and I need to make some decisions on how I'm going to proceed now that Hannah agreed to my terms.

I quietly sneak into my room and grab some clothes before slipping out. I stuff my house keys and phone in my pocket then put my earbuds in and leave the apartment. I run my usual path through the city and toward the seawall. Running has always helped me clear my mind. It gives me the opportunity to think with no outside factors or pressures. The feeling of my feet hitting the concrete and the light breeze in my hair is therapeutic.

Step one was getting Hannah to give this marriage an honest try, but now I need to show her we can work. Hannah has always had a way of pulling me in. She's the one woman I've always wanted and told myself I can't have. I know why Hannah hates me, and it's my own fault for never correcting her assumptions, but at the time, I thought it was better for her. If it wasn't for the fact we're now married, I don't think I'd be trying to convince her that her view of me is wrong. I wasn't deserving of her then, and I'm still not, but I'm going to fight for this.

I slow outside a local coffee shop a block away from my apartment and step inside to order coffee and breakfast for Hannah and me, hoping this can help us get off on the right foot.

I place the drinks and food bag on the kitchen counter and head to my bedroom to wake Hannah. When I knock on the door, I don't get a response. I slowly open it and see the bed is empty. As I step into the room, Hannah walks out of the en-suite washroom in nothing but a towel. I freeze.

Fucking hell. As if she wasn't temptation enough fully dressed.

Her long blonde hair is hidden in a towel sitting on top of her head, showing off her slender neck. Water still clings to her skin. What I wouldn't give to lick it right off her. She raises an eyebrow at me as she cocks her hip.

I clear my throat and say, "I brought coffee and breakfast home."

She nods, and I back out of my bedroom, closing the door behind me. I won't cross any lines with her, but how in the world am I supposed to live with Hannah for ninety days and not touch her?

I head into the kitchen, grab two plates, and bring the food and coffee to the table. I usually sit at the kitchen island to eat, but I want to be able to look at Hannah to read her reactions. Her body language has always said more than she does. Don't get me wrong, she's not afraid to speak her mind, but she never says the vulnerable things.

When she comes out of the bedroom, she's dressed in a light-blue sundress that lands just above her knees. The top layer of her hair is pulled back away from her face. She joins me at the table, saying, "Thank you," as she hesitantly takes a sip of her coffee. She looks surprised. I've known her for years now, of course, I've learned at least one of her coffee orders.

She picks at the muffin in front of her as she worries her bottom lip. This is a side of Hannah I haven't seen before. Her body is stiff as she sits on the edge of her chair, like she's ready to bolt.

"I'm off today, so I thought I could go with you to your place so you can pack some of your things," I say.

Her head snaps back as her gaze meets mine. "I can do it myself."

"Hannah, I don't mind helping you. You'll be here for three months. I'm sure you'll need quite a bit. I'll make room in the closet so you can put your clothes in there, and we'll work with anything else you need. I'll do everything I can to make you comfortable."

She stares at me before she finally leaves the muffin alone and crosses her arms over her chest, leaning back in her chair. Her arms are crossed just under her breasts, pushing them up and providing me with a good look at them.

"Okay, Grayson, what gives? Why are you pushing this? Why are you asking for ninety days? Why won't you just sign some fucking papers so that we can go our separate ways?"

I lean back and smirk, because there's the little spitfire I know. She's been too quiet, too agreeable.

"Because I don't like to give up before I've actually given something a shot. I want to give this"—I motion between us—"us a shot. It might not be as bad as you think."

She scoffs and rolls her eyes. "Right."

I lean forward and brace myself on the table. "Because the thought of being married and divorced within the span of a week bothers the crap out of me. Besides, you and I agreed yesterday. We agreed that we'd give this a shot, and when time's up, I'll sign the papers. Are you backing out already?"

She holds my gaze for what seems like minutes before her shoulders slump and she lets out a breath. "No, I'm not backing out."

"Good. So, why don't I help you pack some things from your place?"

She nods before pushing away from the table. "Just let me grab my purse."

I watch as she goes into my bedroom and comes back out with her purse and a pair of flip-flops.

"Let's go," she says.

I dump the remaining food into the garbage and our plates in the sink before handing Hannah her coffee. That earns me a subtle smile. It's not the one she gives her friends where her entire face lights up and her eyes look as though little stars are dancing in them, but it's something.

I lead her down to my car, and she types her address into my GPS as I pull out onto the street. The car is silent. Hannah won't look at me, let alone talk to me, and her eyes are glued to the passenger-side window. I turn up the radio as some pop song fills the car. Her place isn't far from mine, which doesn't surprise me because of the location of the hospital.

She hands me a fob to get into the parkade, and I find an empty visitor stall. I follow her as she leads us up to her apartment. Unlocking the door, she holds it open as I trail in behind her. Her place is kind of a mess. She has clothes piled on a chair in her living room with an empty laundry basket on the floor beside it, her shoes are haphazardly against the wall of her entryway, mail is stacked on her kitchen counter, and water bottles are on multiple different surfaces.

She kicks her shoes off on top of her existing stack and moves to a door I assume leads to her bedroom. I move further into the living room and notice the lack of family photos. She has one with another woman who looks to be her mother from probably ten years ago and one with a man who looks to be her dad at her high school graduation. Every other picture is of her and her friends. I take in her overflowing movie collection, which looks like it's probably eighty-five percent rom-coms.

She has three different books lying on her coffee table, each looks like a romance novel. Throw blankets lie on every sitting surface, and there's a basket filled with more in the corner of the room. I shake my head at just how different our apartments are.

Mine is organized and mostly clean. There are times it gets a little out of hand, but my laundry gets put away within a day of taking it out of the dryer. I rotate between two water bottles while she has six just in the living room and kitchen and probably has more in her room.

I move to her bedroom door and lean against the doorframe. She's standing at the foot of her bed in front of an open suitcase with clothes everywhere. I watch as she folds something and puts it inside the bag.

"Need help?" I ask.

She jumps a little before looking over her shoulder at me and shaking her head. "Nope, just grabbing my clothes right now."

She returns to her folding, and I push off the door and move back into the living room. I collect her water bottles, dumping the water in the sink, and open her dishwasher, only to find it full. Shaking my head, I unload it, finding my way around her kitchen as I put everything away. When I'm done and I've loaded all her water bottles inside, I start folding her pile of laundry and stacking it in the empty laundry basket. As I'm finishing with the last piece, Hannah walks out with her suitcase rolling behind her and stops in her tracks, mouth agape.

"Did you just fold my laundry?" She looks around the room. "And clean up my water bottles?"

"Yeah. What else do you need to grab?" I ask.

"Ummmm, I have a few more pieces of clothes to grab and my books."

I nod as she goes through the clothes I just folded and grabs a couple of items and her books off the coffee table before returning to her bedroom and coming out with another small suitcase.

"You have everything?" I ask.

"I guess. I can always come back if I forgot something."

I nod and grab the larger of her two suitcases before we leave her apartment.

Back at my place, I bring her bags into my bedroom and head into my closet, moving all my stuff to one side of the large walk-in to give Hannah space for her things. When I walk back into the room, Hannah is sitting on the edge of the bed watching me.

"I've moved all my stuff to one half so you can have the other. You can stay in here and get all your things set up in the washroom. I'll take the couch and move my stuff into the one in the hallway. Just let me know if you need anything."

I grab some clothes out of the closet and dresser and head into the washroom, grabbing my things before moving to the hallway washroom. She spends hours in the room, probably napping before her shift tonight.

I decide to shower before making dinner for us. I turn the shower on and lean against the edge of the counter, hanging my head between my shoulders. Hannah Smith is in my bedroom. She's moving into my apartment.

I am married to Hannah Smith.

That's not a statement I thought I'd ever say. I'm still in shock about the whole thing. I never stopped to actually process it all. I'm married. I'm fucking married. At the same time I decided I wanted to attend medical school, I decided I wasn't going to get married. It wasn't for me. Rebecca proved to me I wasn't cut out for it.

I step into the water, hoping the heat will relax my tense muscles, but it's not helping. I quickly finish and change before leaving the washroom. As I open the door, Hannah comes out of my bedroom, I guess now her bedroom, dressed in her scrubs. She walks past me, and I just watch her. I don't think she realizes how good her ass looks in those pants.

She opens different cabinets, looking for something.

"Can I help you?" I ask.

"I'm looking for a water bottle to take to work. I didn't grab one from my place."

I walk up behind her and reach over her, my chest brushing against her back as I open one of the top cabinets. My entire body is on edge as I reach up and grab one of the bottles then hand it to her. She looks up at me over her shoulder, and I stare into her eyes. They're this soft hazel colour with flecks of gold floating in them.

"Thank you," she whispers, and I step back, giving her the space to step around me and fill her water bottle.

She doesn't say anything else as she leaves. I'm only sure she's gone when I hear the click of the front door. I guess there goes eating dinner together. I quickly make myself something before heading to my game.

CHAPTER 5

Hannah

I need a plan. It's only been twenty-four hours since I landed and Grayson picked me up and I've already found myself ogling him or staring into his eyes. I can't let my resolve break. I need to stay strong. I need to find a way to drive him away so he calls an end to this arrangement before our time is up.

Needing the time to clear my head, I choose to walk to work. When I arrive at the hospital, I make my way to my locker, leaving my bag as I grab my stethoscope and water bottle and head to the nurse's station. I settle into a chair and log into the system, pulling up the files of the patients currently in the ER. As I'm scrolling, I hear Samantha's voice behind me. She laughs as she says, "Trust me, Dr. Maxwell and I would have had so much more fun in Vegas than him and boring ol' Hannah."

My stomach turns as my thumb plays with the rings on my left hand. I haven't taken them off since that morning. I don't know why, it's not like they hold any special significance to me. They only sit there reminding me of the drunken mistake I made. Despite that, I leave them on.

I turn in my chair and find Samantha looking at me. She smirks when our gazes meet then walks off to one of the emergency bays. I shake my head. A month after Samantha started at the hospital, she became one of those mean girls. We were friendly at first, but then suddenly some switch flipped.

My shift drags, and by the time I'm off, I'm beat. In the locker room, I remember I walked here and now I have to walk back. I groan as I lean against my locker. I just want to take my shoes off, grab a shower, eat something, and curl up and sleep. As I grab my bag, I realize I never got keys from Grayson, so I also don't have a way to get back into the building. My place is too far to walk to.

What a way to end a shitty shift.

Stepping out of the locker room, feeling defeated, I try to figure out what I'm going to do when Grayson pushes off the wall across from me. He holds out a cup of what looks like lemonade.

"What are you doing here?" I ask.

"When you left last night, I never had a chance to give you a set of keys, and I realized you walked here. Thought you could use a ride after a long shift."

I stare at him. Why is he doing these nice things for me? And how long is it going to last? I know it can change at any minute.

As I take a sip of my lemonade, enjoying the refreshing coldness, Samantha walks toward us. She eyes me and Grayson suspiciously. When she gets closer, a smile lights up her face and her hand reaches out to squeeze Grayson's forearm. My stomach tightens as my eyes lock on the touch. Seeing her hand on him has me wanting to yank it off. I don't know why I'm feeling this way. I don't even want to be in this relationship, but I am, and he is legally my husband. Seeing her touch him like this pisses me off. It's not something I haven't seen before. I know she has zero regard for others when it comes to what she wants. I learned that the hard way.

"I didn't think you worked today, Dr. Maxwell," she practically purrs.

"I don't. I'm here to pick Hannah up."

Her expression dims slightly before she plasters the smile back on. "Well, I guess that means you can take me to breakfast then."

Grayson's eyes widen, and he shakes his head. "No, like I said, I'm here for Hannah."

Removing his arm from her grasp, he holds his hand out for me, indicating he'll follow me. I step in front of him and feel Samantha's eyes digging into my back. I walk toward the closest elevator, and Grayson pushes the down button. Being near Grayson has always caused my skin to prickle. My senses feel heightened, and I'm hyperaware of his presence. Being with him in silence has my skin crawl-ing, though. I don't like the man. I have no idea what to say to break the silence that wouldn't be awkward.

When we arrive at his car, he opens the passenger door for me and waits for me to get settled and buckled before he rounds the car to the driver's seat. He immediately turns on the radio, like the silence bugs him, too. I take note that it's not a radio station, but rather he's got an early 2000s playlist playing. The drive to his place is quick. I walk in the front door and toe off my shoes, immediately relieved. I slowly move to the couch, allowing it to eat me as I sink into it.

Leaning my head back, I close my eyes. A minute later, I feel Grayson's presence looming over me. Cracking one eye, I look up at him.

His eyes are soft as he looks at me and holds out a protein bar. "You should probably eat this. If you're hungry for more, I can make you something. I'm sure you want to shower after your shift. I can have it done when you're out."

That sounds so nice. My entire body melts at his words, and I whisper, "Thank you. Food sounds good."

I make my way into his bedroom and into the en-suite wash-room, turning the water on to a blistering temperature while I strip out of my scrubs. I wait for the bathroom to fill with steam before stepping under the water. My muscles slowly relax as the hot water runs down my body. When I finish, I join Grayson in the kitchen, where he's taking a pancake out of a pan. He takes the plate over to the table before retreating to the kitchen and returning with bacon and fruit. He's gone all out.

I slip into a chair and slowly pile food on my plate before digging in. I moan around a mouthful of bacon. I didn't realize how hungry I was until I started eating. I completely devour my food while Grayson watches me with a small smile. Spending this much time with him is making me uneasy. Over the last two years, all the time we've spent together has been either because of work or our friends. I guess this is more forced time spent with him as he made me agree to this stupid ninety-day agreement, but what else was I supposed to do? Say no and let him drag this out just to annoy me.

Nope.

This is better. When we have days off together, I can work to avoid him. Olivia just had her baby, so I can go spend time with her and help with baby Cate. I'm sure I can convince Liz to go out with me a couple of nights, or I can crash at her or Zoey's place.

As I finish eating, my exhaustion settles in, a yawn leaves me as I sag in my chair.

"Thank you for breakfast."

Grayson nods and reaches for my plate.

"I can clean up. You cooked," I say.

He shakes his head. "I've got this Hannah. Just go get some rest."

I push up from my seat and move into the bedroom, sliding under the covers. His mattress is the perfect softness where it feels like you're floating, but not so soft you're falling into it. Last night was the best night's sleep I've had in a while, and I'm not sure if that was because I was so tired after the weekend, or because of this perfect bed.

No matter what I do to try to sleep, it's fruitless, and I toss and turn. I groan, knowing the one thing that never fails to get me to fall asleep when I'm tired, but my brain won't shut up.

I slide out of the bed and rummage through my bag, finding just what I'm looking for. I grab my headphones out of my purse and settle back under the blanket. I pull up the last audiobook I was listening to. It was just ramping up, and I figure it can help me alleviate some tension.

I listen as the story starts playing in my ears. When the main male character says, "Fuck it," I turn on my vibrator. I moan once it's in place, biting my hand to try to quiet the sound. God, this male narrator's voice is like liquid gold. It has me melting further into the bed. The dirty talk doesn't hurt either. As the scene progresses, I turn up speed of the vibrator. I feel myself building higher and higher. As the male voice growls, "Come for me," my back arches off the bed and my toes curl into my feet as I come. I bite my lip, holding back the moan that wants to leave me. I come down from the high and clean up in the washroom before climbing back into bed, sleep finally taking me.

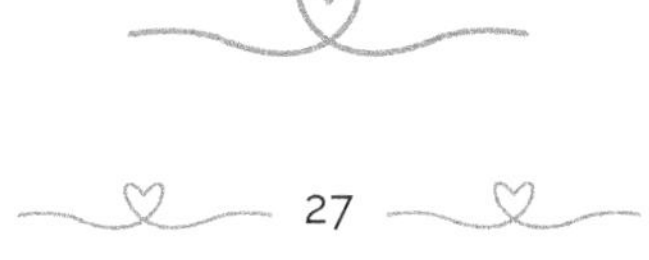

When I wake up in the morning, Grayson isn't home. I have a few hours before I need to head to work, so I slip into leggings, a sports bra, and my runners. Grabbing the extra set of keys Grayson had made for me off the kitchen counter, I head down the street. The sun is warm on my skin as I join the busy sidewalk of people.

I haven't run the seawall in a while, so I start in a light jog in that direction, warming up as I zig-zag my way through the city streets. When I finally catch a glimpse of the water, I pick up the pace, inhaling the smell of the ocean. Growing up in the city, I always enjoyed trips to the beach, trying to get away from the tall concrete buildings. Stanley Park is that little oasis in the middle of downtown that allows a small escape.

I jog past people stopping and taking pictures of the blooming cherry blossoms at the entrance to the park. I smile as I pick up speed, breaking into a full run now that I'm in the park. The feeling of the path beneath my feet is familiar. A gentle breeze comes off the water, and I find a bench at the perfect spot for me to turn around. I settle in, enjoying the view.

"Fancy finding you here," Grayson says as he sits beside me.

I ignore him. I had hoped leaving the apartment would give me time to come to terms with everything. I watch as he taps a finger on his knee. I count the pattern. One, two, three, hold. One, two, three, hold. He repeats it five times before he leans forward, bracing his forearms on his legs.

"I run the seawall every day. It helps me clear my head. I'll run it after a difficult shift, no matter the time of day," he says.

I nod. It feels weird to have him open up to me, even about something as small as his running path or that he runs after difficult shifts.

"I started running when I went to college and just never gave it up. Something about it helps clear my head. It helps me stay grounded when the world around me is beyond crazy."

Not sure what to say, I nod. I push up from the bench and start toward the apartment. He catches up and matches pace with me.

"Hannah, I know this isn't a situation you thought you'd be in right now, but we are. You could at least talk to me."

"You're right," I bite back. "I didn't see myself coming back from Vegas married to you. I think the most frustrating thing is not that I woke up married to you, but that instead of just signing annulment papers, you've made me agree to ninety days."

"Being married to me for ninety days is such a hardship for you? You'd rather be married and end it within seven days than be married to me?"

I see him shake his head out of the corner of my eye. "Grayson, we tried this before. It didn't work out. I don't really believe that people change."

He nods and slows his pace. I keep steady, pulling away from him, thankful for the distance.

All of this has me remembering the very unpleasant feelings of two years ago. Grayson and I had gone on a few dates, done coffee and dinner, and I thought we were building something. That was until I walked in on him and Samantha in a supply closet before Grayson and I were supposed to meet for dinner one night. Her hands were in his hair, and they were kissing. My stomach had turned instantly, and I ran out of the room and made my way to the closest bathroom, emptying the contents of my stomach. I ignored all his texts and calls after and met up with the girls at a bar and got wasted.

The girls know Grayson and I went out a few times, but what I didn't tell them was that I had started to see a future with him. My parents' marriage might have completely fallen apart, and it was hard on me, but it didn't make me lose the desire for true love. Seeing it with Olivia and Josh and then Caleb and Bailey has only made me yearn for it more. I want that person who makes me feel complete. Someone who truly knows every part of me. More and more, I'm beginning to feel like I might never find that.

As if my mother can read my mind, my phone buzzes with a text when I walk in the front door.

MOTHER

Don't forget my birthday celebration is next weekend.

HANNAH

Yes. I'll be there.

MOTHER

You should bring someone with you. You won't be
young forever.

HANNAH

Maybe.

MOTHER

I'm only looking out for your best interest, Hannah.

HANNAH

I'm good, Mom.

I toss my phone on the bed before making my way into the
shower.

Ever since I turned eighteen, my mother has been trying to set
me up or pushing me to date and find someone. Her idea of an ideal
partner is someone who makes a lot of money. She doesn't care
about anything else. I wouldn't be surprised if that's why she
married her third husband. But I want more. I'm not going to settle
for a loveless marriage just because someone can support me finan-
cially. I can do that all on my own. I want someone who will be there
through thick and thin. Someone I look forward to coming home to
after a long day. I want them to get along with my friends and understand just how important they are to me. My girls are the family I've
chosen. I'm an only child and I always wanted siblings, and the girls
are my chosen ones.

When I head into the kitchen, Grayson is already there cooking
something. He turns and looks at me, nodding slightly as he takes
what looks like an omelette out of the pan and places it on a plate
before putting it on the table and returning to the stove, making
another. He looks back at me. "Eat up before it gets cold."

I do as I'm told and dig into the omelette. It's delicious. I'm not
sure where Grayson learned to cook, but everything he's made me so
far has been amazing. Not that I'd tell him that. He doesn't need
anything else to grow his enormous ego.

Settling in beside me, he says, "I'm working tonight, so I can give
you a ride and bring you home in the morning if you'd like."

I still haven't grabbed my car from my place, and I don't want to
have to walk home tomorrow. I accept and finish my food then take
my plate into the kitchen and load the dishwasher.

"What time do you want to leave?" I ask.

"Six thirty."

"I'll be ready," I say before going to the bedroom, grabbing my Kindle, and settling into the bed.

Riding to work with Grayson is awkward. I'm thankful for the music that plays softly in the car as we make our way the short distance to the hospital. As soon as he shifts to park, I throw the door open and make my way to the elevator bank, needing to put distance between us. We've spent way too much time just the two of us over the last few days.

I barely manage to get my arm into the gap of space between the elevator doors and slide in before jabbing at the close door button, hoping the elevator will leave Grayson behind.

I catch a small glimpse of him as the doors finally close. His face is blank, and it has my stomach bottoming out. Grayson is always so carefree and it's usually written all over his face. This stoney lack of facial expression is something I've never seen from him.

The chiming of the elevator as it arrives on my floor pulls me out of my thoughts. I rush into the locker room and deposit my bag into my locker before making my way to the nurses' station and logging in. I stiffen when the sound of Samantha's annoying flirtatious laugh hits my ears.

Grayson's arrived.

For some reason, he is the only person who gets that laugh out of her. Her voice grows louder as they approach.

"You should totally join me for drinks tomorrow. I'm sure you have some stories about Vegas, and I'd love to hear them."

I roll my eyes so hard I can feel them pull inside the sockets. I look up and am met with Samantha's glare. It's one of those thinly veiled ones that if you didn't know better, you'd think she was looking at me indifferently, but I know her. I know the tightness around her eyes and the firm set of her lips as she presses them together.

"Hannah, do you not think that Grayson would have some great stories about Vegas? I know you were probably holed up in your room the entire time, but Grayson must have gotten out and seen the town."

I look at her intensely before my gaze moves to Grayson and I plaster on a fake smile.

"Yeah, Grayson. Why don't you go for drinks with Samantha."

His eyes narrow slightly as if that will allow him to see more behind my words. He shakes his head.

"No, I'm good. I have plans tomorrow."

"Awwww, Grayson." She pouts and grabs his arm. "Why not? We could have so much fun."

He gently plies her hand off of his arm. "As I said, I have plans. Now, if you'll both please excuse me, I'm going to check on my patients."

His eyes dart to me quickly before he moves to bay one and steps behind the curtain.

Samantha huffs as she rounds the counter and sits in a chair beside me. Not wanting to deal with any more of Samantha than I have to, I leave and start checking the stats of the patients in the ER.

At the halfway mark of my shift, I inform Samantha that I'm taking my break and head to the cafeteria. I quickly grab a sandwich and bottle of Coke before sitting at a table in the corner and pulling up my Kindle app on my phone. I'm halfway down the page when the chair across from me is pulled out.

My eyes flick up from my phone, and I see Grayson sitting there. I ignore him, hoping he'll take the hint and leave me alone.

He clears his throat, and I continue to ignore him. He clears it again, and I huff, locking my phone and putting it on the table.

"Is there something I can help you with Dr. Maxwell?"

He offers me a smirk. "I'm just sitting down enjoying my break with my wife."

My eyes widen as I look around to see who could have heard us. Thankfully, it's early morning and there aren't a lot of people around.

"Can you please not say that?" I whisper-hiss at him.

He grins as he leans forward over the table. "You don't want me saying you're my wife?" he says, a little louder this time.

"No, I'd rather like it if you left me alone."

"I want to eat with you, maybe enjoy some conversation."

Why is he so persistent?

"I'm good. Thanks."

"The way I see it, you can either sit here and eat with me while engaging in some conversation, or I can very loudly announce to the entire room that you're my wife. You know how quickly gossip spreads in this place. Your choice," he says, looking very satisfied with himself.

I stare at him, my blood boiling. He opens his mouth wide like he's about to yell something, and I reach forward, clamping my hand over his mouth.

"Fine. You can sit here and we can talk," I grit out and watch the smile in his eyes grow as I remove my hand from his mouth.

Sitting back in my chair, I take a bite of my sandwich as Grayson takes a bite of his. If he wants a conversation, then he's going to have start it. I'm not putting any effort into this.

"Do you have anything planned for this summer?" he asks.

"So far just the group camping trip."

He nods. "Has Liv picked a spot yet?"

"Yeah, she managed to snag a spot right on the lake in Osoyoos. She booked it for the first weekend in August, arrive Thursday and leave Monday."

"Sounds good. I'm sure it will be fun."

He takes a sip of water and watches me. I take another bite of my sandwich. The faster I eat, the faster this can be over.

"Bucket list thing to do?" he asks.

I think for a second, trying to decide just how much I want to reveal to him. Deciding to keep it to something small, I say, "I want to swim beneath a waterfall."

He absorbs my words, and we spend the rest of our lunch break eating in silence. Returning to the floor, I power through my shift until it's time for me to clock out. I know that means I have to spend a car ride with Grayson, but at this point, I'm just ready to shower and climb into bed and sleep.

I meet Grayson at his car where he's leaning against the passenger side. He opens the door for me and helps me in before taking us home.

CHAPTER 6

Grayson

Over the next two days, I drive Hannah to work, convince her to eat with me during our break, and then we come home and both crash. Saturday afternoon, I go to knock on the bedroom door to let her know that I have lunch ready. As I raise my fist to knock on the door, I hear her voice.

"Yeah, I'll be at the game tonight... Yeah, sounds good... Okay, love you, too, Liv."

I grin knowing she'll be at our hockey game tonight. I knock on the door, and Hannah pulls it open within seconds.

"Lunch is ready," I say, and she nods before following me to the dining table. "I can give you a lift to the game tonight," I say, and she stiffens.

"It's fine. I can manage," she says.

"Hannah, I don't mind. There's no point in taking two vehicles to and from the same place."

"I haven't told the girls yet. I don't want to show up and leave with you."

I take a deep breath, reminding myself that she's worked long shifts almost every day since she's come back from Vegas and hasn't had a lot of time to meet and chat with her friends. On top of that, she still isn't fully on board with this marriage. If I don't want to completely push her away, I need to be understanding with her while also trying to get her to warm up to me.

"Okay, we can park at the back of the lot and you can walk in first. I'll give you enough time so that it doesn't look like we arrived together. We can find time tomorrow to go get your car from your place."

She stares at me, her eyebrows pinching before her shoulders slump and she says, "Fine."

It's not much, but I take it as a win.

Knowing how much Hannah likes her space away from me, I decide to go for a run after we finish eating. I run my usual route around the seawall. On my way home, I see a flower shop with beautiful lilies. I immediately think of Hannah. I slow my pace and pull my wallet out, handing the attendant enough for a dozen red lilies and some baby's breath with greenery. She bundles it all up into a bouquet for me, and I walk the last two blocks to my apartment.

When I open the front door, Hannah is in the living room with headphones in as she dances around, singing into a water bottle. I lean my hip against the kitchen island and watch her.

She looks so carefree and happy right now. She hasn't let me see her like that in a long time, and I miss it. I miss the small smiles she used to give me when we'd pass each other in the hallway of the hospital, or the way she'd laugh at a joke that wasn't remotely as funny as her laugh made it seem. I know it's my fault for not correcting her assumptions when she walked into that storage closet Samantha had cornered me in. Now, more than anything, I wish I had. Hannah may, on the outside, seem like she's all snark and sass, like she's the strongest person you've ever met, but I see beneath the facade she puts on for the world. Beneath all of it, she's a soft, caring, loving, supportive person who will do anything for the people she loves.

I knew then, like I know now, that she deserves so much better than me. She deserves someone who can be everything she needs and provide her with the life she wants. I'm not sure that I can. Seeing Hannah cry when she walked into the storage room had me flashing back to when I was eighteen. But now I'm going to give her every-thing I can and hope that it's enough.

She spins and faces me, and when she sees me, she stops in her tracks. I grin as she pulls out her headphones.

I take a step towards her and pass her the bouquet. "For you," I say.

She looks at them for a second, and I swear I see the start of a blush tinge her cheeks as she tucks a stray piece of hair behind her ear and grabs them from me tentatively.

She clears her throat before saying, "Um, thanks."

I move to the kitchen, reach to the back of one of the cabinets, and pull down a vase for her. When I turn back to her, she's still staring at the flowers. I leave the kitchen and move into my room, grabbing some clothes before hopping into the shower.

When I come out of the bathroom, Hannah is cutting the stems of the flowers and arranging them in the vase as she smiles to herself. Her eyes flick to me for a second, and the smile stays on her face.

Another small victory.

Usually when she sees me, whatever expression she's wearing turns neutral or into a scowl. I settle onto the couch and turn on the TV and switch it to Carolina vs Philadelphia playoff hockey game. Hannah sits on the other end of the couch, with her legs curled under her and her Kindle in hand.

We sit in peaceful silence until it's time to leave for my game. I grab my bag and sticks from my office before meeting Hannah at the front door, Kindle still in her hand. The drive to the rink is silent except for the music that plays through the stereo. Hannah faces the passenger door as she reads. I sneak glances at her, watching her subtle facial expressions as she reads. I enjoy seeing how engrossed in her book she is.

Pulling into the parking lot, I find a spot way in the back and park. I round the car quickly and help Hannah out before I watch her make her way to the front door. It sucks having to stand here and watch her and not be able to walk right beside her.

Once she's inside, I grab my bag and stick out of the trunk and head inside. We are the last ones here. When I step inside, I see the whole group standing in a circle. Josh has his arm wrapped around his wife, Olivia, who is wearing their baby girl, Cate. Caleb is holding his little girl, Charlie, while his girlfriend, Bailey, leans into his side. Hannah has joined Zoey and Eliza beside Liv. Matt is talking to Josh about the Carolina game today when I walk up beside him.

After a few minutes, we all make our way to the rink. The girls find their usual spots on the bleachers while we head into the dressing room.

"So, I guess congratulations are in order," Josh says as he claps Caleb on the back.

"Thanks, man," Caleb says.

"What happened?" I ask.

"Caleb popped the question to Bailey," Josh says.

"I win!" I holler before turning to him and saying, "But congrats, man, that's awesome." When Caleb and Bailey first met, I told him he'd marry her and he said they weren't even dating, but I could tell that his sorry ass was falling for her and her daughter.

"Yeah, yeah, you win. I'm marrying Bailey," Caleb says as he shakes his head, but there's still a soft smile on his face.

"When did this happen?" I ask.

"Saturday."

"You didn't say anything when you picked me up from the airport on Sunday," I say.

"Yeah, well, there were other things that had my attention," he says as his eyes flick to my left hand where my wedding ring still sits. Thankfully, no one else notices.

We all change quickly before heading out onto the ice. Hockey has always been a part of me. At the age of five, my dad put me into a program. I loved it. I played all the way through high school. It was my saving grace when everything went down my senior year. Without hockey, I'm not sure I'd be where I am right now. When I got to university, I joined the intramural team, not wanting to take time away from my studies.

Tonight's game moves quickly, and we win 5-2. Our usual Saturday ritual is group dinner upstairs. We all change quickly and Luke, Nick, and Sam also decide to join us tonight. We all take our bags to our vehicles before heading upstairs to join the girls. Josh and Caleb beeline it to their girls, and I notice that Luke moves straight to Hannah. I grit my teeth but don't say anything as he sits beside her. I take the seat across from her, watching them interact.

We order, and I watch as she laughs at his jokes and gives him small smiles. I grip my glass so tightly, I fear it might break. Our food is delivered, and that puts a hold on Luke's flirting. I try to listen as

Bailey tells us about how her and Caleb got engaged, but my attention is stuck on Hannah.

As soon as Luke is done eating, he's back to flirting with Hannah. Rage climbs through me. When he reaches forward and tucks a stray piece of hair behind her ear, I've had it.

"Luke, I highly recommend you remove your hand from my wife if you'd like to keep it."

His eyes widen as his hand drops to his side and Hannah glares at me. The entire table has gone silent, and everyone's eyes are on me.

"You said you wouldn't say anything," Hannah hisses.

"And I respected that until you let him touch you."

She crosses her arms over her chest, and there's a collective gasp from the girls. Zoey is the first up and rounds the table, grabbing her left hand and inspecting the ring.

"How did you hide this the entire game?" she asks as she continues to tilt Hannah's hand, looking at the ring.

"It's easier when you guys aren't looking for it," Hannah huffs.

Hannah's now surrounded by all the girls as they look at it. She narrows her eyes at Bailey. "Why don't you look surprised?"

Bailey's eyes flick to Caleb as he takes a sip of his beer. Hannah's head flips to him immediately.

"I'm not keeping secrets from my fiancée," he says.

"And who told you?" she asks as she glares back at me.

I put my hands up in a defensive position. "Hey, I didn't tell him anything. He saw my ring when he picked me up, but I didn't say who I married."

"Oh, no, Caleb and I figured that out on our own," Bailey says. "He told me that Grayson came back from Vegas married and I knew you also went, we put two and two together."

Thank God, because Hannah's already pissed at me for outing us, I don't need her any more mad.

Everyone takes their seats and the questions start.

"Why didn't you tell us?" Olivia asks, sounding hurt.

Hannah rolls her eyes. "Yeah, I was really looking forward to telling my best friends, 'Hey, I went to Vegas for work and ended up marrying Grayson, you know the man I barely tolerate.' That's exactly what I wanted to do."

Her words hurt even though I expected them. I take a sip of my beer, hoping to hide how her words affect me.

"You know we wouldn't judge you, right?" Eliza asks.

"Yeah, but it doesn't make a mistake Vegas marriage any less embarrassing."

Olivia worries her lip as though she's deep in thought. Her eyes meet mine and a small smile spreads across her face before she looks back at Hannah and I look down at the table.

"You know, maybe this doesn't have to be a mistake," Olivia says, and I could kiss her if we both weren't married.

Hannah's jaw drops as she stares at her friend. "You did not just say that."

"Maybe Liv's right," Eliza says. "They say there's a thin line between love and hate, and if your feelings are this strong, maybe there's a reason behind it."

Hannah's pissed. "Zoey, what do you have to say?"

She blushes slightly before she lifts a shoulder. "I kinda agree with the girls."

"For what it's worth, I do, too," Bailey says.

Hannah balls her napkin and throws it down on the table before pushing back in her chair.

"So glad to know," she says before turning and leaving the restaurant.

I quickly stand and throw some bills on the table to cover both Hannah and my bills. "I'm her ride. I'll talk to you guys later," I say before following behind Hannah.

I have to jog to catch up to her. She stops at the passenger door and turns, glaring daggers at me.

"You promised you wouldn't say anything and give me time to tell my friends."

I step forward, placing my hands on either side of her head, caging her between me and the car. I lean in real close to make sure she doesn't miss a single word of what I'm about to say.

"Spitfire, I did respect that, but then Luke touched you. I'm going to make this abundantly clear, so listen closely. I. Don't. Fucking. Share. You may not want to be in this marriage, but you are. We are married. You are my wife, and I am your husband. And while we're married, no other man will touch you. If I see another man's hands on you, I will break his fucking fingers. Do you understand me?"

I watch her throat bob as she swallows before her eyes meet mine and she nods. I know she wants to push back, to say something, but she doesn't. She just holds eye contact until I reach for the handle beside her. I step back and she follows as I open the door and help her in.

I spend the entire drive wanting to place my hand on the top of her thigh and feel how soft her skin is. To have some sort of connection to her. The emotions running through me have me wanting to claim her more than I did back in the restaurant.

When we pull into the parking garage, Hannah leaves the car before I can even open the door for her. I grab my bag and sticks and make it to the elevator just before the doors slide closed. Hannah has her arms crossed over her chest, pushing up her tits, and it takes everything in me not to stare. This woman has me on the edge of control.

The second we make it into the apartment, she kicks off her shoes and heads into the bedroom, closing the door behind her.

Well, tonight didn't exactly go as planned.

CHAPTER 7

Hannah

When I wake up, my phone is full of texts both in the group chat and from my friends individually.

Fucking Grayson Maxwell and his big fucking mouth. Ugh.

I'm so pissed he went all fucking alpha and declared in front of everyone at dinner that I'm his wife. When he caged me against the car last night, I wanted to bite back, give him a piece of my mind, but then I flashed back to when I was a kid and heard the yelling and screaming from my parents and the anxiety the fighting brought me. So, I bit my tongue, and we rode home in silence, but I know that I'm not doing myself justice by letting him just get his way. I really need to find a way to drive him away and make him sign the annulment papers as soon as possible.

I know I can't ignore my friends and their texts forever, but I hope I can at least make it through the morning before I have to share everything with them.

Grayson is still asleep when I step out of the bedroom, and it's time to start phase one of scaring him off.

I'm no longer going to be a respectful roommate.

I bang around the kitchen as I gather everything I need to make myself a smoothie. I make sure to leave kitchen cabinets open and food scrapes on the counter as I load everything into the blender and turn it on. As the blender whirls, I stare at Grayson, who's now sitting up on the couch and rubbing his eyes.

"Good morning," he says groggily.

"Morning."

I turn off the blender and pour my smoothie into a cup. Then I leave the dirty blender filled with water in the sink. I settle in the corner of the couch and grab the remote, putting on *Love Is Blind* season 1 episode 1. Grayson looks over at me before leaving and going to the washroom. When he comes back out, his eyes bounce between me and the kitchen. With a sigh, he rinses the blender and loads it into the dishwasher, closes the kitchen cabinets, tosses the ends of my fruit into the food scraps bucket under the sink, and takes a wet cloth to the counters.

He makes himself coffee and an omelette before settling at the table. I watch him out of the corner of my eye but say nothing.

He eventually changes and says he's going on a run as he leaves the apartment. I let out a breath as I pause the show.

Okay, I've started step one, make Grayson's apartment a mess, but it's not enough. This morning was just a tiny inconvenience. If I really want him to call it quits, I need to completely take over his apartment.

With a plan in place, I find a water bottle and fill it, leaving it beside the couch before I go into the bedroom. I grab my bag that has my romance books and movies inside and load up my arms before taking them into the living room. I place my movies on the entertainment unit. When mine don't all fit, I take some of his out and put them in a basket underneath. I place my books on every flat surface I can, the side table, the coffee table, the dining table, the kitchen counter, and the shelves.

I take a step back and assess. It's a good start, you can begin to see my presence in the apartment, but it needs to be more.

I check the time then order an Uber to my place so I can grab some things from my apartment and my car. When I step inside, I realize just how much I miss having my own little oasis. It hasn't been long since I moved into Grayson's, but I can't help but want to be back home in my own place. I tell myself that if everything goes well with my plan, I'll be back here in no time.

I load up a few bags with some miscellaneous things and load my car. After parking back at Grayson's, I take up the first load, dropping it all in the living room. Hearing the shower going, I figure I have enough time to go down and get the last load before he's out.

I place throw blankets over the back of the couch and add a basket of them to the corner of the living room. I place candles everywhere, lighting a few as I go. I pull out a stuffed pig that I've had since I was a kid and place it amongst the throw pillows I set up on the couch.

I've just pressed play on *Love Is Blind* when Grayson walks out of the bathroom, his eyes taking in all the changes I've made to his apartment. He opens and closes his mouth as he looks. His eyes land on me, and he shakes his head before walking into his bedroom and coming back out dressed in a pair of gym shorts and a T-shirt.

"I see you've made yourself comfortable," he says.

"I have, thank you."

"Okay, well, I'm going to go hit a few balls with the guys. Text me if you need anything."

I watch as he leaves the apartment again.

Why is he not blowing up? I was rude and woke him up this morning with loud noises, made a mess in the kitchen, which I didn't clean up, and filled his entire apartment with my stuff.

Frustrated, I huff as I turn off the show, grab my Kindle, and settle back on the couch. I need a good book boyfriend to distract me.

Around lunch time, I get a text in the group chat.

LIV

Lunch today? You've got to talk to us Han, we're here for you.

HAN

Sure. I'm at Grayson's so let me know where.

ZO

Sammy's close to you?

HAN

I'll make it work. See you in 30.

I gather my things before heading to my car to meet the girls. I know this is going to be difficult. The girls are probably hurt I didn't tell them, but also I don't know how to fully explain how I ended up to married to Grayson. The night we got married is still a complete blank for me.

Growing up, I always pictured my wedding with the white dress, the decorations, my friends and family. The only thing that wasn't set in my mind was my groom. Not being able to remember that night sucks, because I feel like I've lost the one thing I've always dreamed of. Knowing I'll never get that first wedding back crushes a small piece of my soul. I only hope that when the ninety days are up and I can get this marriage annulled, I'll have that chance of meeting the one person I'll get to spend the rest of my life with.

Outside of the diner, I take a deep breath before getting out of my car and making my way inside. The girls are already there in a booth with drinks in front of them as they talk.

My best friends.

The guilt begins to eat at me. I know these girls would never judge me. They've been there for me through thick and thin. They are the sisters I never had.

I slide into the booth beside Zoey, and the girls look at me, smiling hesitantly. I smile back.

Sammy, the owner and a waitress in the diner, approaches with a cup of coffee for me. We place our orders, and when Sammy leaves all eyes are back on me.

"Sooooo...." I start, my fingers playing with the handle of the coffee mug. I tell them the entire story of how I woke up married to Grayson and our ninety-day agreement. I take a long sip of my coffee before looking at the girls again.

"So, I agreed to give him ninety days, because I just want to get this over with. I don't want him to drag this out. I don't want to be a repeat of my parents," I say, and they nod, knowing exactly what I mean. They've heard the story and know just how badly it affected me. They're silent as they watch me. I can see the wheels turning in each of their heads as they try to understand how I ended up married to the man I've told them I hate.

I'm not sure that's the appropriate word to describe how I feel about Grayson Maxwell. How do you describe that feeling of going from seeing a potential future with someone and wanting to really try a relationship, to being completely destroyed by something they've done? I still don't understand the events of two years ago. I know nothing has come of a relationship between Samantha and Grayson since then, no matter how much she wants one.

After the night of the supply closet incident, he never tried reaching out again. He never tried to explain what happened, or why he did what he did. It got to the point where I was so upset about him not contacting me, I actually changed my cell phone number, trying to convince myself that him not having my new number was the reason he wasn't reaching out. I know that makes me delusional, but I was so hurt.

Liv is the first one to break the silence. "Why ninety days?"

I shake my head and lift a shoulder. "I don't know. He was very specific about that when he was trying to convince me to make this work. I knew if I didn't agree, he could drag this out and fight it, so I agreed."

"What are you going to do for the next ninety days?" Liz asks.

A Cheshire grin spreads across my face. "I'm going to make him regret the day he ever married me."

Liz's eyes go wide as Zoey and Liv almost choked on their drinks, and Bailey assesses me.

"And how do you plan on doing that?" Zoey asks.

My cheeks hurt from the size of my smile as I position myself so I can see all four of their faces perfectly when I say, "I'm going to *How to Lose a Guy in 10 Days* him."

They stare at me for three seconds before they all break out laughing. We've watched that movie as a group so many times; it never fails to be a perfect comfort movie for us when we need a girls' day. They know exactly what I'm talking about.

When their laughter finally subsides, Liv asks, "Are you sure you don't wanna give this a real shot? I know you have issues with Grayson and you guys have a history, but have you ever thought that maybe you don't have the whole picture? I mean, Josh trusts him with his life."

I gnaw on my lip. All these people in my life have nothing but amazing things to say about Grayson, but it's hard for me to reconcile all of that with my experience. As much as my rational brain wants to listen to what my friends have to say, I think the hurt part of my heart is winning. I don't want to feel like I did two years ago. I still want that soul-changing, life-altering love I've always yearned for. In thirty-five years, I want my children to have cherished pictures of me and my husband, completely in love, like Grayson has now.

I don't want to be like my mother, on her third marriage and married to someone I don't think she actually loves. I think my mom is in her marriage for the aesthetics and security of it. She wants that portrayal of being happy and in love and thriving in life and the financial security he provides her.

Watching Josh and Olivia and Caleb and Bailey over the last year has shown me that there are soulmates out there. There are people who will be there for you unconditionally, who will love every part of you. As much as I love my friends and I've loved watching them fall in love, I can't help but feel jealous. To wish it was me finding that person.

I shake my head. "We tried this once. I don't think giving it another shot is going to change anything. When the ninety days are done, we will sign the papers and go our separate ways. Until then, I will endure living with him and try to get him to end this earlier."

Liz asks, "Why didn't you tell us earlier? You know we'd never judge or abandon you, right?"

Liz and I have been friends the longest. We met during eleventh grade in our first period English class. I went through some difficult things with my mom that year, and she was there and supported me through it all. I see in her eyes that me not saying anything to her hurts. I've shared every crazy, embarrassing, painful thing I've gone through with her, and I know she'll always be there for me. The same for Liv, Zoey, and Bailey. I think I was judging myself and was so disappointed in myself that I refused to voice it to the girls.

"Yeah. I'm still struggling with it all. It's been a week since we woke up in the Vegas hotel room, and I still can't believe I made such a dumb mistake. Now, I have to live with the consequences and get myself out of this mess."

After a few seconds, they nod, and we transition the conversation to summer plans. I'm thankful for my friends and their support.

Bailey and Liv leave first, needing to get home to their kids, and Zoey has a family dinner she needs to get ready for, leaving Eliza and me at the table. She stares into her coffee as she takes a deep breath.

Eliza doesn't say a lot; she's usually the observant one offering her opinion when she thinks it's necessary. I watch as she presses her lips together the way she does when she's gathering her thoughts before saying something. I reach out and grab her hand.

"I'm sorry for not telling you before. I know you would never judge me"—I let out a breath slowly—"I'm still not sure I've fully wrapped my head around being married. I'm still not happy that Grayson dropped it like he did."

Her eyes sparkle a bit as she places her free hand on top of mine. "He cares for you, Hannah. I know you may not see or understand it, but he does. I think him getting possessive and not signing the annulment proves that. In time you'll see," she says.

"I'm not sure it's like that—" I start, but she squeezes my hand.

"Hannah, you know I love you. I think you're letting your heart do too much of the thinking right now. Let your eyes and brain do some of the work."

I nod, but I'm not sure I can let my heart take a back seat.

We pay our bills and hug each other before going our separate ways. When I walk into the apartment, I'm momentarily stunned by the sight of Grayson shirtless doing push-ups in the middle of the living room. The muscles in his arms strain as the veins bulge under his skin each time he goes down. I drop my keys on the counter, causing him to look up at me as I move to grab a glass of water.

He doesn't stop, in fact, I think he starts going faster.

His skin glistens with sweat, and I drink my water as my throat seems to get drier the more I watch him. When my glass is empty I fill it again, and I swear to God I see the man fucking smirk. I turn my back to him and finish the water before leaving the glass in the sink and heading into the bedroom.

I'm getting settled on the bed with my Kindle in hand when there's a knock on the door. I ignore it. He knocks again.

I huff as I shout, "Yeah."

He opens the door and leans against the door frame as he stares at me. He's still shirtless, and I watch as a stray drop of sweat travels between his pecks, down his stomach, and to the waistband of his gym shorts that are hanging off his hips. He chuckles, and my eyes snap to his.

"Can I help you with something?" I grit out.

"Yeah." He smirks. "I'm taking my wife out on a date tonight."

I clench my jaw so tightly my teeth hurt. When I open my mouth, he puts a hand up to stop me.

"You agreed. Ninety days, and we do it right. We live together, and we go on dates."

My mouth snaps closed, and I glare at him. "Fine. What time are we leaving?"

"In an hour, figured that should be enough time to get ready."

"Where are we going?"

He grins. "It's a surprise, dress comfortably."

He leaves and closes the door behind him, leaving me staring at the place he was just standing. Figures today would be the day he throws in my face that I agreed to dates. My friends will have even more ammunition when they find out about this.

I grumble to myself as I get out of bed and have a shower. As I stand in the closet afterwards, my eyes catch on something and I grin. I'm not sure why I packed this, but it's perfect for today. If Grayson is going to force me to go on a date, I'm going to embarrass the hell out him.

I grab the items I need and quickly get dressed, taking a quick peak at myself in the mirror before heading into the living room to meet Grayson. He's dressed casually in a pair of shorts and runners with a T-shirt that looks better on him than it has any right to. He looks up from his phone, and shock fills his face before he smooths out his expression. I can't blame him to be honest. Normally, I'd never leave the house dressed like this, but it's all for the shock value and embarrassment so that, hopefully, I can be single again soon. I look, odd, to say the least.

A few years ago, I attended some animal print party and, me being me, went all out. I bought cheetah print leggings, a cheetah print tank top, and happened to find some shoes, too. Packing was a haze, but I managed to grab the entire outfit from my closet, and I couldn't be more glad I did.

Grayson holds his hand out, indicating he'll follow me. I leave the apartment and wait for him to lock the door before me make our way down to the car. He opens my door for me before rounding the car and driving out of the parkade.

He heads south and out of the bustling downtown air. I stare out the window as he drives us closer to the water, realizing he's taking me to the beach. I look over at him, and he smiles softly before his gaze returns to the road. He parks in front of one of the most popular beaches in the area. We get out and he heads to the trunk, grabbing a picnic basket and blanket. I follow him to the middle of the beach, where he lays out the blanket. We kick off our shoes and sit.

A light breeze comes off the water, and I close my eyes and absorb the feeling of it on my skin and the smell of the ocean. After a minute, I open my eyes and turn to look at Grayson, who is watching me. He gives his head a quick shake before he opens the basket and pulls out two little bottles of sparkling wine, a container of cut cheese, another with salami, a bag of crackers, and a variety of fruit. It's everything I would pack to take to the beach.

He unscrews one of the bottles of wine and passes it to me before opening his and taking a sip.

I stare at the food and realize I'm actually hungry. He opens the salami first and holds the container out to me. I grab a slice and moan as I take a bite. Grayson coughs as he adjusts himself.

"Your favourite colour still pastel green?" he asks.

"Umm." I take a bite of cheese. "Yeah," I say hesitantly.

He nods and tosses a piece of cheese into his mouth.

"You still saving for that trip to Paris?"

I nod. "Yeah. Not sure when I'll actually be able to go on it, but still working towards it." I've always wanted to visit Paris. Being someone who is looking for true love, of course I want to visit the city of love at least once in my life. Ideally, I would take the trip with my partner, but if not, a solo trip would be just as fun.

He smiles softly. "Well, I know you'll be able to take that trip soon. I'm sure it will be amazing."

We sit in silence for a minute, the sound of the water lapping at the shore and people enjoying their day out.

"How's your dad?" he asks.

I sigh. "He's good. He's dating someone new. She seems to be good for him. He sounds happier when I talk to him on the phone."

He smiles. "I'm glad."

When Grayson and I tried this two years ago, I told him how I was closest to my dad. My dad was the person I could always turn to when I needed help. When my parents split, it was hard. My mom was super self-involved and tried to make everyone feel bad for her. I was an adult when I learned from someone close to the family the truth as to why they separated. Mom had cheated. Since then, she's gone through more men than I have fingers. She's on her third husband, whom she's already on the rocks with. Over the years, I've pulled away from her, not needing the toxicity in my life.

"Okay, truth or dare?" Grayson asks, and my head swings towards him.

"Neither."

"Spitfire, you've got to give me something here. We're on a date. Let's have fun."

"Fine. Truth."

He tips his head back, staring at the sky for a second before he looks at me. "Most embarrassing moment in college."

Do I go as embarrassing as the time I was dared to streak across campus only to run into my biology professor when he was on his way home and I was five minutes away from my dorm and had to go all the way back completely mortified? Or do I go less embarrassing and say the time I spilt sulfuric acid all over my chemistry homework in front of the entire lab and ended up having to redo the assignment?

Looking at Grayson, I decide to go with the latter. As I'm explaining the story, I have his sole focus. His eyes don't leave me, and it has my feelings all over the place. It makes me want to crawl out of my skin and be anywhere but under his gaze, but it also has me wanting to puff out my chest with pride that the Grayson Maxwell, who could have any woman he wants, who has had any woman he wants, is only paying attention to me. Not the women in bikini's playing volleyball twenty feet to his left, or the woman sunbathing with her ass facing us five feet in front of us. His eyes are only on me. The pride is followed by disgust. Having his attention like this should not make me happy, because I know it doesn't last.

When I finish telling the story, I say, "Okay, your turn, truth or dare?"

"Dare."

I grin, having the perfect one in mind that I know will follow him for months.

I hold my hand out, palm up. "Phone please."

He grabs it, unlocking it with a questioning look before placing it in my hand. I open his texts and find the person I'm looking for.

GRAYSON

You and me, naked party tonight 6pm.

The moment I see that the message has been delivered, I delete it and hand him his phone back. He looks at it, doesn't see anything, and pockets it.

"Your turn. Truth or dare?"

I clasp my hands in front of me as I stare at him. "Dare."

"I dare you to shove as much food as you can in your mouth, let me take a pic, and post it to your Instagram."

I look down at myself and then back at him. A mouth full of food and the most ridiculous outfit plastered all over my Instagram for the world to see is not how I thought this would go.

I reach for crackers, cheese, and salami and stuff as much as I can in and hand him my locked phone. He opens the camera and takes a picture. He's grinning from ear to ear as he looks at my phone. I reach over and grab a napkin, disposing of the gross food because there is no way I was going to be able to chew and swallow that.

He hands me back my phone and watches as I post it with the caption *dares at the beach* with the wave emoji.

We play a few more rounds. As the sun starts to set and the breeze off the water turns cooler, I start to shiver a bit. Grayson notices and wraps an arm around me, pulling me in close. The smell of his cologne mixing with the heat from his body is intoxicating. If things were different and we didn't have the history we do, I'd be wrapping my arms around him and straddling his lap as I go in for a kiss.

I hate that we have this negative history. I wish everything could go back to the moment before I walked into that stupid closet and saw them together. But it can't.

I wiggle out of his hold and put some distance between us. Today has not worked out how I had envisioned. I thought my outfit would make him not want to go out, and when that didn't deter him, I figured I would suffer through the next few hours and go home and curl up with a good book. Of course, Grayson had to go and fuck it all up, because part way through I actually started enjoying myself.

I kicked myself when I was intrigued about the fact that when he was in high school he always thought he'd go to university for, what he now calls a boring job, accounting. Accounting is far off from being a doctor. I chickened out when it came to asking him what changed it all and made him chose medical school. I knew he has a younger sister, but I didn't know she's what he misses most about being home in his small town of Willow Valley.

The way he talked about his sister and their town had me wishing I could go and visit, but that's not something Grayson and I will do. This isn't a real marriage.

When the sun finally sets beyond the horizon, we pack up the basket and blanket and head to the car. We take our time driving through the city before returning home. I'm halfway down the hall to the bedroom when he reaches out and grabs my wrist.

I turn back and stare at where he holds me. Goosebumps have scattered up my arm from the touch.

"Thank you," he says, and my eyes move up to his. "Thank you for the date."

I nod and move into the bedroom, leaning against the door as I shake my head, trying to process the events of the day.

CHAPTER 8

Grayson

Before today, I never would have called myself a masochist, but spending the evening at the beach with Hannah has me rethinking that. When she came out in that ridiculous outfit, I did a double take, but it wasn't going to stop me from taking my wife on a date. Our game of truth or dare went better than I thought it would. I needed to find some way to get her to engage with me. I'm not going to lie, having her move out of my hold when she was cold hurt, but I wasn't going to push the matter. I need to show Hannah that the idea she has of me isn't the real me. At least not anymore. I know she's not going to believe anything I say, so I have to show her. That means patience, no matter how much it kills me.

I change into gym shorts and get settled on the couch. I scroll through my phone until I'm bored. When I look up, I see one of Hannah's books sitting on the coffee table. I pick it up and run a finger over the colourful tabs she has on the pages. I open it and start reading. I've never been much for reading, but these tabs have me interested.

It's a romance novel, which doesn't surprise me one bit, but this one seems dark. It starts out with a guy texting the wrong number and becoming obsessed with the woman on the other end. I make it about thirty percent in before I decide to go to sleep. I make note of the chapter so I can pick up another day.

I'm woken by the sound of crashing cupboards. I rub my eyes

groggily as light streams in through the windows of the living room. I continue to listen to Hannah very loudly moving around the kitchen when I hear her huff. I sit up, and she has her hands on her hips staring up at the top shelf where I keep my water bottles. I take her in before she places her hands flat on the counter and tries to haul herself up. She's unsuccessful. That area of counter is too small, with the stove right next to it on the right and the fridge to the left. She continues to stare, and before she can decide to find another way, I stand and make my way to her, reaching around her and grabbing a bottle down for her and placing it on the counter.

Her body is stiff as I hover behind and over her. She may be five-foot-seven, but she's still short compared to my six-foot-four frame.

I move so my lips brush against the shell of her ear and whisper, "All you had to do was ask."

Goosebumps erupt down her arm as she shutters.

"Thanks," she whispers, and I take a step back before turning and heading to the washroom.

When I come back, she's nowhere to be seen. I grab a water bottle fill it and put my runners on before locking the door behind me.

I run my usual path, and around twenty minutes into my run, I see familiar blonde hair in a high ponytail, black running shorts that hug an ass I'll never be able to forget. After our encounter in the kitchen, I don't want to scare her, so I follow behind her at a safe distance. She moves gracefully as she winds around people moving at a slower pace. She nods to people walking in the opposite direction.

Hannah has always been a little fiery on the outside, giving sass and snarky remarks, but if you just stop and watch her, you can see how it's all a facade. I know it's to protect herself, and I know a lot of that has to do with her childhood and dealing with her parents' divorce. She never told me a lot about it, just that she was seven when they first split. I know she has a much better relationship with her dad than she does her mom, but I want to know why she feels the need to pretend she's not as soft as she really is.

She slows as she approaches the same bench I ran into her at a few days ago. I slow my pace, too, stopping about fifteen feet behind her, and take a seat on the grass under a tree as she sits. I watch her as all she does is stare out over the water. I take in the view, trying to see what she does. The downtown core is directly on the other side of the water. A cruise ship sits docked at Canada Place. Water planes fly over before they land and make their way to the nearby dock. People move in groups as they walk near the water, kids laugh nearby, and the sound of the water lapping against the seawall fills the air. It smells like the ocean. I don't see what has her so enthralled.

I grew up in a small town about six hours east of here. Every day I got to experience the view of the unmarred landscape of trees and mountains. I got to listen to the sounds of the horses as they moved around the fields. I could go to my special place and be almost completely alone as I listened to the sound of running water and birds above.

I want to know what about this view has Hannah so taken with it.

After ten minutes, she gets up and starts to run towards home. I follow, giving her the same distance as before. One day, I hope she'll invite me to go on a run with her. That she'll want to spend time doing something so trivial with me.

I stop at a coffee shop a few blocks away from the apartment to allow her time to herself and grab us each a cup of coffee and something small for breakfast. When I get home, I walk to the bedroom and listen. I don't hear her and pop my head inside and the sound of the shower filters in from the en-suite. I leave her coffee and breakfast on the dresser before closing the door behind me and heading for a shower of my own.

Hannah manages to be out of the house again by the time I finish. I know she's avoiding me, and it doesn't surprise me. I call my mom and check-in. I haven't told her about getting married, because I know how much it's going to crush her that she wasn't there. My parents and younger sister have always been my biggest supporters. When shit hit the fan at the end of my senior year, they were there for every step of it.

Mom updates me on the small town gossip and about the new fire chief who's supposed to be arriving later this summer with the current one retiring. My sister is still teaching first grade and working summer shifts at the local coffee shop, and dad is keeping himself busy running his mechanic shop. He's passed off a lot of the manual labour to his staff, but he still enjoys getting under a car and getting dirty. Mom is still volunteering at the local community centre and managing a local bakery with her best friend Lyla.

Hannah walks in the door as I say, "Bye, I love you, Mom," and hang up the phone.

I watch as she pauses before placing her keys on the counter. She faces me, her hands clasped in front of her as she fidgets.

"Ummm, thank you for the coffee and breakfast this morning," she says.

I nod. She's like a frightened dog. One wrong move, and she'll be running away from me.

"How's your mom?"

I smile. Like I said, softy.

"She's good. She's busy preparing for the big Canada Day celebration. They go all out every year, and she's always been on the committee. She's asked me to go and spend a week there, arrive a few days before and help finish getting things set up."

Her eyes widen slightly. It's my turn to fidget as I shuffle from foot to foot and clear my throat.

"I'd like for you to go with me, if you're up to it."

Her hands stop fidgeting.

"I don't need to know right now. We still have a few weeks. Just let me know closer to."

She stares at me before she nods almost imperceptibly. Good, I haven't completely scared her, but from the look on her face, I can tell she needs time to process and to do that she needs to be alone.

I grab my keys and move to the door. "I'm going to head out for a bit. If you need anything, just text me."

I sneak past her and leave. I have no idea what I'm going to do, but I need to talk so I text Caleb, and he tells me he's with Charlie at her favourite park.

I drive to the park and make my way to the playground. Eight months ago, Caleb met his now fiancée, Bailey, and her daughter, Charlie, while responding to a 911 call at their place. Her five-year-old made the call when her father was hurting her mom. I don't know how those two did it, but they wore him down until he had them moved into his place and was sharing things about his life that he still hasn't told anyone else. He dotes on both those girls. Seeing how soft he's become is kind of gross, but I can't help but be happy that my best friend is happy and sharing his life with a woman he loves.

When I walk up to the playground, Caleb is pushing Charlie on the swing. She spots me and waves with a grin, and I wave back. She's become a big part of all our lives, coming to a majority of our hockey games and our group hangouts.

Caleb tips his chin and says, "Hey, man. What's up?"

"Not much."

His brows furrow. "You didn't meet me at the park for, 'not much.'"

I look down at Charlie, and she smiles up at me and asks, "Where's Hannah?"

I grip the back of my neck and give it a squeeze as I say, "Um, she's at home."

Charlie nods and jumps off the swing, making her way to the slide and running up it before sliding back down. I follow Caleb over to a nearby bench and sit.

"How is your wife?"

Wife. That both fills me with pride and has me cringing. I have no idea what the fuck I'm going to do with Hannah. She tries her best to avoid me and has no desire to work on this. She'll follow through on the agreement, but she won't do anything beyond that. She's biding her time until I sign the paperwork and she can be free of me.

"She's good."

Caleb's gaze burns into the side of my head as I lean forward, resting my arms on my legs with my head ducked. If anyone would have advice as to how to get someone to open up and accept something, it would be Caleb, but I'm not sure I can spit it all out. He remains silent, and it feels like it's sucking all the oxygen out of my lungs. I've kept this secret for so long.

I let out a heavy sigh before I lean back against the bench.

"Two years ago, I asked Hannah out. She said yes, and we went on a few dates. Things were going well. I enjoyed her company. I was ready to give up all other women and try something serious for the first time since I was eighteen. The night I was going to ask her to be my girlfriend, to give me a real shot, she walked into a storage closet in the hospital as I was being cornered by one of the other nurses,

Samantha. It's still a blur. The second I heard the handle begin to move, Samantha was on me. She had her fingers in my hair as she kissed me. It wasn't until I had pushed her off that I saw the back of Hannah's head as she left the room. I chased her down, trying to explain, but she wouldn't hear me out. I decided she was better off. I knew there were some things I couldn't offer her in a long-term relationship. Wanting to try one was selfish. Ever since, I've allowed her to hold on to this image of me as a cheater, because I needed her to realize she's better off." I run a hand through my hair as I say, "I haven't touched a single woman in two years. Not since before I took Hannah on that first date."

Caleb lets out a laugh, and my head whips to him. He laughs harder. "Man, if the roles were reversed, in fact, when I was in a very similar situation, you made a bet that I was going to marry Bailey. I'm not sure what sympathy you're looking for, but I will tell you this. You need to tell her. She needs all the information if she's going to make an informed decision about your marriage. Based on her reaction the other day to you outing your marriage, I'm assuming she's wanting out."

I nod.

"Then she needs to know she doesn't have all the information about the situation."

"There's no way she's going to believe me if I say something to her. My best bet is to show her. Believe me, Hannah is very much a believer in actions speak louder than words."

He watches me for a second before nodding. "Okay, and how do you plan to do that? How do you show her after two years that you aren't the asshole who was hooking up with a nurse in a closet while dating her?"

"I show her I care about her, that I respect her."

"That sounds easier said than done. I don't envy your position."

Charlie comes running up to us. "Daddy, can we go home? I'm hungry."

I feel a knife in my stomach as I watch Caleb reach out and run a hand over the top of her head. Soul crushing memories wash over me, but I push them aside.

"Yeah, Little Bear, we can go home. Say your goodbyes."

She waves at me. "Bye, Grayson."

Caleb pushes off the bench and turns to me. "Good luck, man."

"Thanks."

I watch as he and Charlie walk to his truck.

I need a drink after that heavy conversation, so I hit up a bar near the apartment and then walk home.

When I walk in the front door, Hannah is sitting on the couch with a tub of Ben & Jerry's ice cream while she watches *Lucifer*. She's dressed in a sexy satin pyjama shorts and tank set. She looks at me, and her brows furrow. I grab a glass and fill it with water before chugging the entire glass and repeating the process. My head is dizzy.

I stumble my way to the couch before plopping down beside Hannah. Her scent fills my lungs, and it's the best thing I've ever smelt. I wish I could bottle it up and carry it with me everywhere. My eyelids feel heavy, and as I drift to sleep, I feel a blanket draped over me just before I'm completely out.

Another late-night shift at the hospital has Hannah and I riding in together. We eat dinner together in the cafeteria, and she does her best to engage as little as possible. When our shift is over, I convince her to have breakfast with me at a diner down the street.

As we're leaving through the front entrance of the hospital, a woman in her early fifties walks straight towards us and says, "Oh, just the girl I was looking for. Hannah, honey, how are you?"

Hannah stiffens, and the most fake and painful-looking smile spreads across her face. I watch as brick by brick a wall is constructed around her. Any softness to her is completely gone in the presence of this woman.

"Mom, what are you doing here?"

That explains it. Seeing Hannah's reaction to seeing her mom has horns blaring in my mind. I know she is somehow behind the facade Hannah feels she's forced to put on to portray strength.

"I wanted to see my only daughter. I wanted to confirm you'll be at my birthday celebration on Saturday, all my friends will be there.

Agnes's son will be there, too. You should meet him, he'd be a good man to settle down with."

My instinct is to wrap my arm around Hannah's waist and drag her behind me as I growl *mine*, but I do with gripping my left hand into a tight fist as I push my right hand forward to shake hands and say, "Hi, we haven't been introduced yet, my name's Grayson Maxwell, Hannah's husband. You must be her mother, Mrs. Rivers."

Her jaw drops, and Hannah moves slightly closer to me. The small movement has my heart beating erratically in my chest.

Hannah's mom gathers herself and holds out her hand to shake mine. "Please, call me Lauren. It's nice to meet you." Her eyes dart to Hannah as she glares at her quickly before they return to mine, all softness. "I had no idea Hannah was married. My daughter never told me. I wasn't invited to the wedding."

I wrap an arm around Hannah's waist, and she leans into me. "Oh, we eloped. One of those when you know, you know things. You understand right?" She goes to open her mouth, but before she can say anything, I finish with, "My mother was just happy that I'm happy. She can't wait to meet Hannah."

Her expression completely changes. I knew hearing my mother was happy for us would make her want to put on a good face. The smile she gives me is forced. "Of course. As long as my Hannah is happy, I'm happy."

"Oh, we're extremely happy. And we wouldn't miss your birthday. We'll be there."

Hannah remains silent during the entire interaction.

Lauren gives her a look that says they'll talk about this later. "Well, I'm glad. We'll see you then."

I nod and watch as Lauren walks away. The second she's out of sight, Hannah steps out of my hold, and I want nothing more than to pull her back in and hold her forever. She fits into my side perfectly, like she was made for me.

The bricks are still in place as I watch Hannah, but it's like they're crushing her. Her arms are wrapped around her middle, and I've never seen her look so small. The last thing she needs right now is for me to take her somewhere public to eat. I grab her hand, and she doesn't resist as I lead her through a side door of the hospital that leads to the stairs down to the parkade. Hannah's mom really did a deal on her if she's letting me hold her hand and drag her along. I need to get to the bottom of what is making her feel so small.

I help her into the car and drive us home. She's silent the entire drive and as still as a statue. She doesn't fidget or lean against the door as she stares out the passenger window. She's facing forward, feet flat on the floor, hands folded in her lap. A trauma response. Anger fills me, but I know bursting will do nothing to help Hannah, so I push it down and focus on taking care of her.

When we get back to the apartment, I lead her the couch and prepare her a cup of hot camomile tea with honey and a splash of milk, her favourite. I quickly make a couple omelettes and bring her one. I watch as she slowly picks at it. I'm just happy she's eating.

When she finishes, she places her plate on the table and turns to me. "You don't have to go if you don't want to," she says.

I place my plate next to hers and position myself so I'm looking directly at her. "Of course, I'm going to go. I'm not going to make you go on your own."

She relaxes slightly, but the air still vibrates with tension.

"Are you okay?" I ask.

She nods, but her eyes don't meet mine.

I grip her chin and force her to look at me. "Hannah, are you okay?"

Her eyes are glossy, but she blinks it away. "Yeah, or at least I will be." She inhales deeply before slowly releasing it.

I let go of her chin and stand. I offer her my hand, and she takes it. I lead her into the bedroom and into the en-suite. I open the bottom drawer of the sink where I keep my bath items and start the water for her. I pull out some candles I keep in here, light them, and move to leave the washroom.

Hannah's hand reaches out and very lightly grips my wrist as she whispers, "Thank you."

Just as quickly, her hand lets go, and I leave her there to relax, my wrist still burning from her slight touch.

CHAPTER 9

Hannah

Once Grayson leaves, I lie in the bath and repeat to myself:
She doesn't define you.
You are independent.
You are strong.
Her opinion doesn't matter.

I repeat the four phrases over and over, hoping maybe this time they'll sink in. For years, I've wanted to live up to my mother's expectations, and every time I've fallen short, she's been sure to let me know. I shouldn't be surprised she showed up at the hospital to corner me and make sure I go to her birthday celebration, because, after all, it would be a bad look to not have your only daughter there. It's all about the appearances for her. What I didn't expect was for Grayson to take over the conversation and introduce himself as my husband and promise we'd be at her party.

The death glare I got from her means I'll be receiving a call from her later asking why I didn't tell my only mother I got married. It's really going to sound like, *What am I supposed to tell my friends? How is it going to look when people find out I wasn't at my only daughter's wedding? Why are you so selfish? Why must you always make me look so bad?*

I plunge myself into the water and hold my breath, hoping that it will wash away this feeling of inadequacy. It doesn't. I gasp for air as I pull myself out of the water. Heat builds behind my eyes, but I refuse to cry. Not over her. I get out of the bath and pull the plug before wrapping myself in a towel and entering the bedroom. I stare at the bed, wanting to melt into it and feel the cool sheets against my warm skin with nothing between them. I've always preferred to sleep in the nude, but ever since Vegas, I've slept in pyjamas, knowing this isn't my bed and Grayson is just down the hall in the living room.

Tonight, I decide *fuck it*. I drop my towel and climb into the bed fully naked and relish in the feel of the sheets against my skin. I melt into the bed. I'm not sure how, but I somehow manage to fall asleep quite quickly.

I'm extremely groggy when I wake up what feels like an entire day later, but in reality is only ten hours. I grab my robe and secure it around myself before making my way into the living room to grab a glass of water. Grayson is sitting on the couch with a hockey game on and a beer in hand when I enter. He watches me as I grab a glass and fill it from the sink. Despite it being a big playoff game, his eyes never leave me, watching my every move.

"I'm fine," I say as I place my glass on the counter.

He nods and says, "I was serious. I'll go with you to your mom's birthday."

I want to say no, but I know if I show up without him, I'll get more flak from my mother, so I nod and say, "Thank you."

How am I supposed to *How to Lose a Guy in 10 Days* him if he's going to continue to be this nice? He's not making this easy, and it pisses me off, but at the same time, I can't help but be grateful that he'll be there on Saturday. I move to sit on the other end of the couch, curling my legs under me as I get comfortable.

"I ordered Chinese food. I figured you'd be hungry when you woke up."

Just the mention of food has my mouth watering. "I am. Chinese sounds perfect."

He settles back in the couch, and we watch the game together. He cusses at the refs and adds his own commentary. I have no idea what half of it means, but it makes me smile. He's so into this, and it's not even his team playing. From the team initials on the screen, I can tell it's Edmonton and St. Louis, and from his yelling, I guess he's cheering for St. Louis.

I want to know why, but I don't want to ask him, so I pull out my phone and text Olivia.

HAN

Why would Grayson be cheering for St. Louis over Edmonton?

LIV

Because any true Cyclones fan hates Edmonton.

HAN

Why? They're a Canadian team.

LIV

Girl, team loyalty. We don't care if they're in the same city, province, or country. We don't cheer for them. The only exception might be against Toronto.

HAN

So I should be cheering for Edmonton. Got it.

LIV

I might need to disown you as a friend.

Not really, I love you, but anyone but them.

HAN

So Toronto.

LIV

1, that's just a step too far. That's a transgression I just can't support. 2, they didn't even make it past the first round.

HAN

But you said you'd always love me. 😔

LIV

Cheering for Toronto is just unforgiveable, that might be the only thing we couldn't make it past.

HAN

Okay. Fine. 😒

LIV

Good girl.

HAN

Don't get me started 😈

Now I know how to get under Grayson's skin. We sit and watch the rest of the first period. As intermission ends, the food is delivered and Grayson meets the driver at the front door. The puck is dropped and St. Louis gains possession, then they do what I've heard Liv call a turnover. Edmonton takes the puck and has three players making their way toward the St. Louis goal. A cross-ice pass has the puck in the back of the net, and I'm up and cheering. Grayson's head whips to me as he takes the food from the delivery driver, and I watch as his facial expression sours as he catches the replay on the screen.

He doesn't say anything. He just sets the food on the coffee table and returns to the kitchen. He comes back with a couple of plates and cutlery, and tucked under his arm are a bottle of wine and a beer. He has a wine glass positioned perfectly upside down with the stem slipped between his fingers under the plates he's holding. He holds out his hand, and I take the wine glass and plates, setting them on the table as he opens the wine for me and pours a glass before opening his beer. We make our plates and settle back. I continue to cheer for Edmonton, enjoying the sour look on Grayson's face every time I do.

The game ends 6-4 in Edmonton's favour.

"That was fun," I say and I feel Grayson's assessing gaze on me.

"Since when do you cheer for Edmonton?" he asks.

I gnaw on my lip, holding back the smile that wants to overtake my face. I really want to say since you don't, but I hold my tongue. "Oh, I just thought I'd have some national spirit and cheer for the Canadian team."

His eyes narrow, and he nods slightly. He grabs the takeout containers and shakes his head muttering to himself, "I'm married to someone who cheers for fucking Edmonton."

It takes every bit of me not to break out into uproarious laughter. Who knew cheering for a different team could get this kind of reaction?

I finish my glass of wine and wash my glass before saying, "Thank you for dinner. I'm going to read my book. Good night."

"Good night."

Lying in bed, I find the text from my mom with the details of the party on Saturday before grabbing my Kindle and opening my latest book.

Grayson and I both work the night shift the next two days. I'm not sure how we've managed to be on the same schedule so much as we didn't used to be. Both nights he manages to talk himself out of a very instant Samantha's invite to eat together during their break. Instead, he joins me, making small talk about things of literally no importance. On Saturday, we both manage very short naps before we need to get ready to head to my mom's for her birthday.

I type my mom's address into the GPS, and Grayson drives us. My mom and her husband, Richard, live in an upscale residential neighbourhood. The homes are large, and you can tell just from the look of them that the people living inside have money. Each home in this area is worth between three and six million. Richard's place is on the upper end of that spectrum. He and my mom met and married when I was just leaving home for college when she finished her serial dating phase after her second divorce. I never got to experience the wealth and fancy things she does now, and I would be happy for her if I knew she was in it for more than the money. I don't think Richard is a bad guy by any means, I just don't think my mother is capable of loving anyone other than herself.

Grayson finds street parking half a block from their house. Holding a bouquet of flowers and a bottle of wine, I watch as Grayson gets out of the car, but I can't seem to follow. I stare out the window, taking a deep breath and holding it. A party with my mother is never my idea of fun. She's so good at putting on this face to the rest of the world that shows a loving, caring, supportive person, but I know the minute she gets me alone, she'll find some way to tear me down. It used to be comments about my relationship status, or my body, or the way I presented myself, or talked. I wasn't the perfect little Barbie doll she wanted.

The passenger door is pulled open, and I turn my head to see Grayson watching me with concern.

"Are you okay?"

I can't speak, so I just nod.

He reaches for the bottle of wine, taking it from me, and uses his other hand to hold my now-free one. He squeezes it. "I'll be by your side the entire time. I've got you."

Grayson Maxwell might not be my favourite person in the world, but those words, *I've got you*, bring me comfort and give me the strength I need to get out of the car and make my way to the front door.

Grayson knocks, and I hold my breath, waiting for someone to answer. I let out the breath when Richard answers. He smiles fondly at me and opens the door wider for us to come in.

"It's so nice to see you, Hannah. I'm glad you could make it."

I smile at him. "I wouldn't miss it." Which is true, if only to avoid the wrath of my mother.

Richard's eyes dart over my shoulder, and I shuffle from foot to foot and clear my throat. "Richard, this is my husband, Grayson Maxwell. Grayson, this is my mother's husband, Richard."

Richard doesn't look shocked, so my mother must have told him.

Grayson holds his hand out and they shake. "It's nice to meet you, Mr. Rivers."

"Please call me Richard. We're family, after all."

Grayson nods, and his hand comes to the small of my back. It's a delicate touch, but it's one that lets me know he's here for me.

We follow Richard into the living room, where I see my mother entertaining her friends. She's deep in conversation, but when she spots me, she stops and her show smile spreads across her face. I hate that smile.

"Oh, my darling, you're here," she says as she wraps her arms delicately around me.

"Yes, happy birthday, Mom," I say when she releases me. I hand her the bouquet before grabbing the small, wrapped gift out of my purse and handing it to her. "For you."

Grayson hands her the bottle of wine, and her smile grows.

"Oh, how thoughtful of you. Thank you, Grayson."

The smile Grayson gives her is one I've never seen before. His eyes don't crinkle or light up the way they usually do when he smiles. He's putting on a show. "Oh, the wine isn't from me, it's from Hannah. I just carried it for her. I needed her to have a free hand so I could hold it." Oh, he's smooth.

"Well, anyway, thank you."

Of course, my mother thanks my husband for the items I brought her and not me. Why should I have thought anything else would happen?

She excuses herself to the kitchen and then returns with the flowers in a vase and places them in the centre of the coffee table. She leans over to her friend and says, "Just look at these beautiful flowers my son-in-law brought me. Aren't they gorgeous?"

I close my eyes and take a deep breath. I feel Grayson move in front of me. When I open my eyes, his fingers come under my chin and tips my head back so I look him in the eyes. He's checking in on me. His eyes slowly move over my face, taking in every centimetre of it.

I'm okay, I mouth, and after a second, he nods.

We make our way to the corner of the room where food is set up. We each make a plate before moving to mingle. I find the one friend of my mother's I actually kind of like and join her.

Melody is in her late fifties with pure silver hair. She never dyed it when she started going grey, and she looks stunning. Her hair is pulled back in an elegant bun that sits at the base of her head. Her knee-length plum dress looks amazing on her.

"Oh, Hannah, dear. How are you?" she asks as she wraps me in a hug.

"I'm good, Melody. How are you?"

She waves a hand in front of her. "I'm splendid. Your mother told me you got married recently. You have to tell me all about it."

I stiffen. I hadn't planned on saying much to anyone, just that I got married and introduce them to Grayson.

"There's not much to tell," Grayson says as he looks down at me. "It was one of those when you know, you know moments, and we just couldn't give up the opportunity." The way he says it is like he believes those words.

I give my head a slight shake before smiling back at him then looking at Melody. "We saw the opportunity and jumped head first," I say.

Melody's hand comes to her chest. "Oh, that's so lovely, dear. It was that way with my dear Patrick. We met and married in two weeks, if you can believe it. Married now nearly forty years."

My chest aches. That's the kind of love I want. The love you know in your gut is right and will last through everything life throws at you and is still there forty years down the line. I hold my smile in place, trying to push aside the ache.

Grayson's arm wraps around me and pulls me into his side. I don't resist.

"You two just look absolutely lovely together. I'm so happy you found someone who makes you happy, dear. You deserve all that life has to offer." Melody grabs my arm and squeezes before she's whisked away by another friend.

I will not cry. Even though her words hit home, I will not let anyone here see.

Grayson stays glued to my side as we move around the party talking to people. Everyone asks questions about our marriage and how it happened. My mother's friends have always been the biggest group of gossips. We keep it simple: we've known each other for years, but when our friends started dated, we couldn't help but grow closer and took advantage of the opportunity in Vegas. Only when I need to use the washroom does Grayson leave me.

As I'm leaving the washroom, my mother corners me and forces me into the kitchen, where there are no guests.

"You owe me an explanation," she hisses.

"About?"

She rolls her eyes, something she'd never let someone else see her do. "Your marriage, of course. Don't be daft."

"I married Grayson while we were in Vegas a few weeks ago."

She purses her lips. "And why did you get married in Vegas? Why couldn't you have let me throw you a wedding here? Why did you have to take that away from me?"

"Mother, it was my wedding. I didn't want a big to-do about it." If she knew me at all, she'd know that's a lie. I want the pretty white dress and the friends and family. My dad to walk me down the aisle. The bridesmaids and bouquet toss. The first dance. But of course she doesn't really know me.

She purses her lips harder, gives me a head-to-toe look, and says, "And what are you wearing? You could have put some effort into yourself today. Your hair looks flat, your eyebrows need to be plucked, your dress needs to be steamed, and could probably be a size bigger, so it wasn't so tight. You don't need to flaunt all your assets."

"Okay, that's enough." Grayson's voice cuts across the kitchen.

I turn and see him standing at the entrance to the kitchen with his arms crossed over his chest as he gives my mother the nastiest look. If I looked at her like that, I wouldn't be surprised if she slapped me across the face.

"First of all, it was my idea to get married in Vegas, not hers. She indulged me. Secondly, your daughter is stunning. She just came off working two twelve-hour night shifts and took only a short nap before she got herself ready to be here at your behest. So why don't you apologize to her, and we'll be on our way. She needs to rest after the grueling shift she worked last night."

I've never seen Lauren Rivers look as shocked and embarrassed as she does right now, and it brings me great joy. She gives me a very fake apology before Grayson grabs my hand and leads me to the entryway. We say goodbye to Richard before we make our way to the car.

Grayson unlocks it, but instead of opening the door, he starts pacing, anger radiating off him.

"Grayson," I start, but within seconds he has me trapped against the car, hands on either side of me, caging me in. His chest is heaving as he stares at me.

"Tell me not to. Tell me not to go back in there and give your mother another piece of mind. No one gets to talk to you like that. Ever."

I've never wanted to melt for a man before, but I do right now. My traitorous fucking body. I'm supposed to hate this man.

His body shakes with anger.

I reach up and cup the side of his face. "Grayson, thank you. Thank you for standing up for me." My thumb strokes his cheek. "Can you please just take me home. I'd like to stuff my face with ice cream, watch a stupid rom-com, and take a nap."

He stops shaking, and his features soften as he nods.

He reaches behind me and opens the passenger door, helping me in. I let him do the buckle for me before he rounds the car and drives off. He stops at a grocery store and says he'll be right back. When he comes out fifteen minutes later, his arms are full of bags.

At home, he drops the bags on the kitchen counter and says, "Okay, so we have five different flavours of ice cream, mint chocolate chip, cherry, cookie dough, pralines and cream, and rocky road. Three different types of chips, regular, BBQ, and Doritos. A bottle of wine and some pizza pockets and tater tots. What do you want first?"

I can't help but smile. "Pizza pockets, tater tots, and a giant glass of wine."

He grins. "Coming right up. Why don't you pick a movie and I'll be right in."

I settle on the couch, grabbing a throw blanket, and pull up *What Women Want.* We spend the rest of the day like that. At one point, my feet end up in Grayson's lap as his thumb works up the instep. He eventually moves up to my calves and works silently as the movie plays. I don't know when, but I eventually fall asleep.

CHAPTER 10

Grayson

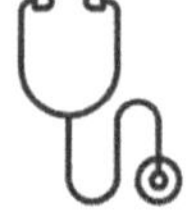

I carry Hannah to bed, tucking her in and plugging in her phone before I head back to the couch. Seeing Hannah with her mom today was a lot. I grew up with parents who loved and supported my sister and me through everything. I can't understand having a toxic parent like Lauren. Thanking me for gifts brought by Hannah pissed me off, but to pull Hannah aside and lay into her about superficial things like the way she looks pushed me over the edge. Hannah is absolutely gorgeous. I've always known she's way out of my league. I was stunned when she agreed to a date two years ago.

I knew Hannah didn't have a good relationship with her mom. I just never understood the extent. The entire time we were in that house, Hannah had that brick wall up. Her smile was fake, and she was on edge. I know it won't be easy, but I need to find a way to convince her to cut off her mom. If Lauren can't support the amazing woman that Hannah is, she doesn't deserve to be in her life.

Scrolling through my phone, I find the group chat with the number I'm looking for.

GRAYSON

You free for a drink?

ELIZA

You asking me out, Grayson? Not a good look.

GRAYSON

No, I'm not asking you out. I want to talk about Hannah.

ELIZA

Is she okay?

Did something happen?

GRAYSON

Kinda. Can you meet?

ELIZA

The Clover, twenty minutes.

I poke my head in and check on Hannah before grabbing my keys and heading to the bar. I've never met Liz one-on-one before, but I know she's Hannah's best friend and will probably have more insight into Hannah and Lauren's relationship than anyone else.

When I arrive at the bar, I see Liz sitting in a corner booth. She waves her hand slightly to get my attention, and I move through the throng of people and take a seat across from her.

"Is Hannah okay?" Liz asks.

"I had the lovely pleasure of meeting Lauren this week. We went to her birthday party today."

Liz slumps in her seat and lets out a deep breath. She leans forward on the table, concern written all over her face. "How bad?"

That tells me this happens a lot.

"I stopped it pretty quickly, but bad." I sigh. "When we first got there, it seemed fine, except she thanked me for the gifts Hannah brought. It was when Lauren pulled Hannah into the kitchen things got bad. She started by going after her for us getting married without her. Hannah told her she didn't want a big wedding, so we took advantage of being in Vegas. But then she went after her appearance. I cut her off, told her Vegas was my idea, and told her to apologize before taking Hannah home. Hannah passed out after we gorged on junk food and watched rom-coms. She was asleep when I left."

Liz bites her bottom lip and furrows her brow while she stares at me. "You didn't hear this from me, but she lied to her mom."

I raise a brow.

"Hannah is a hopeless romantic. She won't tell anyone. She saw her parents' divorce, and frankly her mother's marriages and divorce since then, and feels ashamed to still believe in soulmates and life-altering love. Her mother has done some serious damage to her. Hannah used to have this binder she would update with all the things she wanted for her wedding. It had different dresses, flowers, decorations, venues, all of it. I wouldn't be surprised if she still has it hidden somewhere."

This doesn't surprise me one bit. When Hannah said she didn't want a big wedding, it looked like it pained her to say the words, but what gets to me the most is that her own mother didn't know she was lying. The person who should know her best had no idea.

"I need your help," I say.

"With?"

"I want to convince Hannah to cut her mother off. I know it's going to be difficult and she'll probably fight it, but seeing the facade she had to put on to be around her and the pain she caused, I can't stand by and let it happen. Hannah deserves so much more than that."

She grins at me. "I was right."

"Right about what?"

"You care about her."

I grip the back of my neck. "Yeah, I do."

"How long have you loved her?"

My head whips back, and my eyes widen. That's a brazen question. "I'm not sure what you're talking about?"

She shakes her head. "Oh, cut the crap, Grayson. We both know you're in love with her. You not annulling this marriage right away and trying to protect her from her own mother, prove that. I'm also guessing that this incident she's spent the last two years being pissed at you about is a case of her not having all the information?"

I turn my head towards the bar and remain silent.

She nudges me under the table and leans as far over the table as she can without her ass leaving the bench. "Grayson, how long have you been in love with my best friend?" She nudges me again. "How long?"

I snap. Leaning forward, I say, "Since the beginning, since the first week I met her. Are you happy now?"

She grins. "Yup. Now explain the shitting on love thing then. If you've loved her for years, why have you spent the last year shitting on the love your friends have gotten to experience?"

"Because I told myself when I was eighteen I wasn't going to put myself in that situation again. I wasn't going to allow my heart to be pulled out of my chest and stomped on. There's a reason I let her spend the last two years hating me and did absolutely nothing to stop it, but now that she's my wife, that I get to legally call her mine, I'm saying fuck it and showing her that I care."

My chest is heaving from my rant. It feels good to get that off my chest, to finally have someone else know how I've felt about Hannah over the years. Caleb now knows about the incident and that I haven't touched anyone in two years. Liz knows I've loved her the entire time. It's kind of freeing to not have it all bottled up anymore.

"How do I know you're telling the truth?"

"What do you want?"

"I want to know my friend is safe with you. You broke her heart. How are you going to put it back together?"

I lean back and run a hand through my hair before dropping it to the table. "I don't know what is going to put Hannah's heart back together. All I can do is try. I'm trying to spend as much time with her as possible without smothering her and sending her running for the hills. I hate the night shift. I don't mind working it occasionally, but I have seniority over a good portion of the doctors and chose to take mainly morning and day shifts. For Hannah, I have taken every shift I can to match her schedule. To be able to drive to and from work together, to spend breaks talking to her. Her schedule has been mainly night shifts, and I've worked them. I'm going to keep showing up for her."

"You need to tell her the truth about whatever happened."

I straighten in my seat. "No. She'd never believe me anyways. She has this image of me, this view that she believes to be the absolute truth. If I say something, she's going to think I'm lying, and that's just going to make it all worse."

"You know she won't fully be able to accept your marriage until she gets the truth, right?"

I know she's right, no matter how hard that is to accept. It hurts knowing I probably won't be able to keep her, but all I can do is try.

"When I told her ninety days, I was telling her the truth. If when the ninety days are up, she wants out, I'll sign the papers no fight. I love her. I'm not going to keep her trapped in a marriage she's not happy in. I just want her to give it a shot."

"I'll help you with her mom and getting her to give your marriage a chance."

That surprises me. Isn't Liz supposed to be on Hannah's side?

"She deserves to be happy and be with someone who loves her. So if you continue to show that, I'll help you. What do you need?"

There's one thing that she might be able to help me with, so I give it a shot. "I invited her to go home with me for the week of July 1, my family is doing a big thing. I told her to take some time to think about it. I'd like her to go with me."

"Okay. I'll work at convincing her to go, but know the minute you fuck this up, I won't hesitate to fuck up your life in any way possible."

I know all four of the girls would, so I was prepared for that. "She's lucky to have such good friends."

"We're just as lucky."

I nod. "Thanks for meeting me. I'm going to head home and make sure that Hannah's still all good."

"Take care of her."

With that, I leave the bar and head home.

We get a day off before we both work the day shift. The first half of the shift is peaceful, we move through patients and everything goes smoothly. As I'm finishing my notes in a patients file, Samantha walks up to me.

"Grayson, it's been so long since we've worked together. I've been working day shifts. Haven't you missed me?"

I don't dignify her question with an answer. If I had to name someone I hate, it would be her. She cost me something that could have been great, and that's something I'll never be able to forgive.

Her eyes dart behind me before she takes a step closer and rubs her hand up and down my arm. I stiffen.

She looks at my wedding ring before getting on her tip toes and whispering, "Grayson, we could have so much fun together."

I take two large steps back until I'm out of her reach. "First of all, it's Dr. Maxwell to you. Secondly, you've spotted my wedding ring several times and completely disregarded it. Well, I don't. I won't be cheating on my wife with you, or anyone else, for that matter. So, why don't you keep things professional?"

I turn around and spot Hannah at the nurses' station doing everything she can to avoid looking at us. I walk away before I can say anything stupid, like tell everyone Hannah is my wife.

I'm sitting in the cafeteria when Hannah joins me. She doesn't say anything, just grabs the seat across from me, opens her phone, and starts eating. I know she's reading, it's what she likes to do in her down time. I don't want to push this any farther than she's willing to take it. I know it's a big deal that she chose to sit with me.

When we return to our shift, I can feel Samantha watching me, but I can feel Hannah watching me, too. I enjoy having Hannah's eyes on me. Knowing that somewhere in her subconscious she has some feeling for me that is making her watch me gives me hope that maybe I can convince her to stay after the ninety days.

Hannah

Watching Samantha cling to Grayson had me wanting to puke. It made me flash right back to the moment in the supply closet. Watching him stand up for our marriage without coming out and saying I was his wife had butterflies flying around my stomach. I wanted to smile, but I held back. His back was to me the entire time. He had no idea I was there, so he wasn't saying anything to put on a show for me. I had to reward him in some way without making a show of it, so I voluntarily joined him for our break.

I can't help but watch him for the rest of the shift. No matter what issues I have with him, I have to admit he's great with his patients. He listens to them and gets them out of here as quickly as possible. No one really enjoys being in the ER, but he makes his patients comfortable while they're here.

When our shift is over, I meet Grayson at the car and he takes us home. We go through our regular routine. I shower while he makes us something to eat. We eat together and then he showers before settling on the couch, and I move to the bedroom to read my book before falling asleep.

Home.

Routine.

Two things I never thought I'd share with Grayson Maxwell of all people.

On Saturday, I go with Grayson to his game. I know the girls will be there, and it's become a regular thing for us to all end up at their games.

I feel eyes on us the second we walk in together. We pause outside the dressing room, and Grayson says, "I'll see you after." He looks like he wants to say more but stops himself.

I nod, and he pushes into the dressing room.

The girls are on the bleachers beside the team's bench, and I join them. Charlie spots me and calls my name, and I can't help but smile at the little girl.

"Hi, girlie. How are you?" I ask.

"Good. Did Grayson tell you I said hi?"

My brows furrow. I didn't know Grayson had met up with them. "You saw Grayson?" I ask, looking at Bailey, too.

Bailey shakes her head. "Baby Girl, when did you see Grayson?"

"With Daddy at the park. Daddy pushed me on the swing, and then I played on the slide. Grayson was talking about Samantha and Daddy laughed."

I stiffen. Why was Grayson talking about Samantha? If I was falling into a comfortable spot with Grayson before, this snaps me right out of it. I was right. I can't let myself get comfortable with Grayson, because he's going to pull the same bullshit as before. He must have been putting on a show with Samantha at the hospital because it's the work place. He's probably been seeing her this entire time. How can I be sure of where he's been every time he's left the house that wasn't for a game. I know when his games are, and the girls would have said something if he hadn't shown up.

I thought we were making progress, and here it is all crumpled up in front of me like a scrap piece of paper that's been thrown in the garbage.

"Who's Samantha?" Liv asks.

"Closet girl," I say and watch their eyes widen.

"Don't jump to any conclusions," Liz says. "You don't know what exactly they were talking about. Talk to Grayson about it. It might have been completely innocent."

I roll my eyes, hard. "Grayson has always been a player. I'm not sure how being married to me is supposed to stop that. It's not like he's getting anything from me. So why wouldn't he go get it somewhere else? And why not somewhere familiar like Samantha?"

Liz looks away quickly as she runs her teeth over her bottom lip. That's unlike her. She'd usually say what's on her mind if she thought I needed to hear it, but she's holding back.

"What is it Liz?"

She looks at me for a second before saying, "I really think you should talk to him."

"Why?"

She lifts a shoulder. "Han, he's your husband."

Why is she standing up for him? She's supposed to be my best friend.

"In law only. The minute the ninety days are over, I'm done. Peace out. You know I want to be in a marriage with someone I love and who loves me. I'm not going to be my mother."

She flinches before composing herself. "I would never say you're like Lauren. You know that. I just think that you could clear a lot of this up with a conversation."

Ugh. I'm so frustrated. Why can't she just say fuck him and commiserate with me? Instead, she's got to be all reasonable. Baby Cate whines in the carrier Liv is holding her in, and I reach for her.

"Aunty Hannah needs some baby time to recover from all this," I say, and Liv helps take her out and put her in my arms.

I stand and bounce her as she stares up at me, all smiles. She is the cutest little baby. She is the perfect little mix of her mom and dad, with Josh's green eyes and lips that will for sure look like her mom's. I turn to walk with her and stop when I see Grayson walking towards us. He looks down at Cate in my arms and back to my face, and the look that crosses his face is pained. He says nothing as he passes me and steps onto the ice for the game.

Every time Grayson looks at me while I'm holding Cate, pain flashes across his face. Once I pass Cate back to Liv, the look leaves his face. He's been good with Charlie and with Cate, so why does seeing me hold her cause that reaction?

I'm in my head the entire game, trying to process everything. I wish this was all as simple as saying I'll never see Grayson again and everything will be fine, but I'm legally tied to him and even after I get our marriage annulled, he's best friends with my friends' husbands. I will never be able to just walk away and dust my hands of him.

The guys win, and when they come off the ice, Luke makes his way to me. He smiles at me, and I smile back.

"Hey, Hannah."

"Hey, Luke."

He grips the back of his neck and says, "So, about last time. I had no idea you and Grayson were even a thing, let alone married. I apologize for crossing a line."

I reach out and grip his arm and squeeze. "Luke, it's all good. I hadn't told anyone yet. Grayson was just—" I pause, not knowing how to describe what he was. I wave a hand in front of me. "It's fine. Really."

He smiles again, and his hand grabs mine that's still resting on his arm and squeezes it back.

"Luke." Grayson's voice carries over the crowd.

We both turn and look at Grayson staring at us, rage filling his expression. Even from twenty feet away, I can feel the anger radiating off him.

"Grayson, nothing is happening. He apologized. That's all."

Grayson stalks towards us, and we both drop our hands. "Luke, make another move on my wife and we're going to have some serious problems."

I give Grayson's arm a slap. "Grayson Maxwell, stop it. He was not making a move. He was merely apologizing for last time. Now stop being an asshole and go change. You reek."

Grayson stares me down before leaning close, his breath dusting over the shell of my ear. Goosebumps erupt over my neck and down my arms.

"I don't share. Keep this up, and I might need to teach you a lesson when we get home. You are mine, Spitfire. Don't forget it."

"Don't call me that," I hiss.

"What?" He grins.

"Spitfire."

"What do you want me to call you? Sweetheart? Babe? Baby? Wife? Honey? Snookums? I'm quite partial to Spitfire, but I could also go with Mine."

The way he growls the word *mine* has me holding back a shiver. It's possessive in all the right ways.

"Hannah is fine, thank you."

"Spitfire it is."

He takes a step back, and I scowl at his back until he disappears into the dressing room.

"He's right, it suits you," Liz says.

I throw my hands in the air and huff before crossing them over my chest. "Okay, what the actual fuck? You four"—I point at Olivia, Liz, Zoey, and Bailey—"are supposed to be on my side. You're supposed to be my friends. Why are you siding with him?"

Eliza, the one who's known me the longest, gives me a soft look. The look is so different from anything she's ever given me that it has me slumping and crossing my arms over my chest.

"Oh, Han, don't pout on me. I'm not picking Grayson's side. I'm telling you the truth. I'll always be on your side, no need to worry." Liz smiles.

"Same," Liv, Bailey, and Zoey say.

"Whatever," I grumble.

Liv laughs and links her arm through mine. "Okay, Spitfire. Let's get some food."

I glare at her, but she just laughs in return. I know these girls are pushing my buttons on purpose to get a rise out of me, but I also know if I need anything, I could count on them. We grab a long table like usual and order drinks and food, Liv orders for Josh, Matt, and thankfully, Grayson while Bailey orders for Caleb. It's not until the guys come up to join us that I notice how the girls strategically placed Bailey, Olivia, and I on the ends of the row, leaving empty seats at the head of the table for Josh and beside Bailey and me.

Grayson pulls out the chair beside me and the hair on my arms stands. He's radiating an energy that has my entire body on fire. Once he sits, his arm goes around the back of my chair, his finger grazes across my shoulders, and I shiver. He leans over and whispers in my ear, "I know about the text to Matt. I'm going to get you back for that."

I bite my lip as I lean forward in my seat, away from his touch. I cannot let this man affect me.

"I'm not sure what you're talking about," I whisper back.

He raises a single brow, and I know he sees right through my act. "Spitfire, you really think I don't know it was you who sent a text to my friend about naked time? I got shit for that the second I walked into the dressing room. Just remember, payback's a bitch."

We join conversation around the table as we wait for the food to be delivered. The entire time, I feel assessing eyes on Grayson and me. I know everyone wants to know what's going on. They want all the juicy details about our relationship, but there is no relationship. We cohabitate and work together. That is the extent of it.

"What are you guys doing for Canada Day?" Liz asks.

"We have the usual family neighbourhood party at my parents," Liv says.

"I'm going with," Zoey says. "The food is just to die for, can't pass on that."

Bailey looks over her shoulder at Caleb and then back to the group and shrugs. "I'm not sure."

Caleb kisses her temple, and she melts into him. I lean back in my chair and can't help the jealousy that rises in me every time I see the simple acts of affection between my friends and their partners. I'm so incredibly happy for them. I couldn't be happier that they are with people who love and worship them. But I'm starting to wonder if I'll ever find that love. Will I ever find someone who loves every part of me the way Caleb loves Bailey and Josh loves Olivia?

Grayson's eyes burn into the side of my face as he watches me. His thumb brushes the back of my arm, and I stiffen. It continues to move in soothing strokes up and down. I can't explain it, but it helps. My body loosens, and my jealousy starts to fade. It pisses me off that I react to him like this, but it's like I just can't help it.

"I'm going to spend the week at my parents," Grayson says, and everyone's eyes land on me.

Liz beams at us. "Oh, Hannah, that sounds fun. It will be a great way for you to get out of your mom's insane party. She can't fault you for visiting family, right?"

I never thought of that. Going to my mom's party alone will not be fun. Spending an entire week with Grayson in a small town with his family can't be any worse. Plus, it might be nice to get away from the city.

"I'll need to see if I can get the time off of work. Nothing's decided yet," I say.

Olivia rolls her eyes. "Hannah, when was the last time you took more than one or two days of vacation? Take the time, the other nurses can cover for you. You do it enough for them, it's time for them to pay it forward."

I chew on my lip, and Grayson says, "She's right. You're always the go-to for the nurses when they want a last-minute shift covered. They owe you."

I don't know how Grayson knows that.

"You deserve some time to relax," Bailey says.

"Honestly, anything would be better than your mom's party. I'm not sure how you've put up with those for so long," Zoey says. She went with me one year after me begging her not to make me go alone. I had just gone through a rough patch with my mom and knew not going would just make it worse. At least if I brought a friend, she couldn't lose the perfect facade she keeps up because she couldn't risk her perfect reputation. It worked, but Zoey still got to see how stuffy the party was and how everyone was there just to gossip.

I grab my drink and take a sip, not wanting to verbally agree with her because she is right. Thankfully, everyone seems to drop the conversation and move on to new things. I'm beat after this week of long shifts and am ready for bed.

Grayson waves over the server as I yawn and grabs the bill. It's not until he says, "Well guys, we should get going," and gets up that I realize he paid for both our meals.

"I could have paid for my own meal," I huff quietly as I stand.

"Spitfire, I can pay for my wife's dinner."

I shake my head and make my way around the table hugging my friends before I follow Grayson to the car.

When we enter the apartment, I head straight to the bedroom but stop when Grayson says, "A week away could be good. You could spend time outdoors, maybe ride a horse, go for a swim. It could be fun."

"If I say yes to spending a week with you at your parents', it doesn't mean anything. It just means I need a week away, and I really don't want to attend my mother's party."

He stares at me for a few seconds before he nods. "Fine. It means nothing."

"Then fine, I'll go."

After all, I'm already married to the man, how bad could a week in a small town with his family be?

CHAPTER 12

Grayson

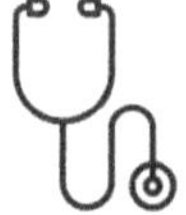

Hannah's yes has me feeling both excited to be able to spend an entire week with her out of the city with no worries about work or anything else and anxious about the phone call I know I'm going to have to make tomorrow. My mom is going to be crushed when I tell her I got married and she wasn't invited to the wedding and hasn't met my wife. She would have wanted to dote on my fiancée and make sure she got everything she wanted when it came to the wedding.

I know when her and Hannah meet, they'll get along better than pigs in shit, as my dad would say. I can't wait for them to meet. Hannah missed out on that loving mother figure I was so fortunate to grow up with. Chloe always wanted a sister, so she'll be excited to have another woman at family dinners to help her gang up on me. I'm not sure how Dad will take the news. I never thought I'd be in a position like this, worried about what they're going to say to me eloping with a woman they've never met. I go to sleep knowing I'm going to need to face the music in the morning.

In the morning, I make myself some coffee and settle back on the couch, staring at my mom's contact pulled up on my phone. Her contact picture is of the two of us at my med school graduation. She couldn't stop crying and smiling. She was so happy that I had accomplished what I set out to do.

I chug my coffee, set the cup on the coffee table, and press the call button. I listen to it ring. As usual, Mom picks up in three rings.

"Hi, Honey. How are you?" Mom's singsong soft voice carries through the phone.

"Um, I'm good, Mom. How are you?" My voice comes out scratchy, and I know she noticed.

"Honey, what's wrong?"

"Nothing," I sigh. "But, Mom, I've got to tell you and Dad something."

"Randy," Mom yells, and I pull the phone away from my face. I can hear the worry in her voice.

"Mom, everything's fine. Please don't worry."

"Honey, when you sound like this, it's something big. I'm your mother. I'm going to worry."

The shuffling of a chair comes through, and then Mom says, "Okay, your father's here. What's up?"

"I'm married." I pause, letting my words soak in for a second before I say, "I'm bringing her with me when I come for the Canada Day celebration."

My phone begins to ring with a FaceTime call from Mom. I quickly put in headphones and answer.

"You got married?" Hurt is written all over Mom's face while Dad is assessing me.

"Yeah, it happened when I was in Vegas for that convention for work."

"That was three weeks ago," Mom says, the hurt now filling her voice.

Shame washes over me as I grip the back of my neck. "Yeah, I didn't say anything because it's complicated, and the last thing I wanted to do was disappoint you."

"Do you love her?" Mom asks.

"Yeah." I nod.

My parents nod back.

"And she loves you?" Mom asks.

I open and close my mouth before I slump further into the couch and say, "No."

"How did you end up married?"

"Drinking in Vegas."

My parents exchange looks, and the pit in the bottom of my stomach only gets bigger.

"Okay, well, at least tell us about her," Dad says.

I sit up, because telling them about Hannah is something easy. "She's gorgeous and smart. She works as a nurse in the ER, she's great with her patients. She's sassy and fiery, but also fiercely loyal. She'll do anything to help out someone in need. She's much softer than she lets everyone think. She loves to run and read romance books. She enjoys camping"—my throat is so constricted I can barely get the next words out—"she's good with kids."

Mom's eyes are glassy, and a small smile pulls at her lips. "What are you going to do?"

I shake my head. "I don't know, Mom."

Hannah walks out of the bedroom and heads into the kitchen. She puts things into the blender while I change the conversation with my parents to our visit.

When the blender turns on, Mom's brows furrow and she asks, "What's that noise?"

"The blender. Hannah's making a smoothie."

"She's there?" I can feel my mother's excitement through the phone.

"Yeah."

"Oh, let me meet my daughter-in-law."

I move into the kitchen and lean against the counter beside Hannah, and when she turns the blender off, I say, "My mom would like to talk to you."

Her eyes widen, and it looks like she's afraid.

I mute my end of the call and place a hand on Hannah's arm and squeeze. "There's nothing to worry about, Spitfire. She's going to love you. She wants to meet her daughter-in-law."

She swallows and then nods, and I take my headphones out, leaving them on the counter before unmuting the call.

I hold up the phone and watch as, piece by piece, Hannah's facade goes up. By the time the phone is in front of us, her perfect smile is up. But I see it for what it is. An act.

"Hi, Mr. and Mrs. Maxwell," she says.

"Hannah, dear, we're family, please call me Melanie, and this is

Randy. We're both so pleased to meet you. I can't wait for you to come in a couple of weeks."

"Me, too," Hannah says.

"Grayson told us you're a nurse. How do you like it?"

Hannah lights up at the question. "Oh, I love it. I enjoy working with the staff and patients. Nothing I'd rather be doing."

Pride fills her voice as she talks about her job, and it makes me happy to know she's doing something she enjoys.

"Well, we'll let you go back to your day. It was so nice to meet you, Hannah. I can't wait to see you in a couple weeks. Welcome to the family," Mom says before hanging up.

Hannah whips around and faces me, crossing her arms over her chest. Feisty Hannah is out to play, and I'm here for it. I smirk, and it only causes her checks to turn red. She's adorable when she's irritated with me.

"What exactly did you tell them about us?"

"The truth."

She huffs. "Your version of the truth and my version are probably very different. So, I'd like words. What did you tell them?"

"I told them we got married in Vegas during the convention and that you're coming with me to visit in a couple weeks."

She narrows her eyes as if she's trying to send laser beams my way in a hope of reducing me to ash. I hold back my laugh.

"Really, that's all?"

"Yes, Spitfire, that's all."

She shakes her head and drops her arms. "Then why was your mom so nice to me if she knows it was just a drunken mistake?"

"Because she loves and supports me. I think she was more hurt that she didn't get to see me get married."

Hannah looks up, and I see that she's on the verge of tears. I reach forward to wipe any tears that might fall, but she takes a step back out of my reach.

"I'm fine." She sighs. "I'm going to go to Olivia's. I'll have my phone if you need anything."

She turns and leaves, closing the door behind her. The conversation with my mother seems to have shaken her, but I'm not sure why Mom accepting her and our marriage would bother her. Hannah's always been a woman of few words when it comes to her emotions. I wish she would open up and tell me what's going on. Why that conversation affected her the way it did. Is it because her mother has always been so hard on her? Is it that she doesn't want my mother to accept her? Hearing Mom welcome her to the family really had it sinking in that I'm married to Hannah Smith. Hannah Smith is my wife.

When it was just our friends who knew, it was easier to let the reality of it not sink in. Her mother was so far removed from us that it didn't really impact my view of our relationship either. Hearing my parents refer to her as family made it all so much more real.

I need a plan. I need her to feel comfortable during this visit to my family. If this trip goes badly, I know nothing can salvage this; no amount of begging or trying will get her to agree to stay after the ninety days.

Giving her some space is the best thing I can do right now. Smothering her and not allowing her to process would drive her away. She built up this facade, and she's not going to allow anyone to break through it. I'm going to have to go step-by-step, slowly pulling away each layer that she built around herself, if I want this to work.

I settle back on the couch and grab her book, opening it where I left off. This man is obsessed with the female main character. Before I know it, I've finish the book. I leave it on the coffee table and see another one she's left on the side table. This one has no bookmark. I read the back, and it seems like it's not as dark as the one I was just reading. Opening it to the first page, I start. As I read, I notice a commonality between the main male characters in both books. They're obsessed with their women. I can relate. That feeling of wanting to be close to them, wanting to reach out and touch them, to spend your every waking hour with them. I feel that with Hannah. She may not know it, but I'm obsessed with her. If she told me to drop to my knees and crawl to her, I would. I would do whatever she asked me to.

A key turns in the lock on the door, and I quickly close the book, place it on the table, and grab my phone. When Hannah walks in, she glances at me before dropping her keys on the counter and heading into her room. Her room. In a matter of three weeks, I have managed to end up married to someone who hates me and lost my bedroom, and now I'm sleeping on my couch. I'm having the worst night's sleep I've ever had, but to have Hannah that close is worth it.

Eventually, Hannah comes out in her pyjamas, grabs a glass of water, and settles on the other end of the couch. She delicately tucks her legs underneath her and positions herself before grabbing a blanket and draping it across her legs. Even as warm as it is, she always has a blanket. This girl would rather open every single window in the apartment and cover herself with a blanket than relax without one.

I pass the remote, and she smiles softly. I don't think she realizes she does it. Usually, when she notices, she quickly changes her facial expression to a neutral one. This soft, acknowledging smile makes me giddy. Not a word I think I've ever used to describe how I'm feeling.

She puts on a reality TV show, and I sit and watch it with her. I enjoy her every reaction to the events on the screen. At one point she stretches out, her feet coming out from underneath the blanket. When she's not looking, I position her feet on my lap and start working my thumbs into the soles. She bites her lip. Her eyes dart to me every once in a while, but neither of us say a word. I continue to work my thumbs into her feet, and she slowly melts further into the couch, slipping towards me. I eventually move up her calf, massaging the muscles and watching her face react.

As I watch her, I realize how close I am. It wouldn't take much for me to lean over and kiss her. To brush my lips over the delicate skin of her neck. To hear her breath hitch as mine dances over the shell of her ear.

I remember our first kiss. I've been no saint. I've kissed many women in my time, but the kiss with Hannah was something entirely different. I never felt so centred.

Ever since the day I met her, Hannah has pulled me into her orbit. After senior year, I was going through the motions. I had a plan. Go to medical school, get a degree, start working in a hospital. I did that. I was floating, just allowing the world to take me where it wanted to take me. When I met Hannah, she sucked me in. I enjoyed talking to her, bantering. I hadn't done that in a long time. Then after our first date, she let me kiss her.

The second our lips touched, she became my anchor.

I wasn't floating anymore. I was attached to her. I know how weird that sounds, that after such a short period of time and a single kiss I had such strong feelings for her. But it was the energy she put out. I recognized it. I recognized the facade, because I was putting on the same one. This illusion that everything's all right, that you're a happy-go-lucky person, when in reality it's all very different.

The only other person who understands how I feel is Rebecca, but after everything, I don't think I can go back and talk to her. I can't be the catalyst of another breakdown. I can't watch her go through all of that again. My parents were always supportive. They were there for me through all of it, but they didn't experience it the way that I did. The way Rebecca did. As much as I love my parents, they're not the people I can turn to for this. I can't turn to Hannah either.

Anyone who watches me sees someone playful who cracks jokes and gives his friends shit. Between the hospital, my friends, and hockey, I'm always surrounded by people, but a couple years ago, it really hit me that I'm lonely. Once I stopped using random women to fill my time to distract me, it was like a sucker punch to the gut. The first time I attempted to flirt with someone after the incident with Hannah, it made my stomach turn. I tried to push past it. I knew Hannah wouldn't give me the time of day again, so I figured why not go back to my life before when I distracted myself from the pain and loneliness. I never got past a chaste kiss with a woman. The fact that my last sober kiss wasn't with Hannah kills me. If I was someone else, I might turn to alcohol, but after seeing the way it affects people and their families, it's not something I could do.

Hannah eventually falls asleep, and I slowly move myself from under her and carry her to the room. Seeing her curled up in my bed pulls at my heart. I want to see her like this every day for the rest of my life. She looks so peaceful, in a way she's never looked while awake. I tuck a stray piece of hair behind her ear and barely stop myself from kissing her forehead.

I quietly leave the room and make my way back to the couch, settling under a blanket with her book before I finally pass out.

CHAPTER 13

Hannah

I spend the next two weeks anxious out of my mind. I told Mom I wouldn't be at her July 1 party because I was going with Grayson to his parents, and she wasn't happy at first. Then I asked how I should explain to her friends that I didn't go with my husband to visit his family because she was having a party. She relented after that. All the girls have said is, *Oh, it will be good for you. You need to get away from the city and your mom. Give him a chance. You never know, he might surprise you. At the very least, you can get some embarrassing stories from his childhood.* The last one from Zoey did make me feel a little better.

Nothing has made the anxiety go away, though. I'm going to drive six hours east to a town I've never visited to meet the parents of the husband I don't want. How could this turn out positively? I've never really been out of the city. I have no idea what to pack, or what I'm supposed to do while we're there. My understanding is that his parents still work. Does that mean just the two of us in his parents' house by ourselves, with very little to do? At least being here, I can leave and go hang out with the girls. There, I'll know no one.

I throw myself onto the bed beside my open suitcase. Why did I agree to this? Because my mom is crazy and I want to avoid her party and being cornered about how I've embarrassed her by not letting her be at my wedding and make a big to-do of it.

Thanks, Mom.

"Looks productive," comes Grayson's voice from the doorway.

I peek my head up and over the side of my suitcase and glare. "I'm going to a town I know nothing about. I have no idea what to pack."

He grins at me. That fucking grin drives me crazy. It simultaneously irritates me and makes me want to take off my panties. That grin is what pulled me in the first time. I drop back onto the bed, not wanting to look at it any more. I listen to his footsteps draw closer until his shadow is looming over me.

"What do you want to know?" he asks.

"Well, what am I supposed to wear? What are we going to do while there?" I throw my hands up. "I don't know, everything and nothing," I groan.

"Bring a variety. You'll want some shorts, some pants, nights get cold. Maybe a dress or two. I'm sure Mom will want to take you out with my sister. If you have some boots, I'd bring those. It can get dusty and dirty. Bathing suit for the lake. As for what we'll do, that's up to you, but I'd bring some books for the downtime."

That's surprisingly helpful. I pop my head up, and he's still standing at my feet. He reaches a hand out, and I take it as he helps pull me up. When I'm on my feet, he holds my hand for a few seconds longer than necessary. His eyes are glued to the connection, and mine lock onto the same place. When he removes his hand, I don't like the sense of disappointment that washes through me.

He takes a step back and grips the back of his neck. "I'm going to finish packing. I'd like to leave at 6 a.m. tomorrow. I don't want to get stuck in any traffic."

I nod and watch him walk out of the room. I step into the closet and grab the clothes I think I'll need, filling my suitcase before grabbing some books and putting those in. I'll wait until the morning to put my bathroom items in. I zip the bag and drag it off the bed then climb under the covers.

I was in a reading slump and asked the girls for some recommendations. I should have read the blurb for this one before I started, because of course my friends sent me a small town, enemies-to-lovers, but the book is too good to DNF. I settle in, determined to finish it and move on to something completely different for the drive tomorrow.

When I first started working as a nurse, I worked the morning shifts, which has made it easy for me to get going in the mornings, even at 5 a.m. I do my full morning getting ready routine before loading my toiletries into my suitcase. I stand in the doorway, going through my mental list to make sure I have everything, when something dusts over my hand that's holding the handle of my suitcase. Grayson offers me a sleepy smile, grabs the bag from me, and rolls it down the hall. Deciding that if I've forgotten anything I'll just purchase it when we get there, I join him in the kitchen. He passes me a cup of coffee and a protein bar.

"It's nothing fancy. I figured we could stop in a couple hours for something better."

I nod and take the items. Taking a sip of the coffee, I have to hold back my moan. How does this man do it? My coffee is made perfectly. Cream, sugar, and a hint of vanilla. I wish Grayson would stop doing these nice things for me. Between bringing me coffee and breakfast when he comes back from a run, carrying me to bed when I fall asleep on the couch, and standing up for me to my mom, he's chipping away at the view I've held of him for so long. I can't forget about the past, but maybe I can move on from it and be civil. I guess time will tell.

We load the car, and Grayson gets us on the highway heading east. He lets me hook my phone up to the car stereo, and I look out the window as we drive. After two hours, Grayson pulls into a parking lot outside a local diner in the last major town before we're driving through the mountains. He holds the front door open for me, and we make our way to a booth in the corner. It's pretty quiet inside, which doesn't surprise me; it's 8 a.m. on a Wednesday morning. I browse the menu and order while the pretty brunette waitress eye-fucks Grayson. He orders a plate of pancakes with eggs and bacon and hands the menu to her, giving her no attention outside of placing his order.

"So, tell me about Willow Valley," I say.

He plays with the coffee cup between his hands as he talks. "It's your stereotypical small town. Everyone knows everyone's business, but they'd give you the shirt off their back if you needed it. They rally around people in need."

I nod and stir my coffee. "What do people do?"

"It's summer, so you'll find the kids around the lake, horseback riding, or at the local ice cream shop. There aren't any major stores. It's all mom-and-pop shops run by the locals, but you can get pretty much everything you need. For the stuff you can't find, it's about an hour's drive to the closest city with a Walmart. There's one school for all the kids, but it's been updated and expanded over the years." He taps his fingers against the table and releases a deep breath. "As soon as we arrive in town, everyone will know, so don't be surprised if someone approaches you and knows your name. The town doesn't get a lot of tourists, and the tourists that do come are typically regulars that come every year."

I nod. The idea of a small town, getting away from the fakeness of the city, appealed to me for a bit in high school Everyone in the city is trying to be someone they're not, pretending that they have more than they do. It wasn't until I met Liz my junior year and then Zoe and Olivia our first year of university that I decided to stay after graduating. They showed me not everyone is fake. My friend group may be small, with the three of them and now Bailey, but I have no problems with that. I want those ride-or-die friends I know will be there with me for anything and everything. I've always said, I'd rather have a few friends I trust with my life than a large group of friends I can't rely on.

"Is there anything I should know for when we get there? Anything I should avoid?" I ask.

His head moves side to side slightly as he thinks. "No. I'd say that everyone will be accepting and be excited to meet you. It's been a while since I've gone home for more than a day or two. I talk to my parents and sister regularly, but going home for extended periods of time isn't easy."

Something in his eyes tells me he means more than just getting time off work and the travel. Something at home haunts him.

"And what am I supposed to tell your parents about us being married?"

He adjusts himself in his seat. "You can tell them what you want.

They're under no illusion that you love me. They know we got married during a drunk night in Vegas."

That surprises me. Grayson has been so set on staying married, I thought he'd want his parents to have a perfect view of our marriage. I would never tell my mom Grayson and I aren't permanent, let alone that it happened due to a drunken mistake while on a work trip. I would never live it down.

"Okay," I say, and he stares at me for a second before nodding.

We eat our breakfast in relative silence before he pays the bill and we're back on the road. Watching the city fade away and the openness of the land untouched by humans is relaxing. By 10:30 a.m., the car is already warm from the sun pouring in. I turn up the AC and crack the window just enough that the wind catches my hair. The air out here feels cleaner. Fresher.

As we wind a corner on the highway, I gasp when a black bear stands on the side of the road with her cubs. Grayson slows as I crane my head to continue watching them. I've never seen a bear in person. It's amazing. When we've continued far enough that the bear is out of sight, I turn to Grayson.

"That bear was just chilling on the side of the road with her cubs," I exclaim.

He smiles and chuckles softly. "Yeah, you see that quite often this far out."

The biggest animal I've seen in the wild is a rare deer in Stanley Park. That bear was huge. She just watched the cars pass by, not a care in the world. The further we drive, the drier the landscape becomes. The grass turns from vibrant green to a dull green-and-yellow colour. We're on the cusp of forest fire season, so I should be prepared to see it, but for some reason, seeing it in person hits differently. I don't know how people living out here do it. I couldn't imagine spending every summer worried a fire might come through town and take my home.

Seeing the *Welcome to Willow Valley* sign has my stomach tightening. There's no going back now. I'm going to spend the next week with my husband's family in a town I've never been to.

CHAPTER 14

Grayson

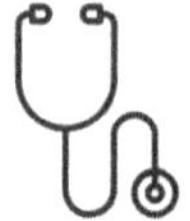

Entering Willow Valley always brings with it an array of emotions. I'm looking forward to seeing my parents and Chloe, but every time I'm home, I'm faced with those memories of the past. Those memories I hope to never relive again.

My grip on the steering wheel tightens while I watch Hannah's leg shake. Neither of us are fully ready for our arrival, but we're here now.

My parent's place is just on the outskirts of town. They live in a ranch-style home my dad inherited from his parents. The house is situated on around fifty acres of land. My grandparents used to have cows that grazed part of the land, but when my parents took over the land after my grandparents passed, they decided it wasn't something they saw themselves doing. My parents have kept up with the extensive garden my grandmother had, though. My dad occasionally makes wine from the grapes that grow on the property. When I visit, my sister and I still go out and pick blueberries off the bushes for pancakes. There is so much out in the garden, I'm not sure how they keep up with it all.

I turn left down the road that leads to the only two houses on my parent's street, and my stomach starts to turn. In a matter of minutes, I'll be introducing my parents to my wife. Hannah's leg starts to shake quicker. The trees that surround both sides of the road abruptly end, and the road forks into two driveways. I turn down the one on the left and follow it until the space opens up and I see both my parents' cars and my sister's. She knew I was arriving today, so I'm not surprised she's home.

Hannah stares out the windshield when I put the car into park.

I reach over and place a hand on her still shaking leg and say, "They'll love you, don't worry."

She half-heartedly rolls her eyes at me and says, "Of course, they will. I'm me. I'm just stressing about the fact that when you inevitably piss me off, I have nowhere to run. I'm stuck six hours from home with you in a town I don't know."

I can see the force behind the smile she gives me. I remove my hand from her leg and leave the car. I grab our bags from the back and meet her at the gate that leads to the house. She reaches for her bag, but I wave her off and I reach through the fence to unlock the gate.

The second the hinges creak, I hear my parents' golden retriever Micky bark. Hannah and I shuffle in quickly as Micky barrels towards me. I drop to knees as he reaches me and licks my face furiously. After a minute, he moves on to Hannah, sniffing around her feet and up her legs.

She looks at me hesitantly, and I say, "He's friendly."

She nods and reaches down, scratching him behind the ears. His tongue lolls out as his eyes close. Yeah, boy, I know. Having Hannah's hands on you is something else.

When Hannah stops, I grab our bags again and walk to the mudroom door. My parents rarely use the front door. You know if someone is knocking there, they aren't family or a close friend. I push open the door, because my parents never lock it, and Hannah and Micky follow me in. Micky runs through the kitchen, probably to go lie in his usual spot in the sunroom.

I toe off my shoes and leave our bags before walking into the kitchen, where I see my dad and sister sitting at the table. Chloe has a book, and Dad has today's paper. Mom is standing in front of the gas stove wearing her signature apron Chloe and I made her for Mother's Day when I was eight. It has our hand prints, and we wrote *Best Mom Ever* on it.

Chloe spots me first and puts down her book before she's running at me. I catch her and spin her around. Chloe and I did not get along one bit growing up. We fought constantly, and we never wanted to spend time together. But as we got older, we started getting along better, and now she's probably one of my best friends.

"I missed you, big brother," she says as I put her down.

I kiss her cheek and say, "Missed you, too, Chlo."

She peaks around me, and her face lights up. "You must be the infamous Hannah Mom's told me about."

Hannah waves and says, "That would be me. Not sure what I'm famous for, though."

Chloe laughs and links arms with Hannah. "We're going to have a great week. I can't wait to show you around and take you to all the best places."

"Oh, Chlo, give the girl some time. She's only just got here," Mom says before she wraps her arms around me. "It's so nice to have you home, Honey." She squeezes me.

"It's nice to be home, Mom."

She pulls back, her hands remaining on my shoulders as her eyes travel my entire body and back up to my face. When she seems satisfied that I'm alright, she pats the side of my face before moving in front of Hannah. "Oh, look at you. You're more gorgeous in person." Mom pulls Hannah in, and I watch as she stands there, stiff as a board. She's not used to physical affection from her own mother based on their interaction that I did see, so I'm not surprised by Hannah's reaction.

"Thank you, Melanie," Hannah finally croaks out.

I walk over to Dad, and we shake hands as he says, "Good to have you home, son."

"Good to be home."

"Well, lunch is almost ready. Why don't you guys take a seat and Chloe and I will finish getting the table set."

Hannah nods and eyes the table, unsure of where to sit. I pull out a chair for her, and she offers me a soft smile as she takes a seat. I sit between her and Dad and watch as my mother and sister bustle around the kitchen.

This kitchen holds so many memories for me. Saturday breakfasts, dying Easter eggs, my graduation party, the night I thought I might pass out as Rebecca and I sat at this very table and told them the news. I give my head a shake as Chloe places a plate in front of me. I glance at her, and she mouths, *Are you okay?* I give her a reassuring smile, and she finishes setting the table as Mom brings over the food.

Mom places a big bowl of cold pasta salad and a plate of barbeque chicken in the centre of the table. I haven't had Mom's pasta salad in forever, and my mouth waters at the sight of it. Once everyone is seated, we dig in.

"So what are your plans today?" Chloe asks.

"I thought after Hannah gets settled I might show her around the property. I'd rather not venture into town today, it was a long drive and I'd like to relax."

"Tomorrow, Incahoots is having a big thing. We should go. It will be nice for you to get out and see some people from high school," Chloe says.

Hannah furrows her brows and asks, "What's Incahoots?"

"It's a local bar and just about the only place in town to do anything after 10 p.m.," I say, and she nods.

"What are they doing?" Hannah asks, seeming genuinely interested.

"Half off beer and nachos, and they have a live band coming in."

"Sounds fun," Hannah says.

"Yeah, Grayson, sounds fun. You guys should come."

The last place I want to be is a bar with all the people I went to high school with, drinking and with a complete lack of filter. When I told Hannah everyone knows everything about everyone, I wasn't lying. The people in this town are the only ones who know about everything that went down my senior year, and I'd like to keep it that way.

"Yeah, we'll see how tomorrow plays out," I say, and that seems to satisfy my sister enough that the conversation can move on.

"I thought we could grill up some steaks for dinner tonight, maybe some baked potatoes the way you like, and some corn on the cob. How's that sound, Grayson?" Mom asks.

"Sounds good."

"Hannah, you'll have to tell me some of your favourite foods so I can whip them up this week."

Hannah wipes her mouth with her napkin and says, "Oh, it's

fine, Melanie. I'm good to eat anything, and please tell me how I can help out."

Mom waves her off. "You're all good, honey, don't worry about it. But please get me that list. I need to know you feel welcome here. We're family, after all."

Hannah is quiet for the rest of lunch. Chloe offers to help Mom with cleanup and dishes while Dad goes back to work and I get Hannah settled.

"Your old room is all ready for you two," Mom says as I wheel the suitcases through the kitchen.

At the base of the stares, I pick up the bags and lug them up. I don't have much time before Hannah realizes we're sharing a room for the next week. Which also means there is likely only one bed.

Opening the door to my old bedroom and turning the light on, I try to look at the room from Hannah's perspective. I have old hockey posters up and a Vancouver Cyclone's flag hanging over my bed. The sheets are black and match the comforter. My old desk still sits against one wall beside the closet. The room is fairly empty of things. I didn't leave much behind when I moved out between donating things and what I took with me.

When I turn around, Hannah is standing in the doorway looking around the room, and when her eyes land on me, she bites her lip. Fuck. I wish I was the one biting her lip. I want to hear her moan for me as I pull it between my teeth.

Her eyes bounce between me and the bed, and I can see the thoughts racing behind her eyes.

"I can sleep on the floor," I say.

She closes her eyes and takes a deep breath. "I can be an adult if you can. We can share the bed, put up a wall between the two sides."

I look over to the bed. Sharing a bed with Hannah and not being able to pull her into me and hold her is going to be pure torture, but it will be better than sleeping on the floor. After weeks of sleeping on the couch, it will be nice to sleep in an actual bed again.

I nod and roll the bags up against a wall. "I'm just going to use the washroom and then we can go for that tour if you're up for it."

"Sounds good," she says, and I make my way into the hallway.

When I return to the bedroom, I find Hannah sitting on the edge of the bed, evaluating the room.

"You ready?" I ask.

She nods and stands before following me downstairs.

I call out, "Taking Hannah on a tour," as we slip back into our shoes and leave the house.

"You always been into hockey?" Hannah asks as we walk towards the garden.

Micky follows us, sniffing around and doing his own thing.

"Yeah. My dad got me into it at a young age. It hooked me, and I never let it go. I played through high school, and when I got to university, I played on an intramural team."

She nods. When we near the large planters full of strawberries, Hannah sucks in a shocked breath behind me. I turn and see her staring at the garden, jaw dropped and eyes wide. I chuckle. Growing up with all of this was normal for me. I forget Hannah grew up in the city, meaning she didn't get to see large amounts of fruits and vegetables growing so close to home.

I walk over to the closest bush and pull the biggest ripe strawberry I can find and walk over to her. She watches me hesitantly as I lift it to her mouth. She licks her lips before she opens and takes a bite of the strawberry. The moan she releases as she pulls away goes straight to my cock. Her tongue trails across her lips, picking up the stray strawberry juice. I hold back a groan of my own.

I bite into the remaining strawberry, allowing my teeth to slowly sink into it before pulling away the stem and throwing it into the dirt below the bush. Hannah's eyes are locked on my lips, and I follow her lead, licking them slowly just as she did. She holds her breath as she watches. I lick the remaining strawberry juice of my fingers, and she shakes her head and turns to face the garden again.

I follow behind her as she examines the plants. She picks at the blueberries and raspberries as we pass them and stops to look at the lettuce, cucumber, and peas. When we've made our way through the garden, I take her towards the pond. It's just past the strip of trees that separates the garden from the pasture the cows used to graze. It's a perfect place in the summer. During the peak of the day, part of the pond is covered in shade when you want to escape the heat while the other is in direct line of the sun. You can spend the whole day out here if you wanted to.

The minute she spots the water, Hannah is running to the edge and toeing off her shoes before stepping into the water. I sit in the grass, Micky lying beside me as I watch Hannah stand in the water, head tipped back enjoying the fresh air. Out here, it's just the sound of your thoughts, the flow of the stream not far from here, and the birds in the trees.

When Hannah turns and looks at me, it's with a smile spread wide across her face and no stress or worry in her expression. It's in that moment I vow to do everything in my power to make sure she spends as much of her life feeling like she does right now.

CHAPTER 15

Hannah

The tour around the property with Grayson was actually relaxing. I never realized how much being in the city stressed me out. The constant noise of cars and people and the claustrophobic feeling of being on sidewalks and buildings packed with people. You can't do anything in the city without being surrounded by noise.

On the walk back to the house, Grayson asks, "So, what do you think?"

"It's gorgeous. It must have been so nice to grow up out here. All the fresh air and space to just be free." I sigh.

This is somewhere I'd love to bring my future kids. Somewhere they can run around and I wouldn't need to be constantly worried about them running into the middle of the road and getting hit by a car. Thinking about kids is a stab in the gut. I'm so far off from it that I have no idea why I'm thinking about it.

"Yeah, it was nice, for the most part. Having everyone know everything about your life, not so much, but we knew that we were safe, and we had more freedom than I'd expect city kids had growing up."

"You and your sister seem close," I say.

He smiles broadly. "Yeah. Growing up, we fought like cats and dogs. Mom was always yelling at us, trying to get us to play nice and get along. It wasn't until I was in high school that we started to get along better. Now, I'd say she's probably my best friend. We text and call regularly."

"I wish I had a sibling," I say softly. I feel Grayson's eyes on me. "Growing up as an only child was lonely. I had no one to hang out with, and it was even worse when my parents split. Spending opposite weeks with each parent meant that it was harder to make friends with the kids in my neighbourhood, because I wasn't around all the time."

Grayson is silent for a minute before he says, "I'm sorry you had to experience that, Hannah. I could never imagine what it's like to grow up with split parents and no one else who understands that feeling."

I nod, grateful for his words, but also needing to move on from the topic. "I'm sure it's nice to be home and spend time with her in person. She hasn't visited you in the city, has she?"

He grips the back of neck. "It is nice to be home. I'm glad I get to spend time with her while I'm here. She hasn't been able to come visit. It's a decent drive and big time commitment. I try to come for a couple of days at least every summer."

Walking up to the house, I see Melanie and Chloe sitting on the back deck and Randy standing in front of the barbeque. We walk into the kitchen, and I wash my hands before moving to the side so Grayson can wash his. I pass him the hand towel to dry his hands and can feel his eyes taking in every inch of me. It has me on edge, feeling like my skin might catch flame under his gaze. Luckily, his sister comes in to grab a bowl of salad, drawing Grayson's attention.

"Come on, you two. Dinner's just about done then Dad's gonna start a bonfire. I bought all the fixin's for s'mores."

I follow Chloe outside and feel Grayson's eyes on me the entire time. I'm eventually going to need to do something about this building tension, because it's got me wound up and I need release. Being stuck here with his parents and sharing a room with Grayson for a week is going to make finding that release very difficult.

After a minute, Grayson joins us at the table, Micky settling under the table at our feet. I enjoy watching how Grayson and Chloe poke fun at each other and how much he truly enjoys being back with his family. They all embrace me as part of the group, asking questions about my work and family.

They don't pry much when I give them the bare minimum on my mom, but I tell them about my dad and some of my favourite memories growing up with him. Some of the hockey games he took me to when I was really young. I remember enjoying it despite knowing nothing about hockey. Getting to spend that time with my dad was everything to me. We did dinner before, and I got to stay up late.

When dinner is over, I change into pants and a hoodie as Grayson warns me about the attack of the mosquitos that happens when it gets late. We create a circle of chairs around the large fire pit they have dug in the backyard. I watch as Grayson helps his dad place logs and light it. His every movement is like second nature to him. It's like watching him on the ice. I'd never tell him this, but out there, he looks so strong and capable. If I hadn't spent the last few years hating the guy, I'd say it's panty melting. I hate to admit to myself that over the last few weeks, he's been wearing me down, and seeing him do these things is having an effect on me.

When the fire is lit and going strong, he grabs a seat beside me. I watch Chloe and Grayson prep their marshmallows and hold them over the fire. I bite my lip, focusing on their technique. Grayson looks over at me and raises a brow.

"You not making one, Spitfire?"

I shake my head. I don't really want to admit that I've never roasted a marshmallow or made a s'more before.

"Come on, you've got to. It's Maxwell tradition, the first night Grayson's home we make 'em," Chloe says.

I adjust myself in my seat. "I'm good."

Grayson sits further back in his chair and leans over the arm to be closer to me. He drops his voice so only I can hear him. "Spitfire, what's up?" I shake my head, but he pushes. "Hannah."

"I've never made one before."

I expect Grayson to laugh or say some quick-witted remark, but he doesn't. I turn and face him, and he's grinning at me. It's all warm and inviting, and it has me wanting to see it more. Ugh. What is this man doing to me? I've gone from hating his guts to wanting to be close to him, to being reminded of why I hated him, and back to wanting to be near him and see him smile at me. This is so draining, emotionally and mentally.

"Spitfire, it's all good." Grayson's words pull me out of my thoughts. "I can show you, and we can have you all s'mored up in no time."

He quickly pulls his marshmallow off his stick and plops it in his mouth before loading it with a fresh one. He passes me the stick and says, "Okay, so you want to hold it over the coals. You want to avoid the flames 'cause it will catch the marshmallow on fire and burn the outside and leave the inside pretty raw. Just rotate it slowly until it's the colour you want it."

I follow his instructions, his hand coming to my wrist every once and a while to get me to spin the stick. His light touch has goosebumps scattering up my arms. I peak over at him, and his attention is focused on the marshmallow, making sure it doesn't burn. I take in his features while I can. He looks genuinely relaxed here.

After a few minutes, I pull it out and it's this beautiful, golden brown around the entire outside. Grayson grabs some graham crackers and lays two pieces of chocolate on one. He places the cracker with chocolate under the marshmallow and the other cracker at the base. He drags it off slowly, and I watch as strings of marshmallow are left behind. He sandwiches it and passes it to me. I take a bite and feel how the heat of the marshmallow has melted the chocolate. It's so freaking sweet, but it's so good. I can't help the moan that leaves me as I take the second bite.

Grayson clears his throat. "Good, right?"

I nod as I finish the last bite. He chuckles and loads another marshmallow and makes himself one. After a while, his parents say their good nights and head inside, leaving just the three of us. Chloe grins before she grabs her blanket and follows her parents as she calls, "Good night. Remember, old house means thin walls."

Grayson shakes his head as he says good night. Despite the heat from the fire, the air is still cold enough that a shiver runs through me when a small breeze comes through. Grayson notices and holds his blanket up and pats his lap. I don't move.

He reaches over and delicately runs his hand over my arm, causing me to shiver again, but this time it's not from the cold.

"Come on, Spitfire. You're cold, don't punish yourself by staying over there."

The breeze comes through again, this time a little stronger. I push up from my chair and position myself on his lap. He brings the blanket over my legs as he wraps an arm around my waist and pulls me in close. I don't know why I crawled into his lap so easily when I could have just gone inside, but something about him today has been pulling me in, making me want to be close to him. I allow myself to relax into him and absorb his body heat.

He runs his hand up and down my thigh, warming me. He smells like smoke from the bonfire, and it does something to me. I pull my hair over my shoulder as I squirm in his lap, and he groans. The sound has me squirming even more. I need release.

His grip on my waist tightens, and he drops his head to my shoulder, running his nose over my over sensitive skin. I bite my lip, holding back my own groan. I shuffle a bit, and his fingers dig into my skin through the fabric of my sweatshirt as he whispers, "Spitfire, you've got to stop that."

I look down and bat my lashes at him. "And why is that?"

His eyes are molten lava as he holds my gaze. "You know exactly what you're doing to me. But if you need me to spell it out for you, you and your sexy-as-sin ass squirming on me has me hard as a fucking rock. As much as I'm trying to respect your boundaries, unless you want me pulling down those leggings and fucking you right here, you need to stop."

My breathing is quick and erratic. That sounds so fucking good. I shift a little more and feel his erection under my thigh and holy fuck, he's big. The thought of him fucking me right here has my panties soaked, but I don't give in. For the next thirty minutes, I remain as still as possible.

When we decide to go inside, Grayson grabs the hose and tells me he'll be inside in a few minutes. I hurry inside, grabbing my pyjamas and a towel before heading into the washroom and turning on the shower. As soon as the water is a decent temperature, I step under it.

My hand trails down my body. I tweak both my nipples before my hand trails further south. I run a finger through my folds and find just how wet I am from earlier. I pump my fingers inside myself a few times before I find my clit. I bite my lip to stop the moan that wants to tear through my entire being. I'm so built up and so on edge, it's not long before I'm coming, and the name I stop myself from calling out when the orgasm tears through me is Grayson's.

I finish my shower and change. When I open the bathroom door, I come face to face with a shirtless Grayson leaning against the wall outside the washroom. I take him in, his broad shoulders and the cut of his abs and how they move as he pushes off the wall. Man, is my husband sexy.

Grayson chuckles. He leans down and whispers in my ear, "Like what you see?"

I'm frozen in place, because fuck yeah I do, but also I'm so not going to admit it to him. "It's okay," I croak, and he laughs.

"If you say so."

"I do," I say more firmly.

He steps back enough to let me pass, and I head into the bedroom. I climb under the covers on my side and settle in. Grayson eventually comes in, leaving the light off, and finds his way to the other side of the bed. The bed dips as he climbs in, and I immediately feel his body heat. He's like a freaking furnace.

I toss and turn, trying to find a comfortable position, all while trying to forget that I'm sharing a bed with Grayson Maxwell. After fifteen minutes of me constantly moving, Grayson's arm wraps around my middle and he pulls me into him. I freeze.

"What are you doing?" I ask.

"Helping you sleep. Now just close your eyes, you're keeping me up."

He doesn't let go, and after a couple minutes, I find myself relaxing into his hold. I fall asleep to Grayson's light snores behind me.

In the morning, I wake up to an empty bed and go downstairs to find everyone in the kitchen. Grayson is helping his mom make pancakes while Randy and Chloe are talking at the table. They all greet me as I join them. Grayson passes the spatula to his mom and pours a cup of coffee, adding cream and sugar and few pumps of a syrup before passing it to me.

I say, "Thank you," and hold the liquid gold in my hands as I settle at the table and take a sip. He somehow makes it exactly the way I like it every time.

He moves around the kitchen with ease. He and his mom work together in perfect sync, like they do this every day. I wonder if he gets all of his cooking skills from her. Every meal he's made me has been amazing.

They place the eggs, pancakes, and bacon on the table and join us. Everyone digs in, and Chloe spends the entire time trying to convince Grayson to go to the local bar tonight.

"If Grayson doesn't want to join you tonight, I will," I tell her, and her face lights up.

"Oh, Hannah, this will be great!" she exclaims.

"I'll go," Grayson says beside me, and I peak over at him. He's watching me with an intensity that has me wanting to squirm in my seat.

"Sounds like a plan, we should leave after dinner, the band starts at 10 p.m., but we'll probably want to get in early and snag a table before it gets crazy."

Grayson nods, and we finish breakfast. The entire time I feel Grayson looking over at me every once and a while. Being so close to him for the last twenty-four hours has me on edge. I need some space. Some distance to clear my head and get back in my right mind and remember why I wanted this marriage to end.

After we clean the kitchen, I run upstairs and throw some things in a bag and grab a blanket and towel before heading downstairs. I tell Grayson I'm going for a walk and I'll be back for lunch. He nods, and I make my way outside.

I walk through the garden, retracing our steps from yesterday until I find the pond. I lay my blanket out in the sun, slip off my shoes, and lie down on my stomach as I settle in with my book, feeling the warm sun on my back. No matter how much I want to, I can't seem to get into my book. My mind keeps wandering to last night and sitting in Grayson's lap. To the feeling of his breath dusting over the shell of my ear as he whispered how hard he was because of me. The feeling of him wrapped around me last night.

No matter what I do, I can't seem to escape the immense physical attraction I have for Grayson. Spending time with him over the last few weeks has only made it worse, because now I think my emotions might be getting involved. I've tried to push it all away, but it won't go away.

Yesterday, Grayson told me no one comes out here, it's all private property and it was always more his spot growing up than anyone else's, so I figure I'll have some privacy. I've never gotten myself off anywhere other than my bed or the shower, and I thought it might be fun to try something new, so I packed a little something in my bag.

I reach into my bag and pull out my vibrator as I roll onto my back. I slip off my panties and tuck them into my bag. I pinch my nipples through the fabric of my dress and lace bra. Images of Grayson dance through my mind. Grayson last year at the beach during our group camp as he came out of the ocean, water dripping down his body. Drops tracing each of his abs. I lick my lips.

Closing my eyes, I remember the feeling of his hard cock under my leg as I sat on his lap last night. His whispered words of fucking me right there beside the fire have me so fucking wet. I position the vibrator and turn it on. I barely contain the whimper that tries to escape me.

I think of Grayson as he hits a player into the boards during a game. The way I feel when his eyes trace every inch of me. I'm so fucking close.

Grayson doing push-ups in the living room. I moan. The memory that sends me over the edge into oblivion calling his name is his words from the day after our wedding, *Hannah, you never look like shit. You look beautiful.*

"Fucking hell."

The sound of Grayson's words have me snapping back to reality. I remove the vibrator and pop my head up to see Grayson standing at the edge of the tree line watching me.

CHAPTER 16

Grayson

Hannah's been gone a while when I decide that, instead of having her come back for lunch, I'll pack a picnic so we can enjoy the outdoors. I make some sandwiches and throw in some cheese, crackers, and cookies before picking some fruit from the garden and making my way through the property. Based on how much Hannah seemed to enjoy the pond yesterday, my guess is that's where she ended up.

I'm almost to the edge of the trees when I hear moaning and what sounds like it might be my name. I continue moving towards the sound and the pond. When I clear the trees, I spot Hannah lying on her back under the sun. She moans again, and her legs move, and I see a glimpse of what I can only assume is a vibrator as she squirms on the blanket. She moans again before her back arches and she calls my name as I watch an orgasm tear through her.

"Fucking hell," I say and immediately know Hannah heard me.

She reaches between her legs and removes the vibrator as her head lifts and she sees me.

I move across the space separating us, and when I'm standing in front of her, her chest is flushed pink as it rises and falls at a quick pace. She watches me as I kneel beside her. She doesn't shy away, and it's such a fucking turn on.

"Want some help?" I ask.

She looks over my shoulder quickly and bites her lip, thinking about the question. Her nod is subtle, but it's there. Does this mean she's finally going to let me touch her? Am I finally going to get my hands on Hannah fucking Smith, the gorgeous woman who's hated me for years?

"Can I touch you?"

She nods and says, "Yes."

I don't hesitate. I reach a hand out and touch her thigh. Her skin is soft as my fingers lightly trail up her leg. She bites her lip again, and it's the sexiest fucking thing. I lean down, allowing my breath to dust over the shell of her ear for a few seconds before I whisper, "It's just us. Don't hide your noises. I want to hear how every little touch makes you feel. Be loud, Spitfire."

My fingers finally reach the apex of her thighs, and I feel the heat radiating off her. My finger dips between her folds. She's fucking soaked. It makes me feral knowing the reaction that I cause in her, knowing that she's this wet from thinking about me. I circle her clit, and she moans.

"Good girl, tell me how you feel."

Her head falls back, and her mouth drops open. I apply more pressure, and she arches her back as another moan leaves her. She's so fucking responsive. I love it. My fingers dip lower. Finding her entrance, I tease her with one finger before slipping in a second. She rides my hand, bucking her hips with my movements. She reaches out and grabs the front of my shirt as she bites her lip so hard I fear she might draw blood.

The heel of my hand finds her clit, and she moans. "I'm close, so close."

"Good girl. Tell me what you need."

"More, I need more," she mewls.

"My needy girl. You want more?"

Her eyes meet mine, and she nods. I pull my fingers out and add a third, her back arches and she moans my name. I kiss her neck and nip it before licking the spot. She arches her head, giving me more access. I pull her earlobe between my teeth, and she clenches around my fingers. She's close.

"Yes, Grayson," she calls as I pick up speed.

Her head thrashes side to side, and she clenches tighter around my fingers.

"Come for me, Spitfire. Soak my fingers the way I know you want to soak my cock."

That does it. She comes, her back arching off the blanket as she grasps my shirt tighter and calls my name. I remove my fingers, and when she comes down from her high, she looks at me and I stick my fingers in my mouth, licking off every last drop of her orgasm. She's the sweetest fucking thing I've ever tasted. I moan loudly as I clean my fingers. After a few seconds, shock fills her face as she registers what we just did.

She pushes up, sitting straight on the blanket before looking back at me. She doesn't say anything as she makes her way to the pond, stepping into the cool water. I sit on the blanket and watch her, allowing her to process everything. When she comes back, she sits beside me and slides her panties back on under her dress.

I grab the picnic basket I brought and start unpacking it. She silently accepts the bottle of water I hand her. We quietly eat, enjoying the sound of the surrounding nature. I know we need to talk about this. I can't let her just fixate on this and ignore it. I know this probably means something completely different to her than it did for me, but for me, it was finally being able to touch the woman I have lusted over—loved—for the last two years.

"So, we should probably talk," I say.

She looks my way but doesn't say anything, choosing to look back at the pond. We watch as a duck flies by before landing on the surface of the water. She stares at it more intently than necessary. She's avoiding this.

"Hannah," I say.

She looks back at me and says, "What's there to say? I got caught up in the moment, that's it."

Her words stab me in the gut. I mask my face, hoping I don't show how they affect me. "Okay, if that's how you feel."

"Grayson, what more can it be? In less than sixty days, we'll be divorced. It was a moment of weakness. I needed release, and you were offering assistance."

I nod, not sure what else to say. We finish our lunch in silence, and I pack up the basket.

"I'll let you relax until dinner. It should be done at 6 p.m.," I say before I walk back to the house, leaving her there.

I'm a broody bastard when I get back, and I know it. Hannah has been messing with my fucking head for years. I thought we were finally getting somewhere, but I guess I couldn't have been more wrong. She used me for an orgasm and ignored me afterwards like it was nothing. Everyone has looked at me like some fuck boy for years, thinking I only used woman for sex and tossed them to the curb when I was done with them. And yes, I did only have sex with some woman, but I made sure they were fully aware of the situation going into it. But with Hannah, I should have known we were both looking at this situation very differently.

To her, I'm the man who broke her heart years ago and she can never forgive.

To me, she's the only woman I've truly wanted since I was eighteen years old. The only woman I've ever truly loved.

Chloe notices my mood when I enter the kitchen and start unloading the picnic basket.

"Didn't go well, did it?" she asks.

I don't say anything. What am I supposed to tell my sister?

Oh, by the way, I'm in love with my wife, but she hates my guts and I brought her lunch and she let me finger-fuck her until she called my name and came all over my hand, but then she told me that's all it was and she still plans on divorcing me.

Yeah, not happening.

"Grayson?" she pushes.

"Don't want to talk about it, Chlo," I say.

"I'm your sister, you can tell me."

"Chlo, not now," I grit.

My sister and I may get along better now, but she still knows how to push my every button and she proves it right now.

"Grayson, what's going on with your wife? There's no way you married some random woman in Vegas, drunk or not. So what's going on?"

I turn around, throwing my arms to the side. "She's not some random woman. She's the woman I told myself two years ago I wasn't allowed to have, because I know I can't give her everything.

She's going to want things I'm not sure I can give her, not after Rebecca."

Chloe's eyes soften as she looks at me. "Maybe you should talk to Rebecca while you're here. Maybe it will help you cope. This is not how you deal with all your emotions. I'm not sure you ever fully moved on, Grayson. If you want your marriage with Hannah to work, I think it's time you face the past."

I know she's right. The only way I can move past it all is to revisit it, but I'm not sure I'm strong enough to do it yet. Chloe knows not to push it any further. She squeezes my arm as she passes me and heads outside. I finish dealing with the picnic basket and head upstairs for a much needed shower to get out of my head.

Hannah barely says a word to me when she gets back. She showers and joins us for dinner. I feel her eyes on me at some points, and I want to reach out and put my hand on her thigh and give it a squeeze, show her I'm here and I'm not freaking out about what happened at the pond, but I don't.

When we finish eating, Chloe drags Hannah upstairs to get ready for the bar. I help Mom with cleanup and I know she's itching to ask me questions. This is the first time we've been alone since we arrived.

Mom is drying a plate as she says, "Hannah seems like a lovely girl."

I keep my head down, paying attention to the dishes I'm washing. "She is."

"I can see why you love her."

I freeze and look over my shoulder to make sure no one else is around. The last thing I need right now is Hannah to hear that. She's already set on running away. Hearing those words is just going to freak her out.

"Oh, Honey, she's not here. Maybe she needs to hear that she's loved. I have a feeling that girl hasn't heard those words enough in her life."

Mom's hit the nail right on the head with that. I wonder if Lauren has ever said those words to Hannah. But I'm not sure hearing them from me will do anything. Knowing Hannah, she'll probably think I'm saying them as a way to manipulate or hurt her.

When we finish with the dishes, I head upstairs and change so we can head to the bar. When I come out of the room, my jaw drops at the sight of Hannah. She's dressed in denim shorts that just cover her ass, a white tank top, what looks like one of my old flannel shirts unbuttoned, and a pair of Chloe's cowboy boots. The image of her in nothing but those boots on my bed with them wrapped around my ears has me half hard.

Chloe gives me a smug look. "You like?"

I clear my throat. "Yeah. You look great, Hannah."

I swear I see her blush.

"Thanks."

Chloe links her arm with Hannah's. "You don't look half bad, brother. Why don't we head out? We don't want to miss any of the fun."

I follow behind Chloe and Hannah, adjusting myself in my jeans as we go. I open the doors to the car for the girls, and we make our way into town. I haven't been to Incahoots since the summer I turned nineteen. It's usually packed in the evening, especially when they have live music.

I find parking right out front, and we head inside. The sound of country music hits my ears the second I open the front door. When my eyes adjust to the darker atmosphere, I take in the space. Not much has changed. There's a bar spanning the left wall, a few shelves of liquor behind it. On the right wall, there's a hallway that leads to the back office and kitchen. A stage sits against the back wall, with a dance floor in front and tables spread across the rest of the open space.

Chloe drags Hannah to a table in the corner with a few girls already sitting around it. I recognize one of them as Chloe's best friend Brinley. When we get to the table, Chloe introduces everyone.

"Girls, this is my brother, Grayson, and his wife, Hannah. These are my friends Brinley, Aspen, Lennon."

Hannah settles at the table and is talking with the girls like they've been best friends for years. Brinley asks something, and Hannah holds out her left hand, and I watch as the girls fawn over her ring. It makes my chest swell with pride that I'm the one who gave it to her. The fact that she wears them all the time even though she didn't want this marriage further inflates my ego.

I'm not even sure why I'm here, other than I knew I couldn't let Hannah come to this bar with a bunch of guys who haven't seen a pretty new girl in God knows how long.

I excuse myself from the table and head to the bar to order a beer for myself and Chloe, and a margarita for Hannah. As I wait for the drinks, a hand claps me on the shoulder.

"Well, lookie here. The Grayson Maxwell, back in Willow Creek. What are you doing here man?"

I turn and come face-to-face with Colby Miller. He hasn't changed much since we were in high school. His blond hair is still slightly disheveled, and he's wearing his patented smirk that got him a lot of action back in the day. Last I heard, he'd married his high school sweetheart, Felicity, and they were expecting a baby.

"Hey, man." I shake his hand. "I'm just in town to spend the week with the family. How's life?"

His smirk drops for a second before it returns. "Life's life."

The bartender places my drinks on the bar, and I grab them before saying, "It was good to see ya, man. I should get back to the ladies. I'll see you around."

He nods, and I head back to the table, dropping Chloe and Hannah's drinks off in front of them before taking my seat. I barely pay attention to the conversation around me. I notice Hannah make her way through her drink quite quickly, and when Shania Twain's "Man! I Feel Like A Woman!" comes blaring through the speakers, she's out of her chair and dragging my sister with her. I watch as they laugh and dance to the music.

I flag down a server and order Chloe and Hannah each another drink and a Coke for myself. The two of them are having a blast.

When the drinks are dropped off at the table, they come over and grab them, Chloe stopping to kiss my cheek and say, "Great big brother," before going back out with the girls.

When the music cuts out and the band takes the stage, I see the excitement written all over Hannah's face. They start playing Brooks and Dunn "Boot Scootin' Boogie", and Chloe teaches her the dance moves. Hannah stumbles over herself a bit in the beginning, but she picks it up, and a smile lights up her face as she moves across the dance floor. They transition to "The Girls Gone Wild" by Travis Tritt, and Chloe moves smoothly into the tush push. Hannah watches her and eventually picks it up. She really gets into it, her hips moving with every beat.

The music changes, and people couple off and begin to two-step. Hunter Davis steps up and takes Hannah's hand, pulling her in, and begins to dance with her. She smiles, but it's not her flirtatious smile. It's the same one she gives Liv and the girls. I sit back, not wanting to cause a scene, no matter how much I hate his hands on her. When he leans in closer to whisper in her ear, I've had enough. I don't care if I make a scene. I don't care if the entire town hears about it before breakfast. I want Hunter Davis's hands off my wife.

Making my way through the crowd, I stop when I'm right behind Hannah. "Davis, I highly recommend you let go of my wife."

Davis grins at me. "No way Grayson Maxwell is married to this gorgeous woman."

Hannah's cheeks pinken before she says, "He is," and holds up her left hand, the light hitting her rings perfectly.

He looks shocked, to say the least.

"Again, Davis, I recommend removing your hands from my wife."

"It's just a dance, man. Calm down."

I'm not in the mood for this. I wrap an arm around Hannah's waist and pull her into me. She giggles when her back hits my chest. Davis goes to protest, but I grab Hannah's hand and spin her before falling into the dance moves with her. She grins as she follows my every move. When the music ends, I drag her off the dance floor, down the hallway, and into the back office. I try the handle and am not surprised the door isn't locked.

I lead her inside, close the door, and spin around, pinning her between me and the door.

"What did I say about sharing, Spitfire?"

Her eyes widen as her pupils dilate. She's turned on, and it only turns me on, too. She fists my shirt as she says, "That you don't share."

I nod. "What else did I say?"

She swallows, and I watch the movement in her throat. "That I'm yours." Her voice comes out breathy.

Hearing her acknowledge that has me needing to take her right here and now. I need to claim her. I need her to know that no other man is going to touch her.

Leaning forward, I drag my nose lightly up her neck and watch goosebumps erupt across her skin. I gently kiss behind her ear before tugging on her earlobe with my teeth. "I think I might need to fuck you so that message gets into your pretty little head."

She nods.

"You like the sound of that? Like the thought of my cock stretching your pussy as I fuck you so hard you won't walk straight for a week."

Her head rolls back as a moaned, "God, yes," escapes her.

That sounds like the best fucking thing in the world, only I'm now remembering I don't have a fucking condom on me. I drop my head into the crook of her neck. "I don't have a condom."

"I'm clear," she whispers.

"I need a condom," I whisper back, and she nods. "So help me God, if you tell me you have one I may need to spank you until your ass is bright red."

She bites her lip as she shakes her head. "I don't have one."

She presses her thighs together and squirms. I drop to my knees in front of her. "This will have to do for now." I reach forward for the waistband of her shorts and make eye contact with her. When she nods, I undo the button and slowly pull her shorts and panties down her legs, exposing her pussy. I help her spread her legs, and her eyes remain on me the entire time.

"You wet for me, Spitfire?"

She nods.

"Such a good girl, wet and ready for your husband."

I lean forward and tease her with my tongue. Her hand comes to her mouth, and she bites down on it, holding back her moan. I bring a finger to her entrance and tease her some more. Her free hand comes to my hair, and she grabs a fist full. I grin at her before I begin feasting on her like a man starved. I taste every inch of her. She bucks against my face, chasing her release.

My finger slowly enters her, crooking to find that sensitive spot inside. The feral moan that tears out of her tells me I've found it. I don't relent. I keep going until she's clenching around my finger and calling my name as she comes.

I help her back into her panties and shorts, leaning down and whispering in her ear, "I want you to spend the rest of the night knowing that it was me who just made you come like that. That I'm the only man who makes you come like that."

She nods, and when she's righted herself, I lead her back into the bar. The look on my sister's face tells me she knows something just happened with Hannah and me back there. We go to the dance floor, and I don't leave Hannah's side until we're ready to head home.

When I climb into bed, I pull Hannah into me just like I did last night. I make a mental note that tomorrow I need to make a run to the store and grab some condoms, because I'm not missing a chance to fuck my wife like I did tonight.

CHAPTER 17

Hannah

In the morning, I wake up with Grayson wrapped around me. I pretend to be asleep, enjoying the feeling of his hard chest pressed to my back. I can smell hints of the cologne he wore last night. Last night. Memories of him pulling me away from that Davis guy and dancing with me before he took me into the back office flood my mind. I thought hearing Grayson claim me and act as possessive as he did would be a turnoff, but I was completely wrong. His words alone had me wet, add in his close proximity, and I was a goner. I've never had a man eat my pussy like it was his greatest accomplishment the way Grayson did.

His refusal to have sex with me without a condom does stick out. I've never gone without, but I've only ever had men beg to go without, never one insist the way he did. I understand the precaution, but now I'm left wondering if it's a me thing or a him thing. Was it because I had been drinking and he wanted to make sure I knew what I was agreeing to?

His lips dust over my shoulder, and I squirm in his arms remembering the way his lips felt against my skin in the field yesterday. His erection presses into my ass, and his grip on me tightens.

"Spitfire," he grits. His morning voice does things to me, making me squirm more. "I don't have a condom, and the more you do that, the more I want to fuck you."

I twist my head to look at him over my shoulder and say, "Then fuck me."

He stares at me, and his grip around me relaxes. He rolls on to his back and stares at the ceiling. I've apparently gone and stepped in it. How have we gone from me wanting nothing to do with Grayson to me lying here sad because he won't fuck me?

"I'm sorry," I say and move to slide out of bed.

He reaches out and grabs my wrist, halting my movements. He sits up and runs his hands down his face.

"You have nothing to apologize for, Hannah. I just won't go without one. I trust you're clear if you say you are. I am, too, just so you know. And please know, I want nothing more than to fuck you right now. I've been thinking about it for a while. This is just a boundary I'm not prepared to cross right now."

I reach out and squeeze his arm. "I respect that. I won't say anything more about it."

I climb out of bed and grab a change of clothes on my way to the washroom. Grayson swaps spots with me when I come out, and I head downstairs to the kitchen to grab a cup of coffee. I'm surprised to find the kitchen empty today. I pour myself a cup from the coffeepot and make my way onto the back porch with Micky following me and settle in a chair as I look out across the property. I close my eyes and enjoy the quiet. Sitting here, I can hear my own thoughts. There's no one else around talking up a storm with friends, or the sound of traffic as people honk their horns.

The sliding glass door opens, and Grayson steps out with a cup of coffee and passes me my phone.

"It was blowing up, figured it was the girls wanting to check in and make sure you're safe."

I smile, saying thank you as I take my phone and scroll through my messages.

DAD

Hey Han. Hope you're doing well. Would love to catch up some time this week. Give me a call when you get a chance. Love you.

LIV

Update please. I need to know that you haven't
killed Grayson yet.

ZO

Please don't kill him. I don't think I have enough to
bail you out if you do.

LIZ

Any sign of life would be great.

LIV

Han you good? You've been there for a day.

BAILEY

Maybe she's too busy sleeping with him to
respond.

ZO

Get it girl. You deserve it.

LIV

Please tell me that's the case. You could use some
good orgasms.

HAN

I'm alive and no I haven't been fucking Grayson.

LIV

Awwwww.

ZO

I'm disappointed.

BAILEY

Anyone else notice she didn't say anything about
the good orgasms?

LIZ

I did in fact notice that. Han, I believe you're
holding out on us.

I gnaw on my lip. Of course, they noticed my lack of denial about orgasms. But if I tell them things with Grayson have taken a kind of turn, they're going assume that means this marriage is going to work out. I still plan on signing the papers after the ninety days, but why not get some mutually beneficial orgasms out of it in the meantime?

LIV

Your lack of response is answer enough. You're
getting some.

ZO

Oh, it must be good.

HAN

Fine. Yes, something happened. It does not mean
that anythings changed though.

LIZ

Sure, you keep telling yourself that.

HAN

I mean it. Two orgasms does not a relationship
make.

ZO

Two. We talking all at once or separate occasions
because that makes a difference.

BAILEY

Details. You wanted all the details about Caleb. I
expect the same.

HAN

When we get home we can have a girls' night.

I lock my phone and slip it into the pocket of my shorts.

"I have to head to the grocery store before they close and grab a
few things. Did you want to go with me? We can watch the parade
afterwards if you want. It starts at 11 a.m., and then there's different
community activities we can check out," Grayson says.

"Sure, sounds fun." It does. While we're here, I want to experience all the small town things I've never been able to. We finish our
coffee before heading to the car.

It only takes a few minutes until we reach the town's downtown
area. I'm not sure you can really use the word downtown to describe
it, though. It's small and looks like it's only a few streets with almost
everything situated on Main Street. Grayson parks outside the
grocery store, and we head inside. While he grabs his items, I grab
some snacks and meet him at the checkout. When we've finished, we
leave everything in the back of the car and Grayson grabs a couple of

collapsable lawn chairs. We walk a few blocks up the road, and I see people starting to gather on the side of the road. People are sitting in lawn chairs, kids are bouncing up and down, some of them holding water guns. Grayson selects an empty spot and takes the chairs out. As we settle in them, a woman in her late forties approaches us.

"Oh, Grayson, I heard you were in town making a fuss with your wife. This must be her." She reaches a hand out to me, and I shake it. "I'm Trixie," she says.

"Hannah." I smile at her.

She pats the top of my hand with her free one before releasing it. "Well, it's so nice to meet the woman who locked down our boy Grayson. We weren't sure what was going to happen after everything him and Rebecca went through, but we knew he's a strong boy."

I give her a fake smile and say, "It's nice to meet you, too."

Who the hell is Rebecca, and what the hell happened between them?

"Well, I just thought I'd come say hi. I'll let you two enjoy the parade."

As she walks away, I watch Grayson shift uncomfortably in his chair. I can tell right now is not the time to have this conversation, so I push it to the side to ask him later once we're back at the house.

When the parade starts, the excitement from everyone is palpable. Kids run into the street, grabbing pieces of candy, and when the fire trucks make their way past, the kids spray the firefighters with their water guns. I can't help the smile that spreads across my face. When the parade ends, we pack the chairs back into their bags. Grayson throws them over his shoulder as we make our way off Main Street and down one that has tents set up with tables underneath showcasing different items. It's a little market set up down a few blocks. Grayson lets me drag him from stand to stand as I check out everything.

I find a gorgeous pair of earrings and a matching necklace that were handmade by a local woman. I also get a print of black bears drinking from a nearby river. Halfway down the market, Grayson's hand slips into mine and I intertwine my fingers with his. We stop at a booth that has a bunch of silly things to take pictures with. I grab the pair of maple leaf glasses that have the word *CANADA* printed above them and wrap a red-and-white boa around Grayson's neck.

He pulls me into his side, and we take a few selfies. I make faces at the camera, and he follows suit. I giggle as he sticks out his tongue and bugs out his eyes. He pokes his fingers into my side, tickling me and causing me to squeal as I squirm and fight to get away from him. I finally escape his grip, and he holds his hands up and makes a tickle motion with his fingers and I giggle as I take another step back. I find a few photos I like and post them to my Instagram.

Enjoying small town life on Canada Day!

We take the items off and continue making our way through the booths. We're at the second to last booth where I'm looking at a beautiful amber necklace when a woman asks, "Grayson?"

Grayson becomes very still next to me, his grip on my hand tightening. We turn and come face-to-face with a beautiful brunette woman. She's about an inch shorter than I am and has a few more curves. She looks hesitant as her eyes bounce between Grayson and me. Her eyes finally stop on me, and she reaches a hand out as she introduces herself as Rebecca.

Is this the Rebecca Trixie was talking about earlier?

"It's nice to see you, Grayson, how have you been?"

Grayson gives my hand a quick squeeze before he says, "Good."

She smiles. It's a soft genuine smile that causes the corner of her eyes to crinkle.

"I'm glad." Her eyes come back to me. "I heard you got married. It was talk of the town last night after what happened with Davis in the bar."

He grips the back of his neck. "Yeah, it's quite new. We got married about six weeks ago."

"That's great." She shuffles from foot to foot before she asks, "Have you visited the site yet?"

Grayson shakes his head. "No. I'll go before we go home."

She nods, and I feel so completely lost. What is their connection, and what site is she wanting Grayson to visit?

A little brunette boy, followed by a tall man who looks like his father, comes waddling up to us as he calls, "Mama! Mama!"

Rebecca spins and crouches, picking the boy up. "Hi, baby," she coos.

The energy radiating off of Grayson right now has me knowing I need to get him out of this situation. I don't know what he's feeling, but he's not well.

"Well, it's been nice meeting you. We should probably get going. We have some things to prep before tonight," I say, and that snaps Grayson out of his fog.

He says goodbye, and we make our way back towards the car. We make the walk in complete silence. When we get inside, he leans his head back against the headrest and closes his eyes as he takes deep breaths. I've never seen Grayson respond to any situation with such a visceral reaction. I give him his space to process, because I know sitting here in the car in the middle of town is not the place to try to have a conversation with him about what just happened.

After a minute, he starts the car and begins the drive back to his parents' place.

When we get there, he helps upload the bags into the kitchen before turning to me and saying, "I just need a few minutes. I'll be back," and walking out the back door.

CHAPTER 18

Grayson

Once I'm out the sliding glass door, Micky's quick on my heels as I make my way across the backyard to the tree line. When I'm past the first few trees, I drop to knees, the weight of everything bringing me to the ground. My lungs are tight, and it's hard to take in air. I grasp at my chest as a sob leaves me. I haven't cried in years, but I can't help it. Being home and seeing Rebecca, especially seeing her with her husband and son, it's too much. Everything I've bottled up for years is being pulled out of me at once, and it's almost more painful than the initial pain I felt over ten years ago.

There's a reason I never stick around town for very long when I come to visit my parents, because the longer I'm here, the higher my chances of running into Rebecca are. She's a reminder of my failures that I've tried my best to never revisit. After a few minutes, my sobs subside and I settle on the ground and lean against a tree. Micky nudges my hand and lies at my side, his head resting on my thigh. I have no idea how I'm going to last the rest of the week here. I can't devolve into this mess every time I see her. But this is a small town; there's no way I can avoid her.

Knowing I need to return to the house, I push off the ground and clean off my pants before I make my way out of the trees. When I step into the backyard, I see Hannah and Chloe sitting on the back deck laughing while playing cards with drinks. Dad is prepping the barbeque, and Mom walks out of the house with a plate of food and joins the girls. Micky runs and joins them, begging for food as soon as he's at their feet. As much as I wish I could enjoy this, Hannah here with me and my family, for the rest of my life, seeing Rebecca reminded me I don't have that luxury. Maybe when we get back to the city, I should just sign those papers like Hannah wants and we should go our separate ways. It will be better for her. She'll be able to find a man who can be everything she needs him to be and not the broken failure I am. Hopefully, it will allow her to find the sense of peace she had at the pond the other day.

I join Dad, and he asks me to grab the burgers from inside. I find them on the kitchen counter and reach for them as I hear the sliding glass door open behind me.

"You good?" Hannah asks.

"Yeah, all good."

Her hand reaches out and grabs my arm. It's a comforting gesture she's never done to me before, and it has me wanting to breakdown and tell her everything, but she doesn't need my burdens on top of her own.

"Grayson, you can tell me. Are you sure you're all good?"

I turn and plaster on my practiced fake smile. "Yeah, all good, Han."

Her brows pinch, but she drops her hand, and I take the burgers out to Dad. She comes back a minute later with a refreshed drink for herself and hands me a beer. I accept it and take a long drink. The entire time I'm with Dad, I feel Hannah's eyes on me, but I keep my perfected all's good attitude. Dad tells me about the shop, and we talk about some of the cars he's worked on recently. He never begrudged me for not wanting to take over the shop; he knew my career aspirations lay elsewhere. But we have always enjoyed talking about cars. It was something Dad and I did just the two of us when I was growing up. Neither Mom nor Chloe were ever interested, so every once in a while, Dad would take me to the shop with him and we'd spend the day together.

When the burgers are done, Dad and I join the girls.

When we've all made our plates, Mom says, "I heard the two of you were down at the parade earlier."

Hannah smiles. "Yeah, it was great. I didn't get to see them growing up. We don't have them in the city. I enjoyed watching all the kids have a blast collecting candy and spraying the firefighters."

"I'm glad you had fun. You'll have to come see it every year," Mom says.

Hannah's eyes dart to me, and I watch as her smile stays in place, but the warm genuineness of it fades. "Sounds great."

I'm grateful she doesn't tell Mom she won't be here next summer because she's planning on divorcing me.

"What else did you guys get up to while in town?" Chloe asks.

"We did the little street market. There were so many cool booths. I got a gorgeous necklace and matching earrings, and we took some funny photos." Hannah pulls out her phone and passes it to Chloe, who then passes it to Mom. Mom passes it to Dad, and I catch a glimpse of the screen and see that her phone is open to Instagram, not her photo app. Did she post pictures of us to her social media? Why? If she believes this marriage won't last past this summer, why is she sharing photos of us to her friends and family in such a public way?

I take a sip of my beer as I try and mull over what this could all mean. She let me hold her hand as we wandered around the market, and now she's posting pictures. Does this mean she doesn't hate me as much as she did before?

"Grayson?" Dad's voice pulls me from my thoughts.

"Hmmm," I say.

"The guys will be here at 6:30 p.m. to go with you to get the barn ready before we do the fireworks."

I nod. "Sounds good."

When we finish, I volunteer to clear the table and Chloe offers to help. In the kitchen, she faces me, resting against the counter as she takes me in. She knows something, probably from the small town gossip.

I sigh. "You know."

She nods. "Yeah, Brinley saw you guys at the street fair. She wanted to give me the heads up."

I'm not surprised it was Brinley. She's been Chloe's best friend since high school, which also means she was around when everything went down. If you were in this house, there was no escaping it, no matter how much you may have wanted to.

"I'm fine," I say.

She shakes her head. "Grayson, you're not fine. When you got home, you abandoned your wife with no explanation. I'm also guessing that if I were to ask Hannah if she knows about Rebecca, she'd say no. How long do you plan to keep this secret from your wife? It's eating at you. You keep saying you're fine. You've said for the last fucking decade that you're fine, but you're lying. You never come home for more than a couple days, and don't give me any more of the you can't get enough time off work bullshit you keep spewing. You avoid this town because you know there's a chance of running into her and having to confront your past. Well, it's time. I miss my brother, and I'm tired of the bullshit. It'd be nice for you to come visit more. Mom and Dad miss you, too. Do you know how much it pained Mom to guilt you into coming for a week this year when she knows how much it hurts you?"

The emotions that fill Chloe's eyes have my knees wanting to give out.

"I love you. You're my big brother, and you've always supported and loved me. You've always been there to protect me. Now I'm going to do the same for you, because if you don't pull your head out of your ass, you're going to lose your wife. You need to face it all and tell her."

I stare at her, not sure what to say. She's just offloaded a ton on me, and I don't know how to process it all.

After a few seconds, I pull her into me and kiss the top of her head. "Chlo, you know I love you more than anything, right?"

She nods against my chest. "Back at you."

We stand like that for a minute before we break apart and finish the cleanup in silence. When we join everyone back on the deck, Mom pulls us in for a card game. One of Mom's favourite things while we were growing up was family game night. Cards, board games, charades, we did it all. Mom was really big on doing things together. I guess that's why Chloe and I ended up so close as we got older.

I watch Hannah as we play, and she's having a blast. I realize she must not have done this a lot. With her parents being divorced and her mom being her mom, she wouldn't have sat around a table laughing while playing games just because they wanted to spend time together. Realizing how different Hannah's and my childhoods were is like a stab to the gut. She deserved so much better.

Around 6 p.m. we clear the table and begin preparations for everyone to arrive for our family's annual Canada Day evening backyard bash. When Ryder, Leo, and Colton show up, the four of us make our way to the barn where we keep the horses. A year after I got a full-time position at Vancouver Memorial, I started paying for full-time care for the horses. I knew Mom and Dad were getting too old to do all of it every day and Chloe was working. It would have gutted Chlo to have to send the horses somewhere else to be taken care of properly, so I took care of it.

The guys bullshit as we walk across the property to the barn. We've been friends since childhood, and I know they've stayed close with my family since I've left. Chloe told me the three of them offer to help with the horses every Canada Day. I'm still lost in my thoughts by the time we reach the barn.

"Grayson," Ryder calls, pulling me out of my head.

"Hmmm?"

"Leo was asking you about your wife," Ryder says.

"What about her?"

"Well, let's start with the fact that you just showed up in town married. We know your parents didn't attend a wedding, so why don't you tell us how you ended up married," Leo says.

I walk past them and pull the barn door open.

"Look at him, once again ignoring the big things," Colton says.

"He did it with Rebecca, and he's doing it again," Ryder adds.

I turn and glare at Ryder. "Don't you dare compare my marriage to Hannah with the situation with Rebecca, they're two entirely different things," I bark out.

"How? You're ignoring both situations," Leo couters.

"Firstly, Hannah and I aren't eighteen. Secondly, marrying Hannah wasn't a mistake. We may have been drunk in Vegas, but I will never say that marrying her was a mistake." I shake my head and move to the horses, grabbing a brush from the wall on my way. I start brushing Miley, Chloe's favourite horse. The guys follow suit and start working on the other horses.

"How else is it different?" Colton asks.

I run the brush over Miley's fur a few times, trying to find the words to put to the situation. "I don't regret Rebecca, but we were young and let things get away from us. With Hannah"—I let out a deep breath—"we're adults, and since waking up married, I've thought this out. I'm not some teenage boy full of hormones. Hannah's strong and fierce, funny and smart, too. She's fucking gorgeous. She's extremely independent and loyal to a fault. She's softer than she lets everyone see. She's someone I want in my life."

"Are you happy?" Ryder asks.

I stop brushing Miley and really mull over his question. I'm not sure it's an easy yes or no answer. I'm happy that Hannah is living at my place, but it sucks that she's in my bed while I'm sleeping on the couch. I know I asked her to give our marriage a shot, but now I'm wondering if I shouldn't just sign the divorce papers so she can find someone who can give her everything she deserves. The things that might destroy me if I tried to give them to her.

I look up and find all the guys watching me. "It's complicated," I say.

Colton asks, "How?"

"There's just a lot of history that we're working through."

"What would make your answer a yes?" Ryder asks.

I think about his question as we work together getting the horses brushed and their blankets put on before closing all the doors and windows to the barn to help keep it as quiet as possible for them once we start setting off the fireworks.

The more I think about Ryder's question, the more I wonder if I can ever answer yes to being happy with Hannah, because I don't think I can ever truly make her happy. If we continue trying to make this marriage work, she's going to be the one unhappy. Knowing that she's not happy is going to kill me. Hannah deserves the world. She deserves someone who will kneel at her feet and worship her like the goddess she is. Someone who can give her everything she wants in life.

When everything is locked up, we make our way back to the house where more people have gathered for dinner as we wait for it to get dark. I find Hannah with Chloe and her friends playing corn-hole, laughing and drinking. Hannah tosses her head back as a loud and beautiful laugh leaves her. Her blonde hair cascades down her back in soft curls, and the sun shimmers off it. When she looks at me, it's with an unadulterated smile, and I tell myself that for the rest of the week we're here, I'm not going to worry about our future; I'm going to enjoy the present.

Hannah

Grayson's been off ever since our run in with Rebecca, and I don't know why. I'm assuming there's history between them, but I have no idea what that history is. As nosey as I am, I don't want to go asking his family about it. It's something Grayson will have to tell me when he's ready and wants to. I'm not gonna lie and say it's not heart-wrenching knowing he's seen me at my worst and knows how shitty my relationship with my mother is, yet he has this secret he hasn't even mentioned to me before. I had never heard the name Rebecca in relation to Grayson until the parade.

I don't know why it bothers me. It shouldn't. My plan was always to divorce Grayson as soon as possible, but he's making me see another side of him and it's chipping away at this view I had of him.

When the guys leave for the barn, Chloe drags me to the yard where her friends have just shown up. She convinces me to join them for a game of cornhole.

"Okay, we're gonna play twenty questions cornhole," Chloe says. "You get a beanbag into the hole, you get to ask anyone a question and they have to answer truthfully, or they drink."

Everyone nods and grabs a drink from the bucket beside the deck. Brinley goes first and tosses the beanbag. It slides across wood and hangs just over the hole but doesn't fall in. Chloe laughs and makes her throw. It lands right in the centre of the hole.

She taps her finger against her chin as her eyes bounce between all of us before they finally settle on me and a wicked grin spreads across her face.

"Hannah, fuck, marry, kill, Grayson's friends, Matt, Caleb, and Josh."

I nearly spit out my drink. I cough and pat my chest. "You realize one is a friend's brother, the other is that same friend's husband, and the other is a friend's fiancé?"

She nods, her smile not fading.

I figure if this is her starting question, then they're just going to get worse, so I might as well answer. I don't want to be wasted before the fireworks even start.

"Marry Caleb, fuck Matt, kill Josh."

She tilts her head, assessing me. "Not how I thought you'd answer that."

I tip my head back and laugh. "And how did you think I'd answer it?"

"I don't know, just thought Matt would be your kill," she says.

I shrug. "Fuck boys do make for the best fucks."

Their jaws drop before they all bend over, laughing.

"Is that how my brother managed to hook you?"

The question sobers my mood. I turn to Aspen and say, "Your turn."

She gets the message and tosses her beanbag. When it slides into the hole, she turns her gaze to Brinley. "Why did I see you sneaking out of Ryder's truck yesterday morning, outside your office?"

Chloe spits her beer out while Lennon's eyes bug out.

"You and Ryder?" Chloe asks incredulously.

Brinley holds her hands in front of her as she shakes her head vigorously. "No. Nope. I'm not sleeping with him. He was on his way to the station for his shift and saw me walkin' to work because my car wouldn't start. He just picked me up and dropped me off at work."

"You're tellin' me Ryder Daniels gave you a ride to work out of the kindness of his heart?" Aspen asks.

Brinley shuffles foot to foot and tucks her hands in the back pockets of her jean shorts as she shrugs. "Yeah, I guess. He pulled over and told me to get in, I did, and we made the drive into town in silence."

"Huh," Aspen says, still looking confused.

Lennon tosses her beanbag and misses, and now it's my turn. I've never played cornhole but assume it can't be that difficult. I pull my arm back and toss the beanbag underhand the same way I watched the girls do it. I watch it slide across the wood and just when I think it won't go in, it drops into the hole. I jump up and cheer while the girls laugh. I turn and face Lennon. I spotted her wedding ring the night at the bar and she only mentioned her husband briefly that night.

"Lennon, what's one secret that you've never told a soul, not even your husband?"

Her eyes widen as she gnaws on her lip. She looks around the group for a second before grabbing her drink and chugging as the girl's jaws drop.

"You're keeping secrets now, Len?" Aspen asks.

Lennon looks anywhere but their faces as she takes another sip, looks at Brinley, and says, "Your turn."

Brinley gnaws on her lip before she nods and tosses her beanbag. We watch it slide in, and she turns to Aspen.

"What's going to happen when Beau comes back to town in a few months?"

Aspen looks at Brinley like a deer in headlights. "Beau's coming back?" she whispers

Chloe and Brinley look at each other before looking back at Aspen.

"You didn't know?" Chloe asks.

Aspen shakes her head, and I ask, "Who's Beau?"

"No one," Aspen quickly interjects.

The conversation moves on, and we laugh as the more we drink, the worse our throws become. We're laughing at Aspen's lastest attempt when arms wrap around my middle and hot air dusts over the shell of my ear. Grayson's scent fills my nose, and I find myself relaxing into him.

"Having fun?" he whispers, and I nod. "I'm glad," he says before placing a delicate kiss behind my ear that has me melting like fucking butter on toast into him. He chuckles and runs his nose down my neck.

"Get a room," Chloe calls.

His nose leaves my skin briefly before his mouth replaces it as he trails soft kisses down my neck. Goosebumps erupt across my skin, and I close my eyes as I lean my head to the side, allowing him more access. He steps back and leaves me hanging. I turn and stare at him. The fucker winks and walks away, leaving me all hot and bothered, standing here with his sister.

"Glad to see you're having fun," Brinley says on a laugh.

"That was not fun," I say, frustrated as hell.

Chloe and I leave the group to help her parents set up the food for everyone. It's buffet style, with chairs scattered around the yard for people to sit. It's very family style, and I love it. I grab a plate and make my way down the line, adding different items before I make my way to a chair at the edge of the yard. Even with my head down, I can tell it's Grayson who pulls a chair up right beside me and settles in. I look over at him and raise a brow.

"Can't leave my wife to eat alone," he says.

"Oh, but you can get her all worked up in public and then fuck off?"

He leans over the arm of his chair until he's as close as he can possibly get and whispers, "If you want that ache between your legs to go away, Spitfire, all you have to do is ask. I'd be more than happy to oblige and watch you come undone as you call my name again."

I squirm in my seat, his words having their desired effect. I twist and lean in close, matching his position. When my mouth is beside his ear, I let out a soft breath, allowing it to dust over his ear.

"Don't make promises you can't keep," I whisper in a low, husky tone before my teeth scrape across his earlobe.

"I keep my promises," he says with a wink before settling back in his chair, his plate positioned just so on his lap.

I let out a soft laugh.

"You laughing at me, Spitfire?"

I bite my lip and bat my eyelashes at him. The grin that spreads across his face is feral and has me wanting to jump out of my chair and drag him to our room.

"I think someone might need to be taught a lesson."

I bat my lashes more dramatically. "Are you gonna spank me?"

He adjusts himself in his seat. "Do you want that?" he asks, his own voice growing deeper with arousal.

I nod.

His eyes eat me up before we dig into our food, both of us sitting in his parents' backyard surrounded by his friends and family while incredibly turned on. My only hope is that tonight he'll actually fuck my brains out like I want. I need sex. I need good sex. At this point in time, my only hope for that is with Grayson. A little voice in the back of my head warns me that it might be a little more than wanting a good orgasm when it comes to me wanting to fuck Grayson. I push it aside, not wanting to think that maybe my emotions are coming into play.

Slowly, Chloe and the girls join us along with the guys that joined Grayson in the barn earlier. When we finish eating, it seems like everyone has decided it's time to interrogate Grayson and me.

"So, Hannah, what made you decide to marry Grayson?" a guy I've been told is Ryder asks.

I don't really want to out to his friends and family that it was a drunken mistake, so I say, "We were in Vegas." Wanting to take an equal jab at him, I ask, "What made you pick up Brinley from the side of the road?"

Grayson raises a brow while Leo and Colton look at Ryder.

He shrugs a shoulder. "Saw her walkin', and my mom raised me right. You pick up a stranded lady on the side of the road."

Aspen leans forward in her chair and looks at Ryder. "Did she also teach you to fuck anything that walks?"

"Just enjoying life. No one doesn't know what they're getting from me when they climb into my bed."

Silence fills the air before Chloe breaks it. "So, Hannah. What's it like working with your husband?"

"It's nothing different. We haven't told anyone yet that we're married, but when we work the same shift, we take our breaks together." They don't need to know it's because of me that we haven't told anyone, or that Grayson basically blackmailed me into sharing every meal at the hospital with him.

"Oh, don't forget you get to see my beautiful face all the time," Grayson chimes in.

"How could I forget," I say with a laugh.

"It's nice being able to spend more time with Hannah. We work such crazy shifts that having some overlap allows us to see each other."

"Grayson," Randy calls from across the yard.

He pushes up from his chair, grabbing my plate and kissing the top of my head before making his way to join his dad. That simple action of kissing the top of my head before he left has my insides in knots. How can I continue to hate a man who shows me affection like he does? I'm beginning to think maybe Liz's comment about a thin line between love and hate might be true.

CHAPTER 20

Grayson

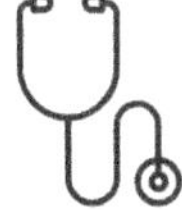

Realizing how natural it was to kiss the top of her head as I walk away has me confused. How in the world have we gone from her hating me and not wanting to spend time with me, to it feeling like the most natural thing in the world to share that act of affection with her before parting? I look over my shoulder at her, and she's engrossed in conversation with everyone. She's fit in so easily with my family and our friends.

I follow Dad to the side of the house where he's kept the fireworks for tonight. We gather the supplies and move them to the open section of the yard where we'll light them later. I drag the hose out and make sure it's properly set up before we start stuffing the tubes. As I'm stuffing the last tube, I see familiar brown hair out of the corner of my eye, and my entire body becomes on edge. I turn and watch as Rebecca and her husband and son make their way toward the centre of the yard.

Her little boy finds the kids who have gathered in the yard to play. My parents' place has always been open to everyone for the holidays. They're known for their fireworks show every Canada Day. I shouldn't be surprised they're here, but I haven't been in town for the holiday in so long that it never crossed my mind.

I close my eyes and rub a hand over the ache in my chest as a hand slips into my free one and squeezes. Hannah's soft, floral scent fills my lungs, and the ache subsides little by little with each deep inhale of it. When I open my eyes, I meet her worried gaze. I offer her a slight smile, but it does nothing to ease her worry. She squeezes my hand again, and I squeeze back.

"Are you okay?" she asks.

I nod. Her eyes continue scanning me, and I open my arms. She wraps hers around my waist and hugs me. I hold her like it's the last time, because for all I know it is, and I need to absorb all of it. I bury my nose in her hair, and my entire body relaxes into her.

I don't know why Hannah has always seemed to calm me, but she does. I have no explanation for it. It's like she's the eye of the storm that is my mind. She may be sassy and fiery, but when it matters, she anchors me.

When we separate, her hand comes up and cups my cheek as she stares into my eyes. The rest of the world falls away as I stare at her. Her hair isn't as perfect as it was this morning. The humidity has flyaways around her face, and sweat forms around her hairline, but she's the most beautiful thing I've ever seen. My hands come up and cup her face.

I lean in, and before our lips touch, I whisper, "Stay with me tonight."

She nods, and I move my lips and kiss her cheek. Ryder comes and joins us and takes over the preparation of the fireworks so I can spend the night with Hannah watching them instead of lighting them. I lead her to the edge of the group and lay a blanket out and lie down. She joins me, and I pull her into my side. Rebecca and her family are on the other side of the yard from us. I want her to be happy. That's all I've ever wished for her, but being near her drags me into the past. Having Hannah by my side helps me stay focused on the present. As we lie here, the sound of nature and my family and friends around us, I realize more and more that I want to spend every Canada Day like this, with Hannah in my arms. In order for that to ever be a possibility, I would have to bare my soul to her. Tell her about everything and hope she stays despite me not being able to give her everything she wants. I resolve to tell her before we head home.

As the first firework goes off, the little gasp that escapes Hannah has me grinning from ear to ear. She makes little sounds as bigger ones light up the night sky, and I wrap my arm tighter around her.

We watch as the different colours explode above us. I turn and look at her as a large red one explodes and the light dances across her face. She's stunning as she grins. I tuck a stray piece of hair behind her ear. She turns toward me slightly, and all I want to do is kiss her. I want to smash my lips against hers and devour her, but if I do, I'm not sure I'd be able to stop. I have this need to consume her. To have her forgetting every other man she's ever been with until all she remembers is my touch. My taste. The way I make her come.

Another firework goes off, and Hannah turns to watch it. After the last few explode above us, we get up and help clean up before making our way back into the house. I hop in the shower, allowing the water to wash away the craziness of the day. As I tip my head back, the shower curtain moves, bringing in a cold burst of air. I look to see what caused the movement and immediately see Hannah naked in front of me. She has her hair pulled up in a messy bun on top of her head, exposing her slender neck. My eyes slowly trail down her body, taking in every inch of her perfect skin. My breathing quickens as I stare at her. My eyes can't find one spot they want to linger. They need to eat up all of her.

Her eyes do the same as she steps into the shower, pulling the curtain closed and standing within inches of me. She smiles seductively at me, and I'm harder than I think I've ever been in my life. She grins as she reaches forward and takes hold of my erection, slowly sliding her hand up and down my length. I hold back a groan as I watch her.

She goes onto her tip toes and whispers in my ear, "I think I owe you a few orgasms."

I grip her wrist, stopping her movements, and she gives me a confused look.

"Spitfire, this is not tit for tat. If this is something you want to do, then that's fine. Amazing, really, but don't do anything because you feel like you owe it to me or you have to. Every orgasm I've given you and will give you is because it's something I want to do. I want to watch you come undone for me. I want you to feel good."

Her gaze softens before it turns to molten heat. "I want to watch you come for me, Grayson. I want to be the reason you lose control."

She drops to her knees in front of me, and my mouth goes dry. She licks her lips before she leans forward and licks my cock slowly, base to tip, her tongue flicking over the sensitive crown. This time, I can't hold back the groan, and her responding grin is wicked. She leans forward and wraps her lips around me, and it's like I've died and gone to heaven. The feeling of her hot mouth around me is like heaven and sin all wrapped in one. She slowly takes every inch I have to offer until I'm hitting the back of her throat.

Holy shit, she has no gag reflex.

She swallows around me, and my hand slams against the shower wall to hold me up. She's relentless as she works her mouth up and down my length. Tears begin gathering at the corner of her eyes, and I wipe them and try and pull away, but she takes my hand and places it on the back of her head as she nods.

Holy. Fucking. Hell.

She wants me to fuck her mouth. She looks at me with pleading eyes, like she wants me to use her for my pleasure, and if that isn't my deepest desires come to life, I don't know what is. I grip her hair as my hips thrust forward, and she moans. The vibrations travel up my spine and have me on the edge already. I'm not going to last long. A few more thrusts and her moaning have me falling over the edge, spilling down her throat. I watch as she swallows every fucking drop of cum.

She releases me and runs her thumb over her bottom lip, picking up a stray drop of cum before licking it off. I lean over, gripping her chin tightly. Her eyes widen, filled with arousal.

"You're a needy girl, aren't you?"

She nods.

"You a needy little whore for your husband's cock?"

She nods again.

"Use your words," I demand.

She swallows so forcefully I see the movement of her throat.

"I'm a needy little whore for your cock, Grayson," she practically pants.

"Good girl."

She melts into my hold at the words. She likes the praise and degradation.

I need to fuck my wife, but I'm not having our first time be in this tiny shower. Reaching behind me, I turn off the water and forcefully pull open the shower curtain. I quickly wrap her in a towel before doing the same to myself and pop my head out of the bathroom door and check the hallway. Seeing it's all clear, I usher her into our room, and the second the door is closed, I pull both our towels off and toss them to the floor.

"Get on the bed." My voice comes out low and commanding, and she immediately follows directions. I grin at how quickly she moves. When she's lying flat on her back, I run a finger slowly up the inside of her right leg before switching to her left and repeating the motion.

"What do you want?" I ask.

"To come," she pants as she squirms under my touch.

"How do you want to come?"

My finger moves up her stomach to her breasts, and I circle a nipple. I watch it harden without even being touched. Her back arches, and she bites her hand as she releases a low moan. She doesn't respond to my question. I pinch her nipple, and she mewls.

"How do you want to come?" I ask again.

"Your tongue. I want to come on your tongue," she rushes out.

That I can do. I position myself on the bed and kiss my way up her right leg painstakingly slow. When I reach the one place she's aching to be touched, I let out a warm breath and watch her squirm even more before moving to her left leg and repeating the process. When I get to the apex of her thighs again, she's glistening. She's so fucking wet and ready for me. I take my first taste of the night, and it makes me ravenous. I devour her, not leaving a single inch of her untasted. As my lips wrap around her clit, her hand finds my hair, and she holds on tightly. I bring my finger to her entrance and tease her. The growl she releases has me chuckling, and her grip on my hair tightens.

"I said I wanted to come on your tongue, not be fucking teased," she says.

My little Spitfire is out to play. I oblige her this time, because I want to see her come undone. I want to watch her writhe as she calls my name. I slowly push my finger inside and find that spot that sends her back off the bed. Adding another finger, I massage the same spot as she tightens around my fingers. She's right on the edge. She's just about to fall off the cliff when I stop. Her eyes fly open, and she glares at me.

I grin back. "Beg for it, Spitfire. You want to come, you're gonna beg me for it."

Her eyes harden as I scrape my teeth slowly over her clit and pull my fingers halfway out. I continue to move them inside her, but never go in more than halfway, and never massage that one perfect spot.

I see the fight in her, she doesn't want to give in, she wants to be in control, but after a minute, she's finally done with my teasing. "Please, Grayson. Please make me come."

Her begging is like music to my ears and I push my fingers in all the way and wrap my lips around her clit again. Within seconds, I have her coming. She holds a pillow to her face to suppress the loud moans that leave her. When she comes down from the high, she removes the pillow, her breathing still coming out as pants, and I remove my fingers. She closes her eyes as she tries to catch her breath.

"Look at me," I say, and her eyes fly open. I hold my fingers to her lips and say, "Open."

She does as she's told, and I place my fingers in her mouth. Her eyes never leave mine as she sucks every last drop of her cum off them. I haven't even had sex with Hannah, and she's ruined me for all other women.

She opens her mouth, and I remove my fingers as she watches me reach into the nightstand and grab one of the condoms I bought earlier today. As I hold it up to my mouth to rip it open, her mouth parts and her pupils dilate even more. I remove the condom and roll it down my painfully hard cock as I lean down and whisper in her ear, "You need your husband to fill you up and fuck you, don't you?"

"Yes." Her voice is breathy and barely audible.

I position myself between her legs and run the head of my cock against her clit. She watches the movements, her teeth digging into her bottom lip. I slip the tip into her, and she releases her lip as she stares at where I'm filling her. I push forward slowly, and I see the indecision in her eyes, whether to watch as I stretch her tight little cunt or to allow herself to fall back and revel in the feeling. I push forward another inch, and she gives in, her head falling back as she moans my name. The best sound I've ever heard is my name coming from her mouth in moans of pleasure.

I push all the way in and bury my head in the crook of her neck, breathing in her scent. When I've gathered myself, I hold myself up. My hand finds her hair, and I grip tightly. I hold eye contact with her, that feeling more intimate than the fact that I'm buried balls deep inside her.

"I'm going to fuck you hard, the way you deserved to be fucked. I'm going to make sure you feel me buried in your pussy when you wake up. I want your eyes rolling into the back of your head when you come."

"God, yes," she moans.

I slowly pull out until just the tip is left inside of her before I thrust my hips forward, fast and hard. Her back arches as her eyes roll, and I repeat the motion. I continue, picking up speed as I go. I revel in the feeling of being inside her as the sound of slapping skin fills the room. It only turns me on more. I bite her neck, and she mewls.

"Who's fucking you?" I pant.

"You."

Not the answer I want. "Who am I?"

Her eyes open, and she stares at me.

I grip her jaw tightly. "Who the fuck am I, Spitfire?"

I can tell the second she realizes the answer I'm looking for.

"My husband."

"Say it again. Who's fucking you?"

Her back arches and she scratches at my arm.

"My husband."

I reach between us and slap her clit. "Good girl. Now tell me how needy you are."

Her arms splay out at her side as she reaches for anything to grab. "So needy. I need my husband's cock. I need it so badly." Her voice comes out in heavy breaths as she squints her eyes closed.

I nip at her neck. "Such a needy girl. Such a good girl."

My words send her over the edge and turns her head and bites my forearm as she spasms around my cock. I know she's going to leave a mark and I love it. I want to be claimed by her. I fuck her harder, sending her higher up the bed until I'm coming, too. I can't get enough of her as we ride out our highs together. I roll off her, panting.

I leave the bed, slipping into some shorts and venturing to the washroom. I return with a warm, wet cloth and help Hannah clean up. She smiles softly at me before I help her up and wrap her in my robe that still hangs on the back of the bedroom door. Grabbing the towels, we head back into the shower, where this time we actually clean ourselves.

Hannah lets me wash her hair. I massage the shampoo into her scalp before rinsing it and working her conditioner into the ends. I really take her in as she stands in front of me. Her shoulders are relaxed, and her eyes are closed. She's comfortable. She feels safe right now, allowing her guard to come down. Knowing she doesn't feel the need to put her walls up right now and feels safe with me is everything.

While I let the conditioner sit in her hair, I wrap my arms around her and hold her close. I place gentle kisses along her neck, and she tilts her head granting more access. I watch as the corner of her mouth tips up, and she lets out a satiated sigh. She squeezes my hand that rests on her stomach.

"Careful," she whispers.

I place a few more kisses on her shoulder. "Of?"

She releases another contented sigh as my lips continue trailing over her skin. "You're starting to convince me you're not as bad as I thought."

Her words drop like a weight in my stomach, reminding me how I made her feel all because I knew she deserved better than me.

I spin her until she's facing me and cup her face. "I think we should talk and clear some things up, because I need you to know some things."

She worries her bottom lip between her teeth and nods slightly. I kiss her forehead and spin her back around to rinse the conditioner out of her hair. Wrapped in towels, we head back to the room. I climb into bed and Hannah follows suit. I pull her into my side, needing her close when I finally tell her the truth.

She trails her fingers over my chest as I run my fingers through her hair, working myself up tell her.

"I've never slept with Samantha."

Her fingers stop, and she lifts her head and looks at me. She doesn't say anything, but her eyes bore into me. She adjusts herself to face me better and asks, "What do you mean?"

I swallow harshly. "That night you walked in on Samantha kissing me in the supply closet was just that. She kissed me. I pushed her off as soon as I could, but I guess it was too late, because you had already walked in. I tried to catch up to you, to talk, but you were gone. I decided it was for the best. You deserved better, so I wasn't going to try and explain it to you." I run a hand over my face. "I wanted you to be happy, and I didn't think you would be with me, so if that meant you hating me and finding someone who could give you everything you want and deserve, I could live with that. For you."

She stares at me, mouth agape, as a tear falls down her cheek. She wipes at it furiously before she falls back on the bed and stares up at the ceiling. She closes her eyes and takes a deep breath. I brush the stray hairs on her face back and tuck them behind her ears.

"You okay?" I ask.

She nods. "Yeah." Her voice comes out soft, and I brush my thumb over her cheek. She leans into the touch, and I smile softly. She opens her eyes, and I can't read the emotions swimming in them. She lets out a slow breath.

"You let me hate you." A tear falls down her cheek, and I wipe it away. "You did that for me?"

"Yeah, I did that for you."

Her eyes bounce all over my face. "Why?"

I kiss her cheek and whisper, "You'll figure it out," before pulling her into me and closing my eyes to sleep.

CHAPTER 21

Hannah

I wake up in the morning sprawled across Grayson's naked chest, his arm wrapped around me. My mind is still reeling after last night and the bombshell he dropped on me. I'm not sure how the hell I'm supposed to process it. I do know I need to talk to the girls.

I slowly slide out of Grayson's hold and wrap myself in his robe before making my way downstairs, pouring a cup of coffee, and making my way to the back deck. Confirming I'm the only one out here, I settle in a chair and text the group chat.

HAN

I need help!

LIV

Are you okay?

HAN

Physically, yes.

LIZ

Mentally?

HAN

I'm not sure.

ZO

Group call?

HAN

Please!

The phone rings, and when I answer, the screen splits and is filled with the faces of Liv, Zo, Bailey, and Liz. I squint at the screen for a second.

"Bailey and Liv, you're still in bed. Do we need to do this later?"

Bailey shakes her head. "No, Caleb just went to go make us coffee."

"Josh got up with Cate this morning. They're in the nursery."

"What's up?" Liz asks, and I run my teeth over my lip.

"Han?" Zoey asks, concern filling her voice.

"You know how I said I caught Grayson and another woman in the supply closet at work?"

They all nod.

"Well, Grayson told me last night that he never slept with her and that she threw herself at him and when he couldn't catch up to me afterwards, he decided it was for the best so I could find someone who could give me everything I deserve."

The girls all stay silent.

"None of you are going to say anything?" I ask.

"Babe, you're not going to like what I have to say," Liv says.

I sigh. "Just say it."

"I told you so. I told you there was more to the story. I know it sounds cliché that some woman threw herself at him, but seeing the way he looks at you, I don't think he would cheat. Not then and not now."

I cross my arms over my chest. She's right, I don't like what she has to say.

Zoey laughs. "Oh, Han, are you pouting because Liv said I told you so?"

I roll my eyes, and she just laughs again. "Bailey, Liz. You're both awfully quiet," I say.

"I agree with Liv. In the short time I've known you guys, Grayson just doesn't seem the type to cheat," Bailey says.

The bitchy side of me wants to snap at her, but I know Bailey's heart is in a good place, just like the rest of theirs, but it doesn't mean I have to like it. I've spent so long hating him that learning it's been all for naught is not easy for me to grasp. Admitting you were wrong is never easy.

"Han, I know you. No matter what we say, your opinion isn't going to change. You need to really think about this on your own. Really pay attention to what's going on," Liz says, and I narrow my eyes at her. She's being cryptic, but she's also right and fuck her for that. No matter what they say, I need to see it to believe it.

The sliding glass door opens behind me, and I turn to see Grayson walk out in nothing but a pair of shorts, holding two coffee cups. He smiles. "Mornin'. I see you have coffee already."

I look down at my cup, and it's almost empty. He notices my gaze, places the fresh cup in front of me, and kisses the top of my head.

"Well, good morning," Liv says.

He grins wider and adjusts himself so he can be seen in the camera of the phone I have propped on the table.

"Good morning, ladies."

"Having fun, I take it," Zoey says, smiling so wide I'm sure her cheeks hurt.

"How can I not? Gorgeous wife, beautiful weather, tons of open space, and no work. Living the dream."

My cheeks are flaming hot. Hearing him call me his wife to my friends is still so weird, but it also gives me the warm and fuzzies. The first thing on his list of positive things was me. It might have been a comment about my looks, but I also know he sees more of me than that.

"Well, ladies, Hannah and I have some plans today, so we should probably get going."

I look at him with confusion, and he just winks at me. The girls laugh and each call have fun or bye before hanging up.

"Plans?" I ask.

"Yup. So you might want to drink up and get dressed."

"And where are we going?"

"Surprise."

I raise a brow at him, and he chuckles. "You're going to like it. Promise."

I quickly finish my coffee and take my cups to the kitchen.

Grayson follows closely on my heels. As I rinse the cups, I feel his heat behind me as his arms trap me between his body and the counter. His lips find my neck, and the sound that comes out of me has me rolling my eyes at myself, because I sound so fucking needy. His lips dust over my exposed skin, and goosebumps erupt in their wake. His hand comes up and moves my hair off my shoulder, exposing more skin.

"In case you didn't catch my comment earlier, you're fucking gorgeous. Every fucking inch of you is perfect," he whispers, and it takes everything in me to not melt into him.

"You're also smart."

Kiss.

"And strong."

Kiss.

"Loyal."

Kiss, and I melt, my back pressed against his hard chest.

"Spirited."

Kiss.

"Funny."

I turn in his arms and stare up at him. The smile he's giving me now isn't cocky or arrogant, but soft and full of something entirely different. He leans down and kisses each cheek and my forehead, but never my lips. It hits me that, despite us being intimate in different ways, he's never actually kissed me. He's kissed every part of my body but my lips.

I'm pulled from my thoughts when his teeth scrape my neck, and I moan. His hands find the backs of my thighs and lift me until I wrap my legs around his waist. He trails his lips everywhere, or almost everywhere, as he carries me to our room.

He drops me on the bed, and I watch as he quickly shucks his shorts to the floor before reaching for the belt of my robe and pulling it free. I slip out of it as he climbs on the bed. He reaches into the nightstand and grabs a condom, placing it beside him before he lies on his back.

"Come sit on my face," he says, and I could not move any quicker.

I throw a leg over his chest and shimmy up until I'm in position. Before I can lower myself, his arms wrap around my thighs and pull me down so he can feast on me. I grab the headboard to steady myself and allow the pleasure to overwhelm me.

Grayson knows exactly what he's doing. Every movement of his tongue has my orgasm building and my body tightening. I bite my lip as a moan is pulled from deep inside me.

"I want to hear you, Spitfire. No one's home. I want to hear how I make you feel."

His lips wrap around my clit, and I throw my head back as the most feral sound leaves me. I feel him grin against me as he continues to suck on my clit, drawing more and more sounds from me, each one growing in volume and unhingedness. His teeth scrape over it, and I'm sent crashing into oblivion as my orgasm tears through me. When I come down from the high, Grayson rips open the condom and rolls it down his impressive cock. My mouth waters at the thought of him stretching me as he fucks me.

"Ride me, Spitfire. Use me. I want to watch you use me to get off."

God, this man. He's giving me things without me having to ask. Lifting myself, I grip his cock and position it before slowly sinking down. I relish the sensation of him stretching me. When he's all the way in, he grips my hips and helps me grind against him, my clit getting that friction it so desperately needs. My head drops forward, my hair cascading with it. He reaches up and delicately tucks it behind my ears.

Grayson has my mind all over the place, how he can be so gentle all while also being so primal.

He leans forward and wraps his lips around my left nipple, sucking before his teeth scrape across it and release it. He moves to the other, repeating the same thing. I clench around him, hovering on the cusp of another orgasm. His hand leaves my hip, and his thumb finds my clit. He circles it gently before applying more pressure. It's like he's been given some all-seeing map to my body, and knows exactly how to get me to come. Exactly what I need.

He applies more pressure and then pinches it, and I come in the biggest orgasm I've ever experienced. I scream his name. The muscles in my legs, abdomen, and arms all spasm as the orgasm tears through me. I can't even hold myself up, Grayson has to.

How could something so quick and vanilla send me over the

edge like that? I've had kinkier sex that hasn't even been close to that. I'm starting to wonder if my reaction to Grayson's words earlier made it better. Am I starting to develop actual feelings for my husband? Are feelings making the sex better?

Grayson helps roll me until I'm on my back and kisses my cheek.

"Watching you come undone for me is the best thing I've ever witnessed," he says before climbing out of the bed and returning with a warm washcloth. My body feels like mush, and all I want to do is melt into the bed and sleep.

Grayson grabs my hand and pulls me into a sitting position. "Nope, we've got plans today. No sleepin'."

I pout, and he just chuckles before kissing my forehead and turning to get himself dressed.

"Wear a swimsuit," he calls before leaving the room.

I huff as I get up and change, throwing a spare pair of underwear into my small bag before joining him in the kitchen. When I walk in, he grins and grabs a few bags off the counter before walking out the front door. I follow behind him, curious about what he has planned for the day.

Outside, he leads me in the direction of the barn where the horses are kept. I look down at my shoes and wonder if I can ride without boots. I look at Grayson, and he's wearing jeans and riding boots, despite the warm weather. I hurry to catch up with him.

"Can I ride with this?" I ask.

He looks at me and smiles. "I thought today, you'd ride with me."

My cheeks flush at the thought of being pressed up against him for God knows how long on the back of a horse. I nod, and his smile grows.

He pulls the barn door open, and there are few people inside tending to a couple of the horses. Grayson walks up to one of the animals, running his hand gently over her snout, and she whinnies at him softly.

"Hannah, this is Rosetta. Rosetta, this is Hannah."

I walk up beside him and cautiously reach a hand out and pet her the same way Grayson did. She doesn't give me the same happy whinny she gave Grayson. I feel her watching me like she's judging me. Grayson chuckles beside me. I give him a little shove, and he laughs harder as Rosetta kicks her head up and walks in place.

I glare at him, and he walks up behind me and wraps his arm around my waist and settles his chin on my shoulder. He reaches out and pets Rosetta again. "It's okay, girl. Hannah's a good one."

She calms a bit, and Grayson kisses my temple before grabbing a saddle and getting Rosetta set. When it's all secure, he puts his backpack on, puts his foot in the stirrup, and lifts himself, throwing his other leg over her back. He does it with such grace you wouldn't be able to tell he's lived almost the last decade in the city. When he's on, he removes the bag, settling it in front of him before offering me his hand and removing his foot from the stirrup.

My eyes bounce between his outstretched hand and the piece of metal.

"Come on, Spitfire. I've got you."

I roll my eyes and carefully place my foot in the stirrup and grab his hand. I count to three in my head and bounce on each count before tightening my grip on his hand and pulling myself up. I miss getting my leg over Rosetta and land back on the ground. I huff out a breath.

Grayson squeezes my hand, and I look at him. His face is full of reassurance.

"You've got this. Take a deep breath. Swing your free leg when you're halfway up."

I nod and take a deep breath, my nose filling with the smell of hay and dirt. Releasing the breath, I try again. This time, I manage to get my leg over and wrap my arms around Grayson's waist.

"Good. You're gonna need to sit as close to me as possible, and don't squeeze your legs. I'll guide Rosetta, but she's a good one, she'll get us there in one piece."

I shuffle forward a bit, and he passes me the backpack to put on. His strong thighs squeeze, and Rosetta begins moving at an easy pace. When we exit the barn, the warm summer air hits my skin as a small breeze comes through carrying the scent of the nearby wildflowers. Grayson leads us towards the tree line, but in a direction he didn't take us on the tour of the property. As we get closer to the trees, I see a worn, narrow path. It looks like it's only wide enough for a single horse or two people to walk side-by-side.

We ride in silence, the only noise the birds singing in the trees and the wind in the branches. It's weird to be comfortable in silence with Grayson. I used to hate it. It made my skin itch, and I'd fill the void with anything and everything, needing it as a distraction. But over time, I've found that I haven't needed to do that anymore.

After about thirty minutes, the sound of fast rushing water hits my ears, and the air becomes misty, water sticking to my skin. We continue riding, and when we come through the last few trees, I gasp as I take in the sight in front of me. Water cascades down rocks, forming a pond below that funnels into a stream surrounded by a small patch of green grass. Smaller falls are on each side of the large one in the centre. The trees above open enough to allow the sun to shine through them and reflect off the water. My smile is so large my cheeks hurt.

Grayson offers me a hand, and I climb off Rosetta before he does the same. He ties the reins loosely around a low-hanging branch of a nearby tree. He slides the backpack off my back and places it at the base of the tree. He leans in close, heat radiating off of him as he whispers, "Your bucket list item. Welcome to Wisteria Falls."

My jaw drops as I turn to look at him over my shoulder. He grins before pulling his shirt over his head and stepping out of his jeans, leaving him only in his swim trunks. I follow suit, tossing my clothes with his and joining him at the edge of the pond. Dipping my toes in, I shiver. The water is much colder than the hot summer air, but it's refreshing. We slowly make our way into the water until neither of us can touch the bottom and we're swimming. Grayson swims over to the waterfall, and I watch the powerful muscles in his back as they ripple with each movement of his arms.

He stops in front of the rushing water and turns to me, calling, "You coming?"

I make my way over to him, and he reaches for my hand before we dive under the water and come out behind the waterfall. I'm grinning when we come up, and the look on Grayson's face has me wrapping my arms around his neck and my legs around his waist. His hands find my ass as he holds me close.

"Thank you," I whisper.

"You're welcome."

I stare into his deep-blue eyes, finding myself getting lost in them. He's holding secrets I can see he wants to release but can't. He tucks my hair behind my ear and delicately runs his thumb over my cheek. I lean into his touch, savouring the way it feels. A stray tear runs down my cheek, and I brush it away before climbing out of his hold.

It hurts knowing I missed his gentle touches and what we could have been because of fucking Samantha and her throwing herself at Grayson. But it's not just on her. I didn't stop and let him explain. I've deprived myself of something that could have been so good, because I had let my mom's horrible marriages jade me. I was so quick to believe Grayson would cheat on me, because I couldn't let myself believe I deserved a happy relationship. All I had known was my parents' failed marriage and my mother's multitude of relationships. I shouldn't have let her failure guide my thoughts.

Grayson swims behind me and pulls me into his chest.

"What's wrong?"

I take a deep breath and plaster on a fake smile and turn in his arms. "Nothing."

His face is solemn, and he cups mine. "Hannah, you don't have to hide with me. You can talk to me. I won't push you, but I'm here. When you're ready, I'll listen. No matter what it is."

I nod, and he releases my face and backs away. That small gesture of giving me space tells me that he knows me. He can read my emotions and what I need. Maybe I shouldn't be writing this marriage off as an immediate divorce. I only wonder if we can really succeed outside of this little bubble we have right now.

CHAPTER 22

Grayson

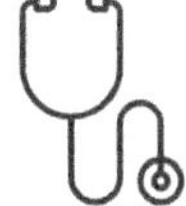

We continue swimming in silence. I watch as Hannah floats on her back, smiling when she gets close enough to the waterfall that the mist hits her face. When she rights herself, she gives me a soft smile before swimming to the shore, and I follow behind her. I grab towels out of the backpack and hand her one. When I've dried off, I grab our stuff and move to a spot in the grass that's in the sun, laying out my towel and settling on it before pulling out the food I packed. Hannah joins me, and I pass her a sandwich.

"This place is gorgeous," she says before taking a bite.

"Yeah, it's one of my favourite places on the property. No one really comes out here, so I can just be alone with my thoughts."

Her eyes are soft as she looks at me. "Thank you for sharing it with me."

I clear my throat quickly and say, "Of course." Hannah still doesn't know I want to share everything with her.

"So, Chloe doesn't come out here?"

I shake my head. "Not really. We each have our own little places that we like to visit. I've brought her here before when we were younger, but it's not really the place she likes to come."

Hannah adjusts herself and stares out over the pond and the waterfall. "I could spend hours out here and never get bored," she whispers. I knew this would be a place she'd appreciate nearly as much as I do.

When we finish eating, we lie back on our towels, staring up at the sky. Birds fly overhead as they move from tree to tree. Hannah's hand reaches for mine, and she entwines our fingers. My breath catches. It's such a small act of affection, but here, where no one else can see and it's not for show or for anything other than to be close to me, it means everything.

I turn my head and look at her. She looks so peaceful, a small smile on her face as she just enjoys being out here. My phone eventually rings, and I look over and see my mom's face flash across the screen.

"Hi, Mom," I answer.

"Hi, Honey. I just thought I'd check in. I'm getting everything ready for dinner and wanted to make sure you two are joining us."

"Yeah, we'll be back for dinner."

"Okay, Honey. Well, it's getting late, so if you're in the woods, I'd start to head home soon," she says in her overprotective, motherly tone.

"Yes, Mom. I'm only twenty-nine and grew up on the property."

"Grayson, I will always be your mother and will always look out for you."

I sigh, knowing her heart's in a good place. "Thank you, Mom. I love you."

"I love you, too. Now get home safe."

Hanging up, I check the time and realize we've been out here for hours. Time with Hannah is flying by, and while I love that we can just enjoy each other's company, I worry that the ninety days will be up before I know, and it scares the crap out of me.

"We should probably head back," I say as I sit up and pack the last of our things.

She nods and reaches over and grabs fresh underwear out of her small bag. She looks at me. "Do you mind?"

I shake my head.

"I mean, will you turn around?"

"Spitfire, we're way past you hiding yourself from me. I've seen all of you and love every inch of your body."

She stands while holding eye contact with me and unties her bikini top, dropping it on the towel in front of her before doing the same with her bottoms. She's so confident as she stands in front of me fully naked.

"Enough of a show for you?" she asks, sass filling her voice.

I rise up on my knees and shuffle towards her, stopping right in front of her. Her breathing picks up, her chest rising and falling faster. "I'll never get enough of you," I whisper before kissing her hip. I move back slowly before standing to my full height and placing a finger under her chin, tipping her head back. "Like I said earlier, you're gorgeous."

Despite wanting to take her right here and now, I turn around and throw the towels and her swimsuit into the backpack and go check on Rosetta. Hannah joins us, and she has an easier time getting on this time. We make the ride back to the house in silence, much like the ride here, but this time, it feels different. It feels like Hannah is holding something back, like she has questions she's not asking.

When we get back to the barn, I help her off before I follow suit and get Rosetta back into her stall and brush her.

Hannah leans against the wall and watches me, when I finish and join her she says, "You're good with her."

I smile and look over my shoulder at the horse I've grown attached to over the years. I remember when we got Rosetta, she always preferred me when we would all go to the barn. It was like an instant connection, and every time I come home, I make sure I go for a ride with her and spend time brushing her. She's also a great listener. Around her, I'm always relaxed and I can verbalize things I would never talk about with people. When everything happened with Rebecca, I was out here with her a lot. We'd go for rides and would head to the pond. I found solace in her presence. I know some people may think it's weird, she's a horse, but she's a living soul. I will be forever grateful for her.

"She saved me. I'll always be grateful to her. I make sure to come see her every time I'm home."

Hannah and I stare at each other. Her brows furrow, but she doesn't ask me the questions I can see swirling behind her eyes.

"Mom's making dinner, we should probably head up," I say, and she falls instep beside me as we leave the barn.

Walking up the stairs to the back deck, Hannah grabs my wrist, and I stop in place and face her. She smiles. "Thank you for today. I had fun." She goes up on her tiptoes and kisses my cheek before walking around me and inside the house.

I follow behind her and join Mom in the kitchen and set the table. Watching how easily Hannah has integrated herself into my family in just a couple of days has my insides in knots. I have no idea how they'll react when we get a divorce. Mom has completely fallen for Hannah, and how could she not? Hannah is amazing. I fell for her long ago, but these last six and a half weeks have proven to me that I don't think I'll move on from her. When she asks for those papers to be signed, I'll need to put as much space as possible between her and I if I'm to survive it.

After dinner, she says she's going to read her book for a while. She grabs her Kindle and makes her way to the back deck with a blanket. Mom convinces me to join her for a game of cards like when I was a kid, and Chloe joins us while Dad settles in his recliner and watches the news.

We play for hours, and I remember how much I love being with my family when it's just us in our own little bubble. Chloe yawns and Mom starts to pack the cards, saying, "It's late. I'm gonna head to bed."

Chloe nods and agrees, both wishing me a good night before heading upstairs. I go outside to find Hannah. She's curled in a corner chair, wrapped in a blanket, her Kindle in her lap, her hand only popping out to tap the page before finding its way back into the warmth. I walk up to her and before she even notices me, I scoop her up. She squeals, and I settle into the chair with her in my lap. She looks at me, and I grin.

"Whatcha reading?'

She settles into my lap more, finding a more comfortable position. "A hockey romance."

"Hmmm," I say. "What's it about?"

She looks at me, her brows furrowing before she says, "A social media manager of a team and the silent player she's somehow become roommates with."

"Is it any good?"

"Yeah."

I nod and rest my chin on her shoulder to read over her shoulder.

She's right in the middle of an explicit scene, and I'm not sure how she continues reading with a straight face. I'm getting harder as the scene progresses. She adjusts herself a little, and I hold back a groan, the feeling of her wiggling in my lap driving me crazy. She looks at me over her shoulder before her gaze returns to her Kindle.

After a minute, she asks, "Can I flip the page?"

I clear my throat. "Yeah."

She taps the screen, and we continue reading. The scene is amping up, and I don't know how the hell she reads this shit in public, because there is no way someone wouldn't notice how hard I am.

When we finish the chapter, she locks her Kindle and climbs delicately off my lap before saying, "Good night," and heading inside.

I lean my head back against the chair, trying to calm down my dick that just wants release now. My mind can't move away from those scenes, though. All I want to do is head inside and ask Hannah if she wants to recreate them with me. After a few minutes, I know I'm not going to get this erection to go away and I head inside and straight for the bathroom. Luckily, Hannah's done and in our bedroom when I get there.

I turn the shower onto cold and step inside. I look down at myself and decide fuck it, I need to rub one out. Gripping myself tightly, I stroke my cock from the base to the tip, taking my time. I picture Hannah naked at the waterfall and how much I wanted to fuck her there. Hannah riding me this morning. My need for her is consuming. I don't want her to think I only want her for her body, though. The sex is amazing. And I love having sex with her, but I want more.

I remember the feeling her body pressed against mine.

The way she tastes.

Her voice when she calls my name as she comes.

That does it. That sends me over the edge, coming with her name on my lips.

I turn off the shower and quickly dry off before quietly making my way into the bedroom, not wanting to wake her if she's already fallen asleep. Standing at the edge of the bed, I stop in my tracks, noticing she's in bed completely naked. Dropping my towel, I climb in behind her, and pulling her into me. She wiggles against me, settling in, and a contented sigh leaves her. I fall asleep to the sound of her soft breathing.

Hannah's not in bed when I wake up. I dress in a pair of gym shorts and a T-shirt and head downstairs. I lean against the entryway to the kitchen as I watch Mom and Hannah move around, cooking together.

"What was your favourite thing to cook with your mom?" Mom asks.

Hannah stiffens a little, and as she avoids looking at Mom, I know she has a fake smile plastered on her face, hiding the pain from her mom not doing those types of things with her.

"I didn't cook with my mom growing up. I did occasionally with my dad, but he was busy working full time. We'd make dinner together when he was home early and could show me what to do. Mom was never interested, though."

Mom nods as she listens, absorbing Hannah's words. Mom has always known just how to respond to all types of news, and as I watch her, I know she knows all Hannah needs is someone to truly listen to her. Not someone to try to fix problems or tell her it's alright.

"Grayson was always in the kitchen with me when he was young. I'm not sure I could have kicked him out even if I wanted to." Mom laughs.

The smile that spreads across Hannah's face as she turns to look at her is genuine.

"I'm not surprised with the way he cooks."

"Oh, good. He cooks for you," Mom says, her smile matching Hannah's.

"Yeah. He always makes sure I'm fed, especially after a shift at the hospital. My dad will be grateful. He's always on me, making sure that I'm taking care of myself, especially with the shifts I work."

"And how did your parents take the news of your wedding? I know I was a bit shocked when Grayson first told us."

I watch as Hannah's shoulders slump. "My mom didn't take it so well. I haven't told my dad yet. I want to tell him in person."

Mom nods. "How do you think he'll take it?"

"He'll be hurt. I'm his only daughter. I know he wanted to walk me down the aisle, and I took that from him, but he'll be happy as long as I'm happy."

Mom stops what she's doing and wraps an arm around Hannah's shoulders and squeezes her. "Are you happy?"

Hannah's silent for a few seconds before she nods slightly and says, "Yeah. I'm happy."

My heart feels like it might burst from my chest. I work to contain my smile as I push off the wall and make my way towards them.

"Good morning," I say, and both of them look over their shoulders at me and smile.

"Good morning, Honey," Mom says as I kiss her cheek.

I move and kiss Hannah's cheek, my lips lingering a little longer as I whisper, "I missed you when I woke up."

Her cheeks flush pink, and her smile turns shy.

"Whatcha makin'?" I ask.

"Pancakes with fresh fruit, eggs, and bacon," Mom says.

"How can I help?"

Mom shakes her head. "We've got this. Why don't you go see your dad. He's on the back deck reading the paper."

I do as I'm told and grab a cup of coffee before joining Dad. Dad doesn't look up from his paper as I settle in the chair across from him. We sit in silence as I look out over the property. After a few minutes, he folds his paper and sets it on the table.

"You happy, Son?" Dad asks.

I set my coffee cup on the table and contemplate how to answer his question. "Right now. Yes."

Dad nods. "And in general?"

"It's complicated," I say.

He turns his chair so that he's facing me instead of the yard. "How's that?"

"There's just a lot going on. It's stressful."

He stares at me as he clasps his hands in front of him and rests them on his stomach, leaning back in his chair. "Stressed at work or in general?"

Dad's really digging in with the questions. He's usually the silent type. I'm not sure what's changed.

"General."

Dad sighs. "Son, what's going on?"

I continue looking over the yard, not able to look at him. "I'm not sure my marriage is going to last," I finally say.

"Why? Don't you love her?"

I lean forward and rest my arms on my thighs, rubbing the heels of my hands into my eyes. "More than anything, but the feeling isn't mutual." I sigh. "We were drunk in Vegas when we got married. I woke up and thought I finally had a shot with the girl I've loved for years while she woke up pissed. When we got back to Vancouver, she told me she wanted an annulment right away. I convinced her to give me ninety days to show her we could work. It's been forty-one days, and I'm not sure I'm any closer to convincing her."

"I see," Dad says, and it hurts to think I disappointed him. My parents raised me to respect women, and I do. I respect Hannah, even though keeping her in this marriage doesn't exactly show that, but I'd regret it for the rest of my life if I just gave up without a fight.

"After the ninety days, I'll sign the papers if she wants, but I couldn't not fight for her."

"You've always loved hard, Grayson. We've watched it with how you love your sister, mother, and I, and we saw it with Rebecca. Just remember to be kind to yourself. Give yourself grace. Your family will always be here for you, no matter what happens."

I release a deep breath, absorbing his words. Him saying I love hard isn't wrong. I'd do anything for my family. "Thanks, Dad."

He stands from the table, clapping me on the shoulder, and says, "I love you, Son," before heading inside.

Hannah comes outside, and when she's standing in front of me, I grab her hand and gently pull her towards me until I can wrap an arm around her waist and pull her onto my lap. I need her close. She giggles lightly as she settles in.

"Breakfast is almost done," she says.

I reach up and run my fingers through her soft hair before tucking it behind her ear. "Thank you."

She smiles.

"Did you have fun cooking with Mom?"

She leans into me more, and I hold her close. "Yeah. I never got to do that with my mom. It was nice."

I lean in and kiss her temple. "I'm glad."

I soak up every moment of holding her like this, knowing once we leave here, things will probably go back to the way they were before. She gets up, and I follow her inside.

CHAPTER 23

Hannah

After breakfast, Chloe offers to take me on a tour of town. I change into a pair of denim shorts, a tank top, and runners before meeting her out front. When we get in her car, country music blares from the speakers. She turns down the music and pulls out of the driveway. I watch the trees that line the driveway disappear as we turn onto the road. She heads in the same way Grayson took us when we went downtown for the Canada Day celebration. She pulls into a parking lot at the far end of Main Street and parks. When we get out, Lennon, Aspen, and Brinley are waiting for us.

They smile broadly, and we all exchange hugs before we start walking down the street. It's full of the same small town charm I saw earlier in the week, but this time the shops are open and people are walking and popping in and out of different stores. We pass a store that has trinkets in the window and tourist items inside. I pull open the door and head inside. The girls follow as I make my way through the store, stopping to look at the different cheesy items.

I find myself in front of the magnet display and grab one that reads *Willow Valley* over an expansive open landscape. I grab a keychain as well and make my way to the checkout. The lady behind the counter is in her fifties, with her greying brunette hair pulled back.

"You visiting?" she asks as she inputs the items in her old-school cash register.

"Yeah. We're visiting my husband's family," I say.

"Oh, how nice. Who are you married to?"

"Grayson Maxwell."

She pauses for a second before she puts the items in a bag. "So, you must be Hannah. I've heard so much about you."

I feel Chloe come to my side. "Yes, I am."

"Hi, Chloe, dear. I was just telling Hannah here how much I've heard about her. You must be happy to have a new sister."

Chloe links her arm with mine. "I am. We do have plans, though, Mrs. Simpson."

"Oh yes, dear. Your total is $11.50."

I tap my card on her machine and take my bag before Chloe leads me out of the store. When we're outside, I look over my shoulder at the door we just left through.

"Word sure does travel fast here," I say.

Chloe gives my arm a squeeze and says, "Don't let them scare you off."

Lennon falls into step beside us. "Chloe's right. Don't let them scare you. There's not a lot to do in town, so people tend to gossip. You eventually get used to it."

A small laugh escapes me. "Well, I'm not sticking around town, so I'm not sure I'll ever get used to the gossip. It's like high school on steroids."

The girls laugh, and we continue our way down the street when Brinley grabs my hand and pulls me into a store. I try and turn around as soon as I see what kind of store it is, but Brinley holds on tight and pulls me further into the lingerie store. The entire store is wall-to-wall panties, bras, baby dolls, anything sexy you could imagine wearing, and more. Brinley does a quick head-to-toe of me before she starts grabbing different items off the racks. I turn to look at the rest of the girls, and they're trying to hold in their laughs.

Help! I mouth.

"Honey, you're just gonna have to let Brinley do her thing. She's done this to all of us at one point."

We follow Brinley as she sorts through items, pulling off specific pieces before moving on to the next. Her hands are full by the time she comes to me and thrusts it all in my direction.

"Ummmm," I say.

"Go try it on."

I stare at the large pile, things I've never seen before in there. She grabs me by the shoulders and shoves me in the direction of the dressing room. I start with the simplest item. It's a red lace demi-bra with matching panties and garters. I go for the black pantyhose she wants me to wear with them, too. When I get everything on, I stare at myself in the mirror, and Goddamn, do I look fucking hot.

A knock on the door startles me.

"You've gotta show us," Brinley calls.

"No," I call back. I'm not ashamed of my body, because I know I'm fucking hot, but stepping out of this room in lingerie is not at the top of my list of things I want to do.

"We're here to help. How can we do that without seeing it?"

I huff and open the door.

All the girls are sitting on the other side. Aspen whistles, Brinley's jaw drops, and Chloe says, "Damn."

I turn a little as I look at myself in the mirror again.

"Your brother is one lucky bastard," Brinley says.

"Ain't that the truth," Aspen says.

"So, you're getting that one. Next," Chloe says.

I pick the next one, a black baby doll with a matching thong. It's cute, but not jaw dropping the way I had hoped. I open the door, and Brinley does a spinning motion with her finger. I do as I'm told.

"Next," she says.

I pick a more risqué piece next. It's just an elastic-type material that goes around my breasts and nipples, with no fabric actually covering anything. The panties, if you can even call them that, are similar. The elastic material follows the outline of my ass, feeling like it's almost giving it a lift, and the tiny scrap of fabric between my legs barely covers anything.

I pop my head out the door, not opening it fully, and say, "If you want to see this, you're coming in here. I'm not stepping foot out there.

The four of them immediately funnel into the tiny room with me.

"Damn, girl. You look fucking hot," Brinley says.

"I'm not sure about this," I say.

"You have to get this," Lennon says.

"I'll think about it."

They shuffle out of the room, and I make my way through the rest of the items Brinley selected. I go back out and grab a couple of the items in additional colours, and by the time we leave, I've spent hundreds of dollars and am leaving with ten new sets.

As we leave the shop, Aspen's stomach growls. "Sorry, it's been a while since I ate breakfast."

"I could go for some lunch," I say.

The girls agree, and we head to a restaurant just down the block. A young hostess, probably about sixteen, leads us to a table in the centre of the full dining room. As she hands me a menu, her eyes catch on my bags and widen before she scurries back to the host stand. I turn and look back at her and see her head pressed together with another hostess and them giggling.

We order and eat. As we're getting ready to leave, my phone buzzes with a text. I check and see that it's Grayson.

GRAYSON

Can't wait to see you in those new purchases.

I look around the restaurant and don't see him.

HANNAH

Not sure what you mean?

GRAYSON

I've been informed you have some bags that contain some fun purchases.

I look at Chloe. "Have you talked to your brother?"

Her brows furrow, and she shakes her head. "No. Why?"

I look around the table, and all the girls shake their heads. "Well, he has somehow found out about my new acquisitions."

Lennon looks over my shoulder, and I follow her gaze to the hostess. She catches us looking, and her cheeks turn pink as she tucks her hair behind her ear. The rumour mill is fucking strong in this town, but it gives me a great idea. I turn back and look at Chloe.

"You wanna fuck with your brother?"

Her eyes widen with anticipation. "Always."

I tell her about the plan, and we gather our things and leave the restaurant. We continue exploring downtown before heading back to the cars. I hug the girls and thank them for joining us, telling them I hope to see them again. We leave in two days, and I'm not sure if or when I'll be back.

Chloe and I drive back to the house to put our plan in motion. When we get back there, Grayson is sitting on the front porch with his phone and a bottle of water. His eyes are stuck on the bags Chloe and I are carrying. When we join him he asks, "Have fun today?"

I smile. "Tons."

I hand the bags to Chloe, and she heads inside. "I'm going to shower before dinner," I tell Grayson before following Chloe. I hear him get up from his chair and follow closely behind me. When I get into the bedroom, he closes the door behind him and leans against it.

I turn and face him, and his eyes are ravenous. "Why don't you show me those new purchases before your shower?"

I play dumb. "I'm not sure what you're talking about. Your text earlier was a little weird. Was I supposed to grab something while I was in town?'

"I heard you made a stop at a little boutique in town. Saw the bags when you got back."

"Oh, those," I say and turn around, digging in my bag to grab fresh clothes as I try to hide my face. "You mean Chloe's new purchases? Yeah, she got some really good things."

"What?" Grayson chokes out.

I bite my lip to hold back my laugh.

"Yeah. Whoever gets to see those is fucking lucky. She definitely has taste." It's getting hard to not crack, but I need to see his face. I turn around and face him. "She got some things that I'm not even sure how you get into the contraption, but she figured it out."

Grayson throws a hand out in front of him. "Okay, you can stop. I really don't need to know what my sister bought today."

He steps away from the door and sits on the end of the bed, dropping his head in his hands.

I open the door and call, "Chlo."

She comes out of her room, and I open the door a little wider as she hands me the bags.

"Was it good?" she asks.

"Worth every second."

She smiles and heads back to her room before I close the door again. Grayson is looking at me in shock.

I drop the bags beside my suitcase and lean down and whisper in his ear, "Maybe you should learn to let a surprise be a surprise."

I grab my clothes and head to the bathroom to shower, satisfied with the way I left Grayson sitting on the bed.

Hannah

Melanie has us spending the rest of the day playing games, just spending time together.

On Monday, Grayson heads to the shop with Randy, and Chloe heads to work at her summer job at a local café. She's working there to make some extra money before school starts again in September. That leaves Melanie and me at the house. I read for the first part of the day and then help her make Grayson's favourite meal. She wants him to get it before we leave tomorrow.

At the dinner table, I feel a shift in the air. Melanie, Randy, and Chloe aren't ready for Grayson to leave again, and I don't think he's quite ready either. If I'm being honest, I'm not ready to leave. I've enjoyed being out of the city and away from my mother. I miss the girls, though. I'm looking forward to a girls' night when I get back.

When we finish eating, Chloe and Grayson head to the back deck. I stay behind, giving them some space as they haven't had a lot of one-on-one time this trip. Randy retreats to his usual spot in his recliner, and Melanie and I stay at the table.

"Thank you," she says, her voice soft.

My brow furrows. "For?"

She looks to the sliding door before back at me. She reaches for my hand and gives it a squeeze. "Grayson has been through more than I had ever hoped he would have to. It's nice seeing him more open and happy now. Coming home can be difficult for him, but this trip he's been"—she lets out a breath—"different. He's lighter and happier. He's stayed longer than he has in the past. He usually comes for a couple of days and leaves as soon as he can. I can't help but think that you're a major reason for that change. So, thank you."

I squeeze her hand back. "I haven't done anything."

"You really don't realize just how much your presence impacts him, do you?" She watches me and must read my answer. Her free hand comes and pats the top of mine. "You two are good together. I'm happy he found a woman as amazing as you."

I'm holding back tears now. Her positive words are more than my own mother has ever said to me. I inhale deeply through my nose and out through my mouth, gathering myself.

The sliding door opens, and Chloe comes sauntering in and starts grabbing things from the cabinets. "It's getting dark. Gray's gonna make a fire and we're gonna have one last night of s'mores," she says.

I smile as much as I can. "Sounds great, I'll be out shortly."

"Mom?" she asks.

"None for me tonight. You kids have fun."

Chloe heads back outside, and Melanie leaves the table, giving my shoulder a squeeze before she leaves. I head upstairs and grab the first sweatshirt I see. I'm in the kitchen when I realize it's Grayson's. I put it on before stepping outside and joining them. There are only two chairs when I get there, and they're sitting in them, Micky lying between them as he stares at the graham crackers and chocolate resting on the arms of one of the chairs. I look down at Grayson, and he smiles as he wraps a hand around my wrist and pulls me into him. I land on his lap. The chair shakes a bit from the movement, and I hold on to him tightly.

His lips find my ear, and he whispers, "I like seeing you in my clothes." His words send a wave of shivers through me.

He wraps his arm around my waist and gets his marshmallow ready on his stick and starts roasting it.

"You excited to get home?" Chloe asks.

"Yeah. I miss my girls, but I'm gonna miss being away from the noise of the city."

"Well, you'll have to come back when you need an escape. We'd love for you guys to visit more."

Grayson stiffens under me. His chest has stopped moving, like he's holding his breath.

"I'll definitely keep it in mind," I say, not wanting to give her too much hope. I still have no idea where Grayson and I stand, especially after we leave here and are thrust back into our everyday lives.

Grayson pulls the marshmallow out of the fire and, before he can even react, I pull it off between two graham crackers, shove a piece of chocolate inside, and take a bite. He stares at me open-mouthed as Chloe laughs.

"You little thief," he says, his eyes tracking the movement of my tongue as I lick of the stray pieces of s'more on my lips.

I lean forward, holding the s'more in front of him. "What's yours is mine. Right, husband?" I whisper.

He leans forward and finishes the s'more in a single bite. I go to lick the marshmallow of my fingers, but he grabs my wrist, stopping me. I watch his throat as he swallows before opening his mouth and slowly sucking the marshmallow off my fingers. His tongue works around them, ensuring he gets every last piece. I squirm in his lap. He's turning me on beyond belief. His eyes are fire as he stares at me.

When he releases my fingers, he puts another marshmallow on his stick and starts the process again.

Chloe finishes her s'more and pushes up from her chair. "I'm going to head to bed. Early morning tomorrow."

She gives us each a hug and says good night and goodbye, because we likely won't see her tomorrow. She calls for Micky, and he reluctantly follows her inside. When the sliding glass door closes, I move to push off Grayson's lap to move to the other chair, but his grip around my waist tightens.

"Where are you going?" he asks, his voice low.

"The other chair."

He leans in close, his breath dancing across the sensitive skin of my neck. "Stay."

I squirm again.

"You horny, Spitfire? Do you need to get off?" His voice wraps around me, sucking me in and bringing me to the edge of begging. I've never wanted a man the way I do Grayson. I've never needed a man the way I need him. I've never begged a man, but Grayson seems to be breaking all those rules.

"Yes," I breathe out.

He tosses the marshmallow stick into the fire, his hand coming to the waist of my shorts and deftly undoing the button before his fingers snake inside the waistbands of them and my panties. He quickly finds my clit, brushing his finger over it lightly and pulling a moan from me before his fingers snake lower.

"So wet for me," he says before nipping my neck. He fights the sting with a kiss. He pulls out his finger, and I mewl at the loss of feeling. He helps me peel off my shorts and panties, dropping them at our feet, and positions me on his lap, my back to his front, a leg on the outside of each of his. I'm fully exposed, the heat of the fire on my pussy.

"Watch. Use the light of the fire to watch me finger-fuck this perfect little cunt," he says as his fingers dip back in.

My head drops back, and he pulls his fingers all the way out again. "I said watch. If you want to come, you're going to watch how well I take care of your pussy."

I move my head and watch as two fingers enter me. He crooks them, finding that spot that is sure to send me over the edge. He builds me slowly, bringing me to the edge before backing away and letting the orgasm subside. Every time my head tries to drop back, he stops. He's torturing me, but the pain is fucking delicious.

His other hand slides up the front of his sweatshirt I'm wearing and under my tank top until he finds my breast. He squeezes it before pulling down the fabric of my bra, exposing it to him completely. He rolls my nipple between his fingers, and the fingers of his other hand continue to work in and out of my pussy. He nips my neck. My mind has no idea where to focus. He's bringing me pleasure in so many ways, but when he pinches my clit, I moan and my mind is positive that's where it's going to focus.

"You're so fucking pretty when you're all worked up for me," he says.

My insides heat at his words. I roll my hips into his hand, needing more. I need to come. He's been holding me on the edge for so long, I need release.

"Do you want to come?" he asks.

I nod vigorously.

"Then beg me for it. Beg your husband to let you come."

"Grayson, please," I mewl. At this point, I'll do what ever he asks, as long as I get to come.

His fingers move a little faster, but it's not enough.

"Grayson, please let me come. I want my husband to make me come," I pant.

"Such a good girl." His praise only makes me wetter.

His fingers move faster, and he rolls and pinches my nipple as he bites down hard on my neck, and I come. I shatter into a million pieces, my body on fire as I call his name, writhing under his touch.

When I've recovered from my orgasm, he pulls his fingers out and holds them to my mouth. "Open and taste yourself. Taste just how good your husband makes you come."

I do as I'm told and suck on his fingers, my taste hitting my tongue as it works over his fingers, gathering every drop. I've never tasted myself before Grayson, and it's not something I'll ever go around doing, but if Grayson tells me to taste myself, I'll fucking taste myself. When I release his fingers, he helps me off his lap and gently helps me dress. The entire time he helps me, my eyes can't leave the sight of his erection. I've never been a tit-for-tat girl when it comes to orgasms, but my mouth waters at the thought of repaying the favour. Of dropping to my knees and pulling him out and taking him as deep down my throat as I can.

When my shorts are buttoned again, I do just that. The grass is warm beneath my knees as I position myself between Grayson's legs.

"What are you doing?" he asks.

"I'm going to make my husband come," I purr.

I reach forward and grip the waistband of his shorts. He lifts his hips, helping me pull them down his legs. I grip his cock in my hand, and he tosses his head back with a groan. I'm not having any of that. If he made me watch it all in order to come, he's going to do the same thing. I release my grip, and his head shoots up as he looks at me, need filling his expression.

"You're going to watch. You're going to watch how well your wife gets you off."

His expression turns from needy to downright feral. I grip him again, giving his cock a few pumps before I lean forward and lick him painfully slow from base to tip. I circle my tongue around the head, and his hips buck. I stop and pull my hair back in a makeshift ponytail, and he grips it in his hand. I lean forward, wrap my lips around the tip, and suck, hollowing my cheeks before moving down, taking him all the way to the back of my throat and repeating it. His grip on my hair tightens as he moans.

Being with Grayson has made me thankful for the fact I don't have a gag reflex, because he easily reaches the back of my throat. I haven't needed it for most of the other men I've been with, but Grayson is by far the biggest. I reach up and roll his balls, and he twitches in my mouth. He likes it. I apply a little more pressure as I take him to the back of my throat and suck, hollowing my cheeks again. The groan that leaves him has me grinning as much as I can around his cock.

I release him with a pop, my hand replacing my mouth.

"Oh, you're so needy," I mock.

His grip on my hair tightens again, and he tips my head back so that I make eye contact with him. "Yes, Spitfire, I'm always needy for my wife. You want to mock me, see if I let you come next time."

Fucking. Hell.

Grayson Maxwell owning up to how much he needs me, but also putting me in my place is the hottest thing I've ever experienced.

His grip on my hair loosens, and I wrap my lips around him again. This time, I don't go slow or tease him. I work to bring him to the edge as quickly as possible. I know he's close when he twitches in my mouth and starts to pull my hair slightly. I hollow my cheeks two more times, and he comes, calling my name. I take every last drop he has to give me. When he's done, I release him with a pop and run my tongue slowly over my bottom lip, collecting any stray drops.

He pulls his shorts back up and leans his head back, and a laugh leaves him. "Fucking hell, Spitfire. I'm not sure what I'm going to do with you."

I stand and brace myself on the arms of his chair. "Keep fucking me, I guess."

He laughs, and I head inside, needing a shower before I climb into bed.

Grayson's not in bed when I wake up in the morning. He's not in the kitchen or the back deck either, but his bags are packed and by the door.

Melanie spots me and gives me a soft smile. "He's not here. He left early this morning. He said he'll be back in time for you guys to get on the road."

"Oh. Okay." Grayson never mentioned to me that he had something to do before we leave today.

I take a seat at the table, and Melanie pours a cup of coffee and places it in front of me. I smile at her and take a sip. It's exactly how I take it. She must read the confusion on my face because she says, "Grayson left a note beside the coffee pot earlier this week with how you take your coffee."

Just another thing chipping away at me previous feelings towards him.

"We're going to miss you," Melanie says, pulling me from my thoughts.

I smile. "I'm going to miss you, too."

She leans forward, bracing herself on the table. "No matter what happens with Grayson, please don't be a stranger."

Her words hit me straight in the heart. Does that mean she's known all along that I was planning on divorcing Grayson? I can't think of what to say, so I just nod. I finish my coffee and head back upstairs to finish packing my bag. As I'm lugging it down the stairs, I hear the mudroom door open and close and Grayson's heavy footsteps. When I meet him in the kitchen, his eyes are full of pain.

"Hey," I say, almost in a whisper.

"Hey."

He reaches down and grabs my bag and his and takes them outside. Melanie and I follow behind him, stopping on the deck to hug each other.

When Grayson returns, he hugs his mom, and I hear her whisper, "Are you okay?" He nods against her and when he pulls back, he kisses her on the cheek and then leads me down to the car.

Grayson's mood is distant when we get in the car. I watch through the side mirror as we leave Willow Valley and wonder if I'll ever get the chance to return.

CHAPTER 25

Grayson

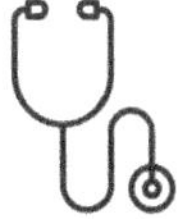

I know Hannah doesn't deserve my distant mood during the long drive home, but I don't know how to kick it. Every time I go and visit that spot, it puts me in a mood that takes time to kick. I had to go before we left. There's no way I'd be able to live with myself if I didn't. In the past, the only people who have had to deal with me after were Mom, Dad, and Chloe, and they understood it. I don't even have the strength to explain to Hannah where I went and why it affects me the way it does.

She's quiet, giving me space, and more and more it shows me I don't deserve her. She's giving me everything I need and asking for nothing in return. It's selfish of me to continue taking from her the way I have been. Every time I visit that spot, it reminds me of the decision I made over ten years ago. It was one I didn't make lightly. It was shaped by pain I don't think I'd survive experiencing again.

Hannah is everything good. She deserves the world handed to her on a silver platter. I want to be the man who does that, and the thought that I can't fucking sucks.

We make a quick stop for lunch in a little highway town before finishing our drive home. It's almost 6 p.m. by the time we get there. When we get upstairs, we settle on the couch; me watching a baseball game and her reading a book. Both of us are silent the entire time. When I yawn, she closes her book, leaving it on the table, and gets up, offering me her hand. I stare at it.

"Let's go to bed."

My eyes dart to the couch where I've been sleeping for the last few weeks.

"Grayson, after this week, we can share the fucking bed. You're tired. Now get up and let's go to bed."

I'm tired and was not looking forward to sleeping on the couch again. I take her hand and push myself off the couch to follow her into the bedroom. She strips and climbs into the bed naked. I follow her lead and do the same. I wrap an arm around her waist and pull her back to my front, kissing her temple, and whisper, "Good night."

She snuggles in, getting comfortable, and whispers back, "Good night."

I wake up in the morning with Hannah sprawled across my chest. She stirs and looks up at me with a soft smile.

"Morning," she says in her sleepy voice.

"Good morning," I say and tuck her hair behind her ear.

She moves and stretches her arms above her head, and I slide out of bed and make a pot of coffee. After a few minutes, Hannah comes out wearing nothing but one of my T-shirts, and it's one of the hottest things I've seen. Seeing her in my sweatshirt the other day had my heart almost beating out of my chest. I knew then that seeing her in my clothing is something I want for the rest of my life, even if it's something I can't have.

I make her a cup of coffee and pass it to her before she settles in a chair at the table. I quickly whip up breakfast and join her.

"What are you doing today?" she asks.

"Not sure."

She nods and continues eating.

I push through and try not to let my mood from yesterday bleed into today. "How about you?"

She smiles. "I'm going to head to Liv's and spend some time with her and Cate."

I force a smile and nod.

"I'll be home for dinner, though," she says.

When we finish eating, she cleans up the dishes, loads the dishwasher, and heads into the bedroom and changes. When she comes back out, she grabs her purse and keys and calls out goodbye before the door closes behind her. I settle back on the couch and put on the sports channel. I don't even realize how much time has passed when my phone rings and I see Chloe's face fill the screen. I slide my finger over and answer.

"Hey, Chlo."

"Hey. How are you? I know you went and visited before you left yesterday."

I sigh. I should have known she'd call and check in. Chloe's a good sister that way, always making sure I'm okay even though I'm the older sibling.

"I'm fine. It was a normal visit."

She's the one to sigh this time. "So, you gave Hannah the cold shoulder your entire drive home then, and likely until this morning."

I open my mouth then close it, because she's right.

"Grayson, you know I love you, right?"

"Yeah."

She takes a deep breath. "Good. Now I'm going to be brutally honest with you. You need to tell her. I know this is a big private thing for you, and that's fine when it comes to your friends, but Hannah's your wife. If you want her to stick around, if you want to stay married, you need to tear down that wall and tell her."

"She deserves better," I whisper.

"Oh, bullshit," she spits. "You're not giving yourself enough credit. I know that you gave Mom a list of ingredients for Hannah's coffee, and when Hannah wouldn't tell her what her favourite foods are, you told her. I saw the note you left beside the coffee maker with Hannah's coffee order. I know you've been there for her when she's needed you."

"It's not enough, Chloe," I almost yell. Her words are tearing at me.

"Have you asked her what she wants and needs, or have you been sitting there making assumptions?"

A lump forms in my throat, because she's right, I've assumed. But it's all from things she's said or things I've witnessed. I can't be that far off.

She sighs again. I can hear her disappointment through the phone. "Gray. You've assumed, haven't you?"

My lack of response is answer enough.

"You're an adult, and I can't force you to do anything, but I will tell you that from the time I've spent with Hannah, I think she'll be more than understanding. She might even be able to help you move on from all of it."

"I'll think about it," I say. I settle deeper into the couch, letting my head rest on the back.

"What did you guys do today?" she asks, and I'm thankful for the subject change.

"I've been at home all day. She went to her friend's place."

"Hmmmm. When do you go back to work?"

"We both work tomorrow," I say.

"Okay. Well, I've got to go. Call me if you need to talk. I love you."

"Love you, too, Chlo."

I hang up and let her words sit with me as I debate whether telling Hannah is a good idea or not.

When Hannah gets home, her arms are full of grocery bags. I jump off the couch and help her carry them into the kitchen.

"Looks like a big haul," I say.

She huffs, catching her breath. "Yeah. I got things for dinner and just to stock the fridge again after being gone."

I start unloading the bags and note some of the things she grabbed. The protein bars I always keep stocked, the orange juice I always buy, she's also grabbed the veggies I usually put in omelettes.

We work together to put everything away, and she grabs a cutting board and gets to work on cutting the chicken breasts.

"What can I help with?" I ask.

"It's all good. I've got dinner tonight."

I nod and take a seat at the kitchen island, deciding to keep her company. "How was your day?"

Her smile lights up her face. "It was great! Baby Cate has grown so much. She's the most adorable little girl. Liv is adjusting to mom life, and Josh just dotes on both of them. I helped her prep a few meals while I was there, so they had some stuff in the fridge. I know Josh is super active with Cate, but with him still working, it can get a little overwhelming, so I helped out how I could. How about you? What'd you end up doing?"

"I just stayed home watched the sports channel. Chloe called to check in and make sure we made it home safe yesterday."

Hannah looks at me. "That was nice. Can you send me her number so I can check in with her? I forgot to grab it from her while we were there."

I try to wrap my head around her asking for Chloe's number. Is she trying to build a relationship with my sister because they're family, or because she wants to be friends with her even after the divorce?

"Yeah," I say and text her Chloe's contact card.

I watch as Hannah moves around the kitchen with grace, cooking. She pulls out plates and cutlery and sets the table, not allowing me to help her at all. When the food is done, she carries it to the table. She grabs us each a drink, and we settle in to eat. She's made a chicken stir fry with rice. We each make a plate and when I take my first bite, I can't help my groan.

"This is really good," I say, also realizing I haven't eaten since breakfast.

She smiles broadly. "I'm glad you like it."

We eat in relative silence, and when we finish, I help her clean up and we settle back on the couch. It's a repeat of last night; her with a book and me watching a game. She adjusts herself, stretching out her legs, and I pat the tops of my thighs, indicating for her to put her legs there. She does, and I begin massaging her feet. The moans that leave her are heavenly. When she starts to fall asleep on the couch, I help her up and we get ready for bed. I pull her into me again, falling asleep with her in my arms.

CHAPTER 26

Hannah

The next two and a half weeks are a blur. We fall back into a regular routine, and it's kind of nice. I've learned I like having someone to come home to after a long day at work, and it's only made better that it's someone who gets it. It's a Saturday, and we're both working the night shift and I'm preparing myself for the craziness. Weekend evening shifts are some of the worst in the ER. People don't have work the next day and do stupid shit while drinking.

We ride in together and manage to make it through the first half of the crazy shift. We take our break together, and when we return to the floor, I see Samantha sitting at the nurses' station like she's waiting. When she spots Grayson, she pushes out of her chair and walks up to him.

"Grayson, I was looking for you. I was hoping to maybe take our breaks together and talk."

"I just took my break," he says, brushing her off.

"Okay, well, how about tomorrow? We're working the same shift then."

Grayson looks up from the chart he's scanning. "I don't think so."

Frustration radiates off her. "We haven't been able to catch up in so long, Grayson," she whines, and I have to hold back my laugh. She sounds like a petulant child.

She looks over her shoulder at me and smirks before she reaches out and grabs his arm.

He looks at where she's touching him before looking at her, his face completely blank.

"Grayson, please," she says while batting her eyelashes.

I reach for my cup of water and take a sip to suppress my laugh.

Grayson's voice comes out with restrained frustration as he says, "Samantha, I highly recommend you let go of me. No, we will not be sharing a meal together. You've seen my wedding ring, and we've discussed the fact that I'm married. You have chosen to ignore it, but I do not. I am married. And like I've said before, I will not be cheating on my wife, so I recommend you quit while you're ahead."

She plasters on a fake smile and says, "Lucky woman."

He shakes his head. "I'm the lucky one by far. She can do much better."

Hearing Grayson defend our marriage like that not only gives me the warm and fuzzies, but also turns me the hell on. Grayson and I haven't had sex since we've returned from his parents'. I don't know why, but I'm all built up now. There's only so much my vibrator can do for me. I need Grayson to fuck me—sooner than later.

Samantha drops her hand before she turns and leaves. Grayson gives me a nod before he heads to bay three to tend to the patient there. I'm on edge for the next three hours, counting down the minutes until our next short break.

When it's time, I find Grayson and stop right beside him, whispering as quietly as I can, "Storage room, fifth floor, east wing."

He gives me a curious look, and I say, "Now." He realizes the seriousness in my words and leaves. I head in the opposite direction, taking the long way there. When I get there, he's already waiting for me.

"Hannah, what's going on?" he asks.

I hold up a condom I snagged on my way up.

His jaw drops. "Here?" he asks.

"Yes. Right here, right now."

He stalks after me, backing me into the wall and bending down to run his nose up the column of my neck. I feel him inhale deeply, and goosebumps scatter across my skin. I reach for his scrubs, undo the tie, and reach my hand inside, finding his cock. I give it a few strokes, feeling it harden in my grip. His hand slips inside my scrubs and panties, and he runs a finger between my folds. I'm fucking soaked for him. Just thinking about his words from earlier has me wet, but having him this close again, inhaling his scent, has me ravenous.

He slowly slips a finger inside, teasing me.

I grip his shoulders tightly. "We don't have time for you to tease me," I exhale.

He pulls his hand out, pushes my scrubs down my legs, and pushes his down until his erection pops free. He grabs the condom from me and tears it open with his teeth before rolling it down his cock. I watch him with rapt attention. It's been too long since I've truly seen him. He turns me around and bends me at the waist. I press my hands against the wall and look over my shoulder, watching his every move.

He grips his cock and runs it through me, teasing my clit, and I chew on my lip before he feeds it into me slowly, inch by inch. I pant as I try not to moan. I chose a closet in the least active part of the hospital at night, but I don't want someone to hear us. Or maybe I do. I don't know anymore when it comes to Grayson.

Grayson grips my ponytail and asks, "What are you?" I know exactly what he wants to hear, and I give it to him.

"Your needy little cock whore."

He groans in my ear as his thrusts come at a punishing pace. He loves when I tell him I'm his. His thrusts are perfect and deep, hitting that spot. Every. Single. Time. His hand reaches around and finds my clit, his finger flicking it twice, and I clench around him.

"Fuck, I missed this perfect little cunt. So needy and wet for me."

His dirty talk does things to me. I clench around him again, on the edge of my orgasm.

"I'm not going this long without sinking into you ever again. You're fucking mine, Spitfire."

"Yes. Yes. Yes," I chant, seconds away from coming.

"You love it when your husband fucks you, don't you? So needy for me."

God, his possessiveness and need to know just how much I need him is not something I thought would do it for me, but it does. It makes me wetter and brings me closer to the edge.

He bites my shoulder, and that's enough to send me over the edge. I bite the collar of my scrub top, hoping that will be enough to muffle the sounds of my screams.

"That's it. Come for me. Come for your husband."

A few more thrusts, and I feel him come, too.

Just as his orgasm is ending, the closet door opens, and we both turn to look and see Samantha standing at the door. She stares at us wide eyed. After a few seconds, she pulls the door closed, and Grayson and I put ourselves together.

Before we step out, Grayson stops me and frames my face with his hands. "Are you okay?'

"Yeah, why wouldn't I be?"

"I just wanted to check, especially with who found us."

I reach up and cup his face. "Grayson, we're doing nothing wrong. Maybe we shouldn't be having sex at the hospital, but it's not like we're cheating on anyone. I'm okay. With that orgasm, better than okay."

He searches my face for a second before letting me go and following me out of the closet. We make our way back to the ER, and after a few minutes, Samantha approaches me. I groan, knowing what's about to come.

"So, you heard Grayson's statement about being married and thought you'd be a home-wrecking whore and go after him anyway?"

I chuckle; I can't help it.

"You think this is funny?" she spits.

"I think your interpretation of it is, yeah."

She glares at me. "You think that it's okay to go around ruining marriages? I never thought you could stoop so low. You really are a no-good whore, aren't you?" Her voice is starting to rise, gaining the attention of more of the nurses and doctors.

Her words mean nothing to me. I know I've done nothing wrong, but from the look on Grayson's face behind her, he's beyond pissed.

"Samantha," he growls.

How he has me going from trying to not laugh, to trying not to melt, is a whole other question. Nurses and doctors alike are watching this interaction now.

Samantha turns around and looks at Grayson. "Grayson, I was just—"

He cuts her off. "You were just what? Sticking your nose in something that is none of your concern? Making a scene at work?"

"It's just... You... I was... You said you were married and wouldn't cheat on your wife. Hannah seemed to be intent on making you."

Grayson throws his head back and laughs. She turns and glares at me.

I stand, wanting to be at even height when I say this to her. "It's not cheating if I'm his wife." I hold up my left hand and my rings, and she pales. I see the shock on the other nurses' and even some of the doctors' faces. "So, no, I'm not a no-good, home-wrecking whore. You caught me and my *husband*." I make sure to emphasize the word for her.

She turns and looks at Grayson. "You married *her*? Why?"

He scoffs. "That's really none of your concern, now is it?"

Tears start to fall down her face before she runs off down the hall. Grayson is in front of me almost instantly as he grips my face. His go-to move when he's worried about me.

"Are you okay?" His voice is full of worry.

I hold his wrists as I look him in the eye. "Grayson, I'm fine. Honestly, I found the whole thing kinda funny, because I knew the entire time just how wrong she was."

He leans forward, rests his forehead on mine, and releases a deep breath. "I'm glad, no one has the right to talk to you like she did." He kisses my cheek before whispering ever so quietly, "And the only time you should be called a whore is when I call you my needy little cock whore."

My knees nearly give out. I want to beg for him right here, but I know it's not the place. I step out of his hold and say, "I'm fine. I promise."

He turns around, and we both see someone from hospital administration standing at the end of the hallway. She jerks her head to the side, and Grayson nods and follows behind her.

As soon as they're out of sight, the nurses join me at the nurses' station.

"You're married to Dr. Maxwell?" Polly asks.

I nod. "Yeah."

"When?"

"How long?"

"I thought you hated him."

Questions are fired at me from all directions.

When they've stopped, I say, "Two months. It's complicated, but no, I don't hate him. Now, I'd really like to get back to work."

They nod and disburse.

Grayson returns after a while and comes straight for me.

"How did it go?" I ask.

"It was fine, they were a little upset we didn't report it to HR sooner. You need to sign this." He pushes a piece of paper towards me.

Declaration of Romantic Relationship

I quickly read through it and sign at the bottom beside Grayson's signature.

"Can you also sign this, please?" He slides a new form in front of me.

Update to Employee Records - Emergency Contact

I read the form and see that Grayson is updating me as his emergency contact.

"Are you sure?" I whisper.

He leans on the counter. "Yeah. It was Caleb, but he has a family now, and my parents and sister are so far. I can change it in a month once I find someone else."

I stare at him and nod before signing the form. I gnaw my lip. My current form has my dad and mom as my emergency contacts, I don't want Mom on there anymore.

"Do you have another form?" I ask.

He pulls out another form and gives it to me. I quickly fill out his information and turn it to him to sign. He slips it in with his forms and heads back the way he came. I settle back in my chair, the events of the day hitting me in full force. We were just outed at work, I was called a whore, and I have been added as Grayson's emergency contact and added him as one of mine. Today will be a day that's hard to forget.

CHAPTER 27

Grayson

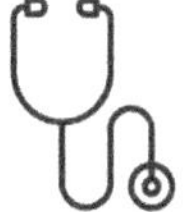

I t's early Sunday morning when Hannah's phone starts ringing like crazy. She silences it and rolls back into my side, but it rings again. She rolls over and silences it again, only for it to ring again when she's back at my side.

"Really?" she groans as she rolls back and looks at it. She sighs heavily and answers. "Morning, Mom."

Running a hand over my face, I climb out of bed, slipping into a pair of boxer briefs, and make my way to the kitchen to make coffee, knowing as soon as Hannah hangs up, she's going to need some.

Her face is full of frustration when she comes out of the room. As soon as she's close enough, I hand her a cup. She manages to give me a soft smile before plopping down in a chair at the table and taking a sip. I don't think I'll ever get tired of the sight of her in my shirt.

I take a seat across from her. "Why was your mother calling?"

Her shoulders slump as she sighs. "She informed me that she's planned a little celebration to celebrate our marriage this Saturday night. She's lucky it's one of my days off, but you're working the night shift on Friday, so I told her you probably won't be able to make it."

She tips her head back before wiping her eyes. Seeing how a single phone call from Lauren impacts Hannah has my blood on fire. She wants nothing more than her mother's love and approval.

"I'll be there," I say.

She looks at me, her tears sitting in her eyes, begging to fall. "Grayson, you don't have to. It's my mother. She should have asked if that day worked for us. I know how hard a Friday night shift is. I'll just go on my own."

"Spitfire, we're family. You're my wife. I'll be there."

My words have her tears falling in earnest. I stand and slide my hands under her thighs, picking her up as she wraps her legs around my waist and her arms around my neck. I carry her to the couch and sit with her wrapped around me. She holds on tightly as she cries, and I run my hand over her hair and kiss her temple. When her sobs subside, she's still holding on. I want to be her rock. That place she knows will keep her safe in the storm.

I kiss her temple again and whisper, "Do you want to go back to bed?"

She nods against me, and I carry her, pulling the blankets aside so she can climb in. I climb in behind her, pulling her in tight. Her head rests on my chest while I run my fingers through her hair as her finger traces over my skin.

"Have you talked to your dad?" I ask.

"No," she whispers. "We're having dinner later this week."

"Invite him on Saturday. It's your party. In fact, you should invite the girls, too. If you're going, you should be surrounded by people who support you."

Her hand stops its delicate movements. Her breath dances across my chest as she lets out a long breath. She nods slightly. "You're right."

I feel the tension slowly leave her body as she relaxes into me. I don't let myself sleep until I hear her soft snores.

This week has been a shit show at the hospital. Samantha called out for a couple shifts, so we were down a nurse, and we seemed to receive all the crazy cases over the last few days. I'm tired as fuck when I wake up from my nap on Saturday. I take a cold shower to help wake me up so I can make it through this party. Hannah's dad agreed to be there tonight, along with all of our friends. I gave the guys a heads up about Lauren so they aren't surprised when they get there.

Hannah's dinner with her dad went about as she expected. He was sad to have missed her wedding and lose the chance to walk her down the aisle, but he said as long as she's happy, he's happy for her.

When I come out of the shower, Hannah's looking at herself in the floor-length mirror. My jaw hits the floor. She's wearing a gorgeous lavender dress that accentuates her every curve as it hugs her body. The dress dips to the middle of her back in a tasteful but extremely sexy way. She's wearing strappy black heels that make her only a few inches shorter than me. Simple makeup highlights her natural features, and her hair is done up, showing off her long neck, and all I want to do is go over and mark every inch of it. I want to write *mine* over every inch of her body.

She notices me staring and smiles at me in the mirror. I can't help myself. I walk up behind her and wrap my arms around her waist as I kiss her neck.

"You look stunning," I whisper between kisses.

"Thank you," she whispers between her quickening breaths.

I give her neck a little nip, and she moans.

I step back and say, "We should get going."

She nods and faces me. With a wicked little grin, her fingers walk up my chest as she leans in and whispers, "I'll get you back for that," and walks away.

I know she'll follow through, and I look forward to it.

When we pull up outside Lauren's, tension radiates off Hannah. Her knuckles are white she's holding her clutch so tightly. I move around the car and pull open her door. I undo her seatbelt and spin her so she's facing me. Placing my hands on either side of her face, I make sure she's looking me in the eye before I say, "Don't let her get to you. I know it's hard, and she's your mom, but you are smart, and strong, and gorgeous. You are a respected nurse. You have friends who love you. She does not get to define your worth, only you do."

She nods, and I kiss her forehead, offering her a hand to help her out of the car. We walk hand in hand to the front door, and I knock.

Richard opens the door, a large smile on his face. He hugs Hannah before offering his hand to me, and I shake it.

"I'm so glad we could do this," he says as he leads us inside.

The party spills out into their large backyard. Tables covered in white linens and food line the edge of the grass. Just to the right of the back door is a bar, with a young-looking bartender serving drinks. Opposite him is a table stacked with gifts.

With my hand on her lower back, I guide Hannah outside. Her mother spots us immediately and comes over, pulling Hannah into a hug. The fake energy radiates off Lauren. It's so practiced that most people can't even tell it's fake, but after seeing the last interaction Hannah and her had, I can see through it. I don't know how Hannah has dealt with her for so long, but I promise myself I'll stand by her and make sure she doesn't need to face her alone.

When she releases her, she turns her fake smile to me. "Oh, Grayson. It's so nice to see you again. I'm glad you could make it. When Hannah said you couldn't because of work, I was so disappointed." She shoots Hannah a look of disapproval that grates every one of my nerves.

I wrap an arm around Hannah's waist and pull her in close. She doesn't resist, her body moulding to mine perfectly.

"Well, when Hannah mentioned it, I knew I couldn't send her on her own, so a little power nap after my long overnight shift and here we are. Hannah was just being an understanding wife when she said I couldn't make it. She knows just how hard the overnight shifts are, especially on the weekend. I appreciate her for it."

Lauren's lip purse for a second before returning to her practiced smile as she tries to hide her distaste for me standing up to her.

"Well, either way, I'm glad you're here. We should really get you mingling with people, so we can get started," she says.

"Oh, we're still waiting for people, we can't truly get things started without them," I say, and the joy I feel at the look that flashes across Lauren's face is indescribable.

"What do you mean you're waiting for people?" she asks, her voice barely hiding her displeasure.

I kiss Hannah's temple and squeeze her hip before saying, "Oh, since this is supposed to be a party celebrating our marriage, we thought it only appropriate we have some of the people that mean the most to us here. My family couldn't make the trip on such short notice, but we did get to enjoy a week with them, so they're okay with that."

Just as I finish, I see Josh and Liv walk into the backyard with baby Cate, followed by Matt.

"Speaking of which, some of them have arrived. Please excuse us as we mingle." My hand moves to the small of Hannah's back as I guide her towards our friends.

When we're out of earshot of her mother, Hannah leans in and whispers, "Thank you. I don't think I've ever seen someone stand up to my mother like that."

I stop us and turn to her, cupping her face and running my thumb softly over her cheek. "I'm not going to let her continue to treat you like you're some screw up because you don't fit some mould she wants you to. You are perfect the way you are. One day, I'll make you see it."

I drop my hand, and we finish making our way over to Josh, Liv, and Matt. Liv and Hannah hug as I shake hands with the guys.

"Thanks for coming," I say.

"Oh, we wouldn't miss this for the world," Olivia says. She peeks around us quickly and quirks a brow. "Although Lauren doesn't look pleased."

"We didn't exactly tell her we invited more people. I'm looking forward to her reaction when Hannah's dad gets here," I say.

Liv's eyebrows raise almost to her hairline. "You invited Bert?"

I nod and grin. "We couldn't celebrate our marriage and not have him here."

Liv shakes her head and holds back a laugh. "You're really looking to stir the pot, aren't ya?"

I look at Hannah, taking in just how beautiful she looks tonight, but also how her beauty is coupled with an anxiety I've only seen when she's near Lauren. I turn back to Olivia. "I'm looking to support Hannah."

I hold eye contact with her and watch her sharp intake of breath, and it's then I know she knows what I feel for Hannah.

We talk for a few minutes until Zoey, Liz, Caleb, Bailey, and Charlie arrive.

Hannah grips my arm as she leans in to me. "I feel my mother's eyes burning into the back of my skull."

I look over my shoulder and see Lauren staring at Hannah, a look of disapproval barely concealed on her face.

"Oh, look at my gorgeous girl," a man in his late fifties says as he walks out of the house and hugs Hannah.

She relaxes and wraps her arms around him as he sways her back and forth.

When he pulls back, he places his hands on her upper arms. "Now, don't you look beautiful."

"Thanks, Dad."

He looks at me, and his smile is genuine as he says, "You must be the Grayson I've heard so much about."

My eyes flick to Hannah, and pink tinges her cheeks. I reach a hand out to shake his. "I am. It's a pleasure to meet you, Mr. Smith."

"The pleasure's all mine, son. It's nice to finally meet you."

"You, too. I'm sorry I couldn't make dinner earlier this week. I was on a bought of night shifts at the hospital."

He pats me on the arm. "No need to explain. I know how crazy your guys' shifts can be. I'm just happy when I can actually see my daughter."

We laugh and socialize with our friends. People come over and offer their congratulations, and we do our best to be polite with these people we don't know. The night is winding down and people are starting to leave when the air around us changes, becoming cold and stiff.

"Albert." Lauren's voice comes from beside me.

His smile is forced, but not fake the way Lauren's is. "Lauren. How are you?"

"I'm good. I'm just going to steal Hannah away for a minute."

Hannah's eyes widen as she looks at me.

I lean down and kiss her cheek whispering, "You're strong."

She nods slightly and follows her mom.

I clock the time the second they walk away and check my watch every five seconds.

"You good?" Liz asks.

"I'm giving her three minutes before I go and check on Hannah," I say.

"I'm sure she's fine. It's just her mom," Matt says.

I look at him with a serious expression. "I'm giving her three minutes, and then I'm going to check on my wife."

Matt laughs. "Separation anxiety, Mr. I-Won't-Fall-in-Love?"

I shake my head. "No, I'm going to make sure that this time when we leave this house, my wife isn't in tears. I'm going to make sure that someone who should love and respect her isn't in there tearing into her because she hasn't conformed to the mould she wants her to fit."

Matt's jaw drops, and I walk towards the house, not caring if the three minutes are up or not. When inside, I follow the sound of raised voices.

"How dare you invite that man into my house?" Lauren shrills. "Why can't you just do as expected? I raised you, fed you, put a roof over your head, and this is how you treat me, by making a fool of me in front of my friends?"

I round the corner as she throws her arms out to the side. Hannah spots me, and I lean against the doorway. I'll step in if I need to, but I want to give Hannah time to handle this.

"Why are you so ungrateful?" Lauren continues.

Hannah takes a few deep breaths, her eyes on me, and I breath with her. That small action seems to ground her a bit.

"This party was supposed to be to celebrate my marriage. I'm not sure why I wouldn't be able to invite my friends or my father," Hannah says, her voice coming out strong and steady.

"Do you really think your friends belong in this life? With my friends?" Lauren says on a huff.

"You mean to say that my polite and respectful friends don't belong here? Or is it because they don't all come from money the way you've married into it?"

Lauren's head snaps back. "Don't talk to me like that, young lady. Don't forget your place. I brought you into this world, and I can take you out of it."

Hannah shakes her head, and her arms flail at her side as tears start to gather in her beautiful hazel eyes.

"My friends are the family I've chosen. They've supported me for years. They are the ones who have been in my corner when you haven't. They are the ones I've called after particularly shitty days in the ER when I've lost children or I've seen a woman come in with her spirit broken after she's been raped. When I've been sick or needed a pick me up, they are the ones I've turned to, because I've learned that I can't rely on you. You continuously taught me that unless I fit into this prefect little mould, you wouldn't support me. Well, Mom. I've finally learned that lesson, and I think I'm better for it. I'm done. I don't want this relationship anymore. I'd rather have Dad and my chosen family than someone as superficial as you. So tonight, when I leave with my husband, know that will be the last time you'll see us. You've lost me."

I'm beaming with pride as I watch Hannah speak her mind. My Spitfire has finally stood up to the one person she's been so timid with. I walk up to Hannah and kiss her cheek before taking her hand and leading her to the backyard so we can say our goodbyes. Neither of us say a word to Lauren as we walk past.

CHAPTER 28

Hannah

When we walk in the front door, I'm still vibrating with energy after the confrontation with my mother. Seeing Grayson come for me, knowing the type of relationship I have with her and his subtle nod as he leaned against the doorway, gave me a strength I didn't know I had. I knew in that moment that no matter what happened, Grayson was there and he'd stand by me.

I follow Grayson into the bedroom, where he perches on the edge of the bed and pulls at his tie. My eyes nearly popped out of my head when I saw him for the first time tonight. He's wearing a suit that fits him perfectly. It's practically sculpted to his ass the way it clings to it, leaving nothing to the imagination. The way his pants fit his legs, it's obvious he plays hockey. His white shirt pulled just enough over his chest and stomach for you to know he's fit without being able to count his abs under it. Six, by the way. He has a very defined six-pack, which I'm currently thinking about licking ice cream off of.

He takes the tie off and tosses it to the chair in the corner before he begins working on the buttons of his shirt. I step between his legs and stop his hands. He looks up at me, a tired look on his face. This man worked a twelve-hour overnight shift and then came home and napped before getting up and going to a party at my mother's so I didn't have to go alone. He convinced me to really make the party for us and invite our friends and my dad. A lump forms in my throat.

I take over, slowly making my way down the buttons. I help him slip out of the suit jacket and then his shirt. I kneel on the ground before him and undo his shoes before slipping them off, followed by his socks. I reach for his belt, undoing it before dragging his pants down his legs and leaving them with the rest of his clothes on the chair.

I stand and run my fingers through his hair, and he leans into my touch. I continue scratching at his scalp, and his arms wrap around my waist, pulling me in close as his head rests on my stomach. His content sigh dusts over my stomach.

He looks up at me, resting his chin on my stomach. "I'm proud of you," he says, and it hits me like a bullet. I didn't know how much I needed to hear those words. My dad's said them to me, and I know he means them, but I needed someone else to say them and mean them. The sincerity in Grayson's eyes tells me just how much he means it.

I tip my head back, trying not to cry and losing the battle. Now Grayson helps me out of my dress. His hands find the zipper at the back and slowly pulls it down. The cool air hitting my newly exposed skin causes goosebumps to erupt. The thin straps on my shoulders slip down my arms, and the dress pools at my feet. I step out of it, and he slips to the floor and deftly undoes the straps of my heels before I step out of them.

He stands and pulls the blankets back and nods at me. I climb in, scooting to the middle, and he follows behind me, pulling me into his chest. His lips brush the top of my head before his fingers run through my hair. We don't speak. We're content in the silence and each other's company, and it hits me like a ton of bricks. This right here, comfortable silence with someone, being able to pull strength from the presence of someone, that's what I've always wanted. That soul-consuming, life-altering love I promised myself I'd search for; I have it.

I'm head over heels, madly in love with my husband. I love Grayson Maxwell.

The stress of the day and the realization have my dams breaking. Tears stream down my face as Grayson holds me tighter, kissing the top of my head. He knows me well enough that he doesn't push or ask questions, he just lets me feel.

I fall asleep wrapped in the arms of my husband, the one man I never thought I'd fall in love with.

I'm distant with Grayson for the next few days. I don't know what to do with this new realization. How the hell am I supposed to act? Am I supposed to just blurt the words out and hope he says them back? Do I want him to say them back? My mind is a complete jumble. Luckily, we have our group camping trip this weekend, so I use packing to distract me.

It's almost a five-hour drive to Osoyoos. We leave mid-morning, so we're there for the 4 p.m. check-in time. I stare out the window the entire drive. At one point, Grayson's hand finds my upper thigh and stays there for the rest of the drive. I try hard to hide my grin. I love when he touches me. I think I must be weird, because I think I might prefer his nonsexual touches, the ones that feel like he just can't survive another second without touching me.

At the campsite, we all set up. Baby Cate is passed around as Liv helps Josh get their tent set up despite his protest that he can do it himself. I walk up to Zoey and take Cate from her, instinctively bouncing as soon as I have her.

I boop her nose and she starts giggling, and I can't hold back my grin. I watch Grayson walk past me and sit as far as away from me as he can get. It's like his mood has done a complete one eighty. I continue playing with Cate before handing her back to Liv for her feeding. I make my way over to Grayson, taking a seat next to him.

"You okay?" I ask.

He nods, but I can feel the tension radiating off him.

I rub a hand up his arm. "You can talk to me."

He looks at me, and his hand covers mine. He stares at our hands, his thumb rubbing gently over mine. "Thanks." His word come out so low I almost don't hear it.

We spend the rest of the day between the water and lounging on towels, enjoying the sun. The guys talk sports, and the girls read. We all fit in nicely. Being here with everyone relaxing and taking time away from our jobs to be with each other makes my words to my mom really sink in. I was right. These people here are my chosen family. These are the people I want in my life.

At dinner, we convince the guys to listen to an audiobook like we did during our last trip. I'm surprised Grayson doesn't make a fuss like he did last year, though. He sits and listens intently to the story. It's only when everyone around the fire starts yawning do we turn in for the night.

We're relaxing by the water after lunch when my phone rings, and a number I don't recognize flashes across my screen. I grab it and step away from the group and answer it.

"Hello?"

"Hannah," Melanie's voice comes through. "Please don't let Grayson know it's me." She takes a deep breath, and worry fills me. My head swings around, making sure no one followed me or is nearby.

"Is everything okay?"

"No." Her voice cracks. "I need your help. I'm going to call Grayson as soon as I get off the phone with you, but I need someone to be with him when I call him. He's going to need you." She releases a long breath that holds so much pain and worry. "Randy's in the hospital. He had a heart attack, they think. Grayson's going to want to come here as soon as we get off the phone, and I know there's no stopping him. He's stubborn, I know. But can you please come with him?"

I hold back a sob. I barely know Melanie and Randy, but in the week we spent with them, they completely embraced me and pulled me into the family. Him being in the hospital is terrifying.

"Yeah, of course. There's nowhere else I'd be." I tip my head back and think. "Is the hospital in Willow Creek?"

"No, it's about twenty minutes west in West Bridgejaw."

"Okay, we're about an hour and a half away. We'll be there as soon as we can."

"Thanks, Honey. We'll see you soon."

"See you soon."

I hang up and give myself thirty seconds to gather myself. I make a beeline to Caleb. I watch Grayson as his phone rings, and I know I don't have much time. I crouch beside Caleb.

"Can you guys take our stuff home with you? We'll grab our bags and as much as we can quickly, but we've got to go right away."

Caleb is immediately on alert but nods. "Yeah, of course. What's wrong?"

It takes everything in me to hold back my sob. "It's Grayson's dad."

That's all Caleb needs before he's up and out of his chair. He makes his way to our tent and is helping pack what he can get his hands on and throwing stuff in the car.

I make my way over to Grayson and see the pain written all over his face as he talks to his mom. I stop in front of him and watch as tears gather in his eyes.

"Yeah, we're on our way," he says and hangs up.

"Han." He doesn't even get my full name out before he's wrapping his arms around me, and I'm holding him back just as tight. We hold each other for a minute before I pull back and grab his face.

"He's going to be okay. We're gonna get in the car, and we're gonna drive to the hospital, and we're gonna see him, and it's all going to be okay."

We both turn towards the tent and everyone is up and helping grab everything that we have laid around the campsite. They've taken our bags out of the tent and loaded them in the car, and Bailey is packing snacks in the front seat for us. We make our way to the car and hug our friends, thanking them for the help. Caleb confirms he'll take the tent with him, and we load up. I offer to drive, but Grayson shakes his head, saying it will help keep him calm. He holds my hand tight the entire drive. Neither of us are able to eat the food they left us, our stomachs both in knots as we worry about Randy.

A highway sign comes into view.

West Bridgejaw 5 km

Grayson's grip on my hand tightens as he takes the exit and navigates the streets towards the hospital. He parks, and we quickly make our way inside, following the directions Melanie gave Grayson over the phone. When we exit the elevator on the third floor, we hang a right and see Chloe and Melanie sitting side-by-side in the waiting room. Chloe is the first to spot us, and she rushes out of her chair towards Grayson. He catches her, and she cries into his shoulder.

Melanie hugs me and thanks me for coming. When Grayson lets go of Chloe, he hugs his mom and Chloe comes to me, wrapping her arms around me.

"Thank you for coming. I don't know how Grayson is going to do with being a visitor in a hospital again. Having you here is what he needs." Her words have me confused, but I know now is not the time to be asking questions.

"I wouldn't let him make the drive alone," I say.

"The doctors were in with him and said they'd come get us soon," Melanie says as we settle in chairs in the waiting room. Being in a hospital for anything other than work is weird. I'm not running around and checking on patients or worried about pages.

"Do you guys need anything? Coffee? Tea? A snack?" I ask.

They shake their heads, and I make my way to the nurses' desk. There's someone sitting at a computer inputting information, and when she's done, she looks up and smiles at me.

"Hi, I'm here to see my father-in-law, Randall Maxwell. I understand the doctors are in with him now, but I'm a nurse out in Vancouver and I was wondering if you could give me any information regarding his status to be prepared."

She looks back at the computer and types something in before smiling back at me.

"He's currently in stable condition. We've administered morphine for his pain. His EKG and ECG were good, and his cardiac panel is clear. His BNP and D-dimer were fine, so we don't suspect a new heart condition, likely some lifestyle changes should be the only thing that needs to change. We're going to continue monitoring him for twenty-four hours."

I nod. "His blood pressure is good? Was he conscious?"

"One fifteen over seventy-nine, and he was awake when the doctor went in."

I nod again, feeling better now that I have more information. "Thank you."

"Of course."

I leave the nurse's station and head back to the waiting room.

Grayson looks up as I join them, and the pain written all over his face has me nearly buckling at the knees. I sit beside him and immediately take his hand and give it a squeeze.

"He's conscious, and his EKG and ECG were clear, and his cardiac panel came back good, too. They don't suspect a heart condition."

Grayson relaxes back in his chair and runs his free hand over his face. I watch some of the worry fade.

"They told you all that?" he asks.

"I just told them that I'm a nurse in Vancouver and here to see my father-in-law. She looked up his file. Nurses stick together. I knew that we'd both feel better with any information they'd give us, so I needed to try."

He leans forward and whispers, "Thank you," across my forehead before pressing his lips there. He holds them there as he wraps his arms around me, and I lean into him, lending him whatever extra strength I can. He pulls his lips away and leans his head on top of mine.

"Randall Maxwell," the doctor calls, and we all stand at once.

"Yes," Grayson says.

The doctor holds his hand out for Grayson and they shake. "My name is Dr. Ritter. I've been looking after your father since his admittance to the ER. We've run all the tests, and he seems to be doing okay for now. I'd like to keep him for twenty-four hours for observation, and then we'll release him. He'll need to make some lifestyle changes, fewer fats, leaner meats, and more exercise. He's in room 3315. You guys can go visit for a bit before visiting hours end."

"Thank you, Doctor," Melanie says and leads us all down the same hallway the doctor walked out of.

When we get to Randy's room, Melanie pushes open the door and gasps lightly before she rushes to his bedside. He's in a hospital bed and gown attached to all the normal monitors. He has an IV in his left hand dispensing saline to help keep him hydrated.

Randy looks confused when Grayson and I walk in behind Melanie and Chloe. "Mel, you didn't have to call them."

"Yeah, she did, Dad. You had a heart attack," Grayson says.

Randy waves his free hand in front of him. "I'm fine."

Grayson grips the rail at the foot of the bed and ducks his head between his shoulders, taking a few deep breaths before he looks back at his dad. "No, Dad, you're not fine. A heart attack is serious. I'm just glad that I was only an hour and a half away. I'm not sure I could have taken it if we were back in Vancouver. You need to take care of yourself. You're going to need to change your diet and start exercising. We can't lose you. I can't lose you."

Grayson is using all of his strength to keep it together. I see the way his muscles shake as he grips the rail. His eyes are full of torment. There's a knock at the door, and a nurse enters with a tray.

"Good evening, Mr. Maxwell. I have your dinner here." She places the tray on the rolling table and moves it closer to him, removing the cover for him. It's a stereotypical cardiac care unit meal. Chicken breast, brown rice, and cooked bell peppers and green beans.

"Thank you," I say before the nurse leaves us.

Grayson's stomach growls, and I realize it's been a while since we've eaten. I reach into my purse and grab a protein bar and hand it to him. He shakes his head.

I position myself so he has to make eye contact with me. "Please. For me."

He takes the bar from me and unwraps it and takes a bite. I smile at him and settle at his side, running my fingers through his hair.

"Randy, you've got to eat," I say.

He grumbles but starts to cut his chicken breast.

"We'll stay with you guys for bit to get Randy settled and work to get a good diet going for him," I say.

Grayson stares at me.

"Oh, we can't ask you guys to do that. What about work?" Melanie asks.

"I'll call the hospital. We're staying. It's not up for discussion," I say.

Melanie wipes at a few tears and gives me a warm smile. "Thank you."

"Of course." I turn to Grayson. "I'm just going to step out and call the hospital and get us the next week off. We can decide later if we need more time." I kiss his cheek and leave the room before heading outside and calling the hospital. I'm able to get both of us the week off with little fuss for a family emergency and then call Liz. I settle on a bench as the phone rings.

"Hey," she answers.

"Hey," I say before breaking down in tears. My chest heaves as all the stress and worry from the last few hours pours out of me. Not only from hearing about Randy but watching the pain Grayson was going through. Watching him in that pain was pure torture, because I could do absolutely nothing for him. I felt so useless when I'm so used to having some control. Not being able to do anything for him was probably the worst thing I've ever experienced in my life.

When my sobs subside and I gather myself enough to talk, I say, "He's okay. They're gonna keep him for twenty-four hours, and we're gonna stay for at least a week to make sure that he gets settled at home. We'll be back before Caleb and Bailey's wedding for sure."

"Okay. How are you?" she asks, concern filling her voice.

"I'm okay. I felt so useless watching the pain that Grayson experienced. I couldn't do anything for him."

"Oh, babe. You're doing everything for him. Being there right now is what he needs. He needs you."

I release a breath slowly as my brain slowly catches up to my feelings. "I love him," I whisper.

"I know." That's all she says, but Liz has always been observant. I guess I'm not surprised she knew before I did.

"I don't know what to do. This is the worst possible timing, and I know he's keeping something from me."

"Han, you know exactly what to do, but for now, just go be with your family. The rest of it will fall into place."

I nod even though she can't see me. "Thanks," I say.

"Any time. I'll update everyone else that his dad is okay, so don't worry about that. Call if you need anything at all."

"I will. I'll talk to you later. Love you."

"Love you, too."

I hang up and sit on the bench for a few more minutes before I head back inside and join my family.

CHAPTER 29

Grayson

Hannah has been my rock ever since Mom called. She's not only made sure I have everything I need, but also that my family's taken care of, too. When we got here, I never thought to go talk to the nurses to see if they could give any sort of update on my dad, but she knows nurses know almost as much as the doctors about patient status, if not more at times. She got enough information to give us peace of mind, and that's all I could ask for.

She holds my hand tightly for the thirty minute drive to my parents' place. The doctors eventually kicked us out, saying Dad needed to rest, and I know they're right, but seeing him lying in that bed and not being able to stay was hard. Hannah assured me we could come back as soon as visiting hours begin tomorrow and said we needed to grab some real food.

After we eat, we head upstairs and crash. The day has wiped me completely, and I sleep straight through until morning.

We're up early so we can arrive at the hospital as soon as visiting hours start. Seeing Dad lying in a hospital bed in a shitty hospital gown will never be easy. He's in his usual good mood when we walk in. The doctor comes in and tells us his overnight observation went well and that they'll be discharging him today. Hannah is doing everything and anything that can be done to help get him out of here quickly. After a couple of hours, we're loaded in the car and begin the drive back to Willow Valley.

Dad keeps the drive full of chatter, either talking Vancouver Cyclone trades with me or sharing memories of my childhood with Hannah. The two of them get along so well, and it has her worming herself deeper into my heart. I already loved her, but seeing her with my family is just another sign she's the one for me. The only person I'd ever settle down with is her.

Dad settles into his chair at home, and Hannah and I walk Mom and Chloe through his new diet and how they need to push him to exercise. Even going for long walks can greatly help him. We confirm we'll stick around for the week to monitor him ourselves to make sure he doesn't have any residual effects from the heart attack. Hannah and I discuss the fact that we're without a few supplies to get us through the week. She writes me a list of what she needs, and I run into town to grab everything. I'm walking out of the grocery store when Rebecca's voice stops me.

"Grayson," she says.

I turn and smile, although it's awkward and I'm not sure it comes across as a smile. This is why I don't come to visit often.

"Rebecca."

"I heard about your dad. I hope he's okay. I know it must be serious if you're here from the city."

I run a hand down my face and take a deep breath. "We were in Osoyoos, so it wasn't that far of a drive. He's doing okay. They discharged him this morning, so Hannah and I drove him back. He's settling at home now," I say.

She nods. "I'm glad." She fidgets with her hands in front of her in a way she only does when she's unsure or nervous. I used to take hold of her hands and kiss her knuckles when she'd do it. Her cheeks would turn pink, and her attention would be focused solely on me and her nerves would go away.

"I was wondering if you'd like to grab coffee with me. Talk?"

My chest feels tight at her word. I haven't spent time alone with Rebecca since the night before she was admitted to the hospital eleven years ago. Chloe's voice fills my head.

Maybe you should talk to Rebecca while you're here. Maybe it will help you cope. This is not how you deal with all your emotions. I'm not sure you ever fully moved on, Grayson. If you want your marriage with Hannah to work, I think it's time you face the past.

Having Hannah at my side through everything with my dad has cemented for me that I need to figure out my shit and find a way to keep my wife. I have a serious feeling that's going to mean facing the one thing I've been running from for over a decade, but Hannah's worth it. She's worth everything.

I swallow past the lump in my throat and say, "Sure."

She follows me to the car, where I tuck the groceries away before we walk to the corner café in silence. We each order a coffee and find a table in the corner. The silence is uncomfortable, and it makes me miss Hannah. With her, we can sit together and not say anything and I don't feel like I need to leave or say something to fill the void.

"How've you been?" I ask.

She smiles softly. "I've been good. I enjoy my work. It lets me be home with Jack as much as possible, and Daniel's able to be around when I can't."

"I'm glad," I choke out.

She leans forward, resting her arms on the table as her hands wrap around her coffee. "You have questions," she says. She's always been able to read me. I don't know if it's that I'm easy to read or just years of being with someone.

I sigh. "Yeah."

"You can ask them."

I can't look at her. Looking at her and asking these questions will probably crack whatever semblance of decorum I have right now. I find a spot on the wall over her shoulder and talk to it.

"I'm sorry." The words fall out of me.

"For?" she asks, confusion filling her voice.

"I failed you," I whisper, and my eyes quickly dart to her.

The look on her face has me unable to look away. She has no idea what I'm talking about.

"After we lost the baby, I failed you. If I had done something"—I run a hand through my hair, trying to gather myself—"anything. I don't know. You went through so much. When your dad called—" I choke back a sob as a tear runs down my cheek. I'm on the cusp of losing it, but I know I need to push forward and have this conversation. "When your dad called and said you'd attempted to take your life, I knew I had failed you."

"Oh, Grayson," she says before shuffling her chair closer to mine. She grabs my hand and holds it tightly.

I look her in the eye, needing her to see how much this has eaten me alive for the last eleven years. I need her to know just how sorry I am.

"Grayson, you didn't fail me. You're the only reason it took me so long to do it. You kept me fighting right after." She wipes at her tears, and my heart feels like it's being ripped out of my chest the same way it did then. "I was so depressed after the miscarriage. I felt like I had failed you and myself. My body hadn't done the one thing it was meant to do. Have a child. I spent every day sitting in my room, going over what I could have done differently so that we could have our baby. That night wasn't the first time I had thought of ending it all. It was you and your love that stopped me each time before. That night was a bad one. It was right after Mother's Day, and I was going through a drawer in my desk and I found a notebook I had forgotten about. I had used it when I first found out I was pregnant. I used it to write different ways to tell you. Seeing it had everything rushing in at once. I couldn't take it. I needed the pain to go away. I didn't want to burden you anymore, because I knew you were in pain, too."

Tears are streaming down both of our faces now. I squeeze her hand to show her I'm still here with her, and she continues.

"When they admitted me to the hospital, they ran a battery of tests. One of them was a hormone test. They said that my levels were far from normal, and it was contributing to my depression. I got in to see a therapist, and I was able to talk through it all."

I nod. It makes sense in my head now that she's saying it. I'm a doctor, I've seen how badly a hormone imbalance can affect a patient. I think the trauma was so ingrained in me that I never thought to examine it more. I wanted to bury it all down as far as I could and never talk about it again. It was the miscarriage that made me decide to go to medical school. I wanted to do my best to be able to stop other people from experiencing the life-altering pain we did. I ended up in emergency medicine, helping stop people from losing those already with us. My heart wasn't able to tolerate prenatal or obstetrics.

"And therapy helped?" I ask.

"Yeah. I still go. I don't think I'll ever be over what happened. We lost a baby we both wanted. We were ready to start a family together, but life had other plans. I'm happy now. Therapy helped me get to a point where I was ready to try to have kids again, and I'm glad I did. I wouldn't give Jack up for anything in the world. My world begins and ends with him. I still have my bad days, but the good days outweigh them now." She smiles. "I take Jack to the tree and tell him about you and the sibling he won't meet. Our baby isn't forgotten. I like to think that they're looking over Jack and whatever future kids you or I might have."

I shake my head. "I don't think kids are in the picture for me."

She squeezes my hand. "And that's okay. Grayson, you don't have to process this the same way I did. You don't have to move on the same way I did. Your grief and pain are valid. I'm glad that you have Hannah to support you."

My eyes leave hers, and she reads my evasive expression.

"You haven't told her, have you?" she asks.

I shake my head.

"When you're ready, you should. Knowing that I have Daniel in my corner on the hard days is my saving grace."

She sits back in her chair, and we finish our coffees before we leave the café. Outside, she hugs me and I wrap my arms around her tight. This hug is more healing than I thought it would be. This hug feels like I may be able to put the past aside and move on, not forgetting it, but not letting it control me anymore.

When we separate, she squeezes my arms and says, "Take care of yourself, Grayson."

"You, too."

I turn and walk back to my car, each step away from the café making me feel lighter.

CHAPTER 30

Hannah

Grayson's weird when he gets back from the store. When I look at his eyes, it looks like he's been crying, but I don't know why. When Chloe gets home, she takes one look at her brother and her eyes widen. She knows something.

Melanie and I make dinner, and it's nice that I can fall into the same rhythm we had a few weeks ago. It's nice to be at this table surrounded by people who all love and care for each other. Realizing these people are my family has been healing in ways I didn't know I needed. Cutting out my mom didn't leave the void I always thought it would. I think the reason it took me so long to do it was because I always thought that, even though we weren't close, finally saying I wasn't putting up with the toxic behaviour anymore meant I'd feel like I was missing something I could never get back. I was wrong. All she did was cause me stress and unhappiness. Being surrounded by Grayson's family has showed me I have everything I need.

After dinner, I curl up on the back deck with a blanket and book while Grayson spends some time with his dad. I must have fallen asleep, because I'm woken up when Grayson lifts me out of the chair to carry me upstairs and place me in the bed. I snuggle into my pillow as he covers me with the blanket before climbing in behind me and wrapping his arms around me.

In the morning, Grayson is waiting for me in the kitchen with a cup of coffee and a serious but hesitant expression. Micky is sitting beside him, his head resting on Grayson's thigh, like he's offering him support. I scratch the top of his head before taking a seat across from them.

"Good morning," I say, accepting the coffee from him.

"Good morning. I was hoping I could take you somewhere today," he says.

I nod. "Okay. Like the waterfall?"

He shakes his head. "No, but it's important to me."

I place my coffee on the table and take his hand. "Grayson, of course, I'll go. Let me just go get dressed and we can leave."

I push up from my chair, and he catches my wrist. "Finish your coffee, and I'll make us some breakfast. Then we can go."

Worry fills his eyes, and I can tell he's stalling for some reason, but I nod and sit back down. He moves around the kitchen and makes us omelettes, just like he does back home, and we eat together in silence. When we finish, I quickly change and meet him at the back door.

We load into Grayson's car, and he pulls away from the house, but he doesn't go down the driveway, instead he takes a right between the fence and the garage and drives down a dirt road I never paid much attention to. He drives for a bit before he stops in front of a gate. He leaves the car wordlessly and opens it before driving through, stopping to make sure he closes it before we continue. The drive is slow and bumpy as he navigates around the potholes. On our left is trees that separate their property from the neighbours while the right side is open fields. A creek runs through part of it, horses stopping to drink from it.

After five minutes, Grayson pulls into a field and parks twenty metres away from a lone white oak. It's large, probably thirty metres tall. Grayson takes a deep breath before getting out of the car. I follow behind him as he reaches into the back to grab something. We meet at the front of the car, and he's holding a bouquet of flowers and a blanket tucked under his arm. He takes my hand, and we walk up to the tree.

As we get closer, I can see a small section has a collection of old flowers. When we reach the tree, Grayson squeezes my hand before placing the flowers on the ground and running his fingers over something that's carved into the bark.

WE LOVE YOU 3-16

I give Grayson space, knowing this place is important to him. He hangs his head for a minute, and then he takes my hand and lays the blanket a few paces away before he sits down. I sit beside him, and we look out across the expansive field.

"Rebecca and I dated in high school," he says, breaking the silence.

I don't say anything, wanting to give him the opportunity to continue.

"We started dating in tenth grade, and it was a whirlwind. It was teenage love. That naive love when you know nothing of the world. It was a couple weeks after Christmas during twelfth grade when she told me she was pregnant. I was scared shitless, but I was also so excited about starting a family. I knew we were still so young, but we loved each other and we were committed to doing everything we could to give our baby the life they deserved. We told our parents, and they weren't stoked because of our age, but they were all supportive, agreeing to be there through the whole thing, helping how they could. I was going to switch my university to online and do classes at night and find a job in town during the day. Once we graduated, we were going to find a tiny little house to move into, and we were going to raise our baby."

He brings his legs up and rests his arms on his knees, his eyes still trained on the horizon, not once turning to look at me. He sighs heavily and continues.

"I had just gotten home with my dad after working at the shop when she called. When I answered, she was sobbing. I could barely understand what she was saying. All I managed to get was that she was bleeding. I rushed to my car and drove straight to her house. Her parents weren't home. I rushed inside and found her in the bathroom on the floor. She was crying so hard she was hyperventilating. It was when I got her to breathe normally that I noticed all the blood."

He wipes at his tears, and I'm unsure of what to do. Do I

comfort him or let him continue? When he wipes at his tears again, I say fuck it and sit up on my knees and shuffle towards him. I use my thumb to wipe at his tears before wrapping my arms around his left arm and leaning into his side. His body relaxes slightly as he exhales, and his right hand finds mine and he grips it tightly.

"She was having a miscarriage," he whispers, and my heart drops. I knew where this was going from how he was talking and my medical background, but that doesn't make it hit any less hard. My own tears gather as I feel the pain my husband has kept bottled up for so many years.

He takes a minute to gather himself and continues. "I rushed her to the hospital in town. It's small, but they were able to help her. They explained what was happening, and I held her as she cried in my arms. We both cried. The baby wasn't planned but was so wanted."

He rubs the heels of his hands in his eyes.

"The doctors watched her for a bit but eventually released her, telling her she could expect cramping and bleeding for a few hours, but it should subside eventually. They kept saying that there was nothing we could have done, and at the time, my brain just couldn't comprehend how something so horrible could happen. I took her home, and her parents were there. I was the one who had to explain to them what happened. I practically lived at their house for the next few weeks. I stayed in the guest bedroom, but I refused to leave Rebecca. We came out here, one of our favourite places, and carved into this tree a reminder of our baby.

"It was hard. Rebecca became a shell of herself. She wasn't the bright, vibrant girl I had fallen in love with. She kept apologizing to me for losing the baby. She kept saying she had failed me, and no matter how many times I'd tell her she didn't, she wouldn't believe me."

He shakes his head as he takes another deep breath, and I know he's nowhere near done unloading all the trauma he's kept inside of him all this time. Another tear falls as he continues.

"It was the Monday after Mother's Day when her dad called me after school. Rebecca had used pills to attempt to take her own life. She left a note apologizing to her parents and me, saying that she couldn't go on knowing she had failed me and the baby. But she didn't fail me. I failed her."

His tears fall slowly as he continues staring out in front of him. I run my hand through his hair, showing him I'm here for him but giving him the time he needs. He leans into my touch, and my heart jumps in my chest, knowing he's finding some sort of comfort from my touch, as he recounts probably the most traumatic thing he's ever experienced. The wind blows through, lightly rustling the branches of the tree and my hair. Grayson's chest rises as he takes a deep breath, like he's letting the wind take away some of the weight he's been carrying.

"I saw Rebecca yesterday. We sat and had coffee and talked, like really talked, for the first time since she was admitted to the hospital that night. I'd been avoiding her for years. She was the reason I hadn't been coming home a lot and why when I did visit, my trips were short. Seeing her and knowing I had failed her all those years ago was devastating. Failing her was why I had decided that love and relationships and kids weren't for me. I still don't think that kids are for me."

He turns and faces me for the first time since sitting down.

"That's why I let you get away after you walked in on Samantha kissing me. I knew I couldn't give you everything you wanted and needed. I figured it was better to let you go before either of us got too attached."

He reaches forward and tucks one of the wind-blown strands behind my ear. I lean into his touch.

"I knew then you were someone I could fall madly, deeply, and completely in love with," he whispers.

My tears are falling in earnest now as I let the weight of everything he's told me settle in. I knew before that I love Grayson, but this solidifies it. I decide to wait until a different moment, one that's about us, to tell him, though. Instead, I encourage him to lower his legs, and I straddle his lap and wrap my arms around his neck, holding him tight to me. His arms find their way around my waist, and his entire body relaxes into me.

When he pulls back and looks up at me, I run my hand through his hair again. "What do you need?"

"I think I need to find a therapist when we get back to the city."

I nod. "Okay, we can do that. What do you need right now?"

He reaches up and cups my face, I lean into his hand as his thumb strokes my cheek. "Right now, I just need you," he whispers.

I lean forward and press my forehead to his. "You have me."

We wrap our arms around each other and just hold each other. I'm not sure if he realizes how serious I was when I said he has me, because he does. Body, mind, and soul, I belong to Grayson Maxwell. This marriage may have started with a drunk night in Vegas, and me wanting to get out of it as quickly as possible, but now I know I want to spend the rest of my life with him.

The rest of the week, we help his parents settle into their new normal. When we leave Thursday morning, I'm trying to figure out what I'm going to do with only ten days left in our agreement.

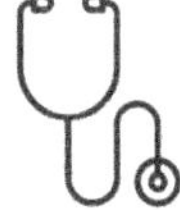

CHAPTER 31

Grayson

I'm dead on my feet when I walk in the door Saturday morning after my Friday night shift. I'm hoping to eat something with Hannah before she heads in for her day shift. I drop my keys on the counter before making my way to the bedroom to find her. The door is cracked as I make my way down the hallway, and her voice filters out.

"The wedding is the day before the end of the ninety days."

I stop dead in my tracks. I knew the ninety days ended the day after Caleb and Bailey's wedding. I've had the date ingrained in my brain since she agreed to this arrangement. I just didn't think she was thinking about it as much. I guess I let myself get caught up in everything. I knew she wanted out of this marriage. I'm not sure why I let it get away from me.

"I don't know what to say," she says. "It's all so much."

I turn around and grab my keys off the counter and head to grab some food.

I'm sitting in Sammy's Diner waiting for my food when Eliza slides into the booth across from me.

She assesses me for a few moments before she says, "So, when are you going to tell her?"

I take a sip of my water, not wanting to have this conversation right now. Hannah's words are still tossing around in my mind as I try to come to terms with the fact that in eight days, my marriage may be over. The thing that makes it sting a little more is the day before I get to stand up with my friend and watch him marry the love of his life.

"I'm not," I say.

Liz sits back in her seat and shakes her head. "Down right dumb, the both of you," she says, and I choke on my water.

"Excuse me?"

"Both of you refuse to see what's right in front of your faces. I can't tell either of you, because for some reason neither of you can understand reason."

I shake my head, trying to understand what she's skirting around, but she changes the subject.

"How's your dad?"

I clear my throat. "He's good. Not a huge fan of his new diet, but him and Mom are enjoying their walks together."

My server places my food in front of me and a takeout bag in front of Liz. She thanks the server and stands.

"Grayson, just remember, don't fuck this up." With those parting words, she leaves the diner, and I'm left staring at her back, wondering what the fuck just happened.

When I return to the apartment, Hannah's gone, and I shower and crash. For the next two days, we're like passing ships in the night, one getting up and ready for work as the other comes home and crashes. Tuesday is the first day we have off together, and the tension in the air is palpable. I don't know what to say to Hannah. I want her more than I did at the beginning of this, but I'm not sure I can put my heart on the line anymore and ask her to stay.

Opening up to her at the tree was hard enough. Reliving that pain all over again had me nauseous. Her touch was like a salve to my heart as I told her my deepest secret. She stayed with me, too. She didn't try to leave or talk me out of my feelings; she listened and held me. I didn't think I could fall more in love with her, but I was wrong.

We sit to have lunch together, and she slides a piece of paper with a list on it across to me.

"I did some research, and these are some of the best therapists that deal with trauma from youth and PTSD. I think one of them could help you. I've added their numbers and where they practice so you can also search them if you want."

She tucks her head as if embarrassed, but my heart wants to beat out of my chest. I haven't found the time since getting back to research therapists like I said I should, but she just took it right off my to-do list for me, finding multiple that would meet my specific needs. Hannah Smith doesn't know it yet, but she holds my heart in her palm, and with every gesture like this, she squeezes it a bit more, making giving her up that much harder.

I place two fingers under her chin and force her to look at me. "Thank you," I whisper, and she nods.

I need to make the most of the last few days I have with her, so I ask, "Can I take you to dinner tonight?"

Her eyes widen as she nibbles on her bottom lip. "Yeah, that would be nice," she says.

We finish eating, and I head out to grab a few things. Returning, I hide them in my office until it's time for us to leave. I've made us a reservation at one of my favourite upscale restaurants in the city. I tell Hannah to dress to the nines, and she spends a few hours getting ready. When she steps out of the bedroom in an emerald dress that lands at her mid-calf and hugs her every curve, my mouth goes dry.

She's stunning.

The dress has long sleeves, and the neckline comes up to her throat. She's completely covered, yet I know what's underneath all that fabric. I've spent my time tracing her body with not only my eyes, but my fingers, my tongue.

I reach down and adjust myself in my slacks and approach her. I hand her the bouquet of lilies and carnations I grabbed earlier. Her face lights up as she takes the flowers and sticks her nose in them, inhaling deeply.

"Lilies are my favourite," she says as she fills a vase with water and settles them inside.

I know, I think.

After locking the door behind us, I take Hannah's hand, needing to touch her as much as possible while I still can.

The lighting is intimate in the restaurant as soft music fills the air, but I barely notice any of it as I stare at Hannah. The way her hair delicately cascades over one shoulder, or when her finger meticulously runs through the condensation on her water glass. My skin heats at the feeling of her eyes on me. Her pupils dilate when I adjust my watch or take a slow sip of my wine. The sexual tension could be cut with a knife, and as much as I want to take her hand and leave with her, I want to draw it out, because I know that when we get home, we'll be explosive.

"What are you girls doing Friday night?" I ask, needing something so my control doesn't snap.

"Liv's parents are taking Cate, and Charlie will be with Caleb's mom, so after we get our nails done, it's a night in with movies, snacks, and booze," she says. I hear the happiness for Bailey and Caleb, but also longing in her voice. I know our Vegas wedding deprived her of what she always wanted.

If I could, I'd go back and make sure it was everything she wanted. Everything.

I take a deep sip of wine and decide to admit to something I haven't told her yet. I didn't think I'd tell her.

"I remember more of our wedding than I let on," I say.

She sits straight, eyes assessing me.

"The next morning it was flashes, but it's come back to me more since then. I remember being super drunk. We'd been at the end of weekend mixer. You weren't going to go, but some nurses convinced you to come. We ended up in some big group together." I smile, thinking about it. "You were wearing this white dress with little green flowers on it and these wedged sandals. Some doctor from a hospital in Edmonton was hitting on you. You smiled at him, and I almost lost my cool."

I take another sip of wine, needing it to continue. Hannah watches me with rapt attention, but I can't tell how this story is impacting her. Is she mad that I didn't tell her? Curious for more details?

"We ended up outside the hotel, and some guy was offering people money to do insane things. You were the first to spot him. I could see the excitement in your eyes. He offered you twenty dollars to get a piggy back from a stranger for five minutes, and you did. You then made me do it. He said he'd give me fifty dollars to marry someone of his choosing. I said no, but you insisted. I was so drunk and wanted to see more of the truly carefree smile you had, so I gave in. He picked you. He took us to some chapel a few blocks down. We stopped at this jewelry store you saw on the way and picked out rings before we got married by an Elvis impersonator. The guy handed me the cash and left. We somehow made it back to the hotel. You insisted we spend our first night as newlyweds together and came to my room. You walked in the door, stripped, and climbed into one of the beds before crashing. I climbed in the other and went to bed, too."

She runs her teeth over her lip as her fingers run up and down the stem of her wineglass. I'm on the edge of my seat, unsure of what's running through her mind, needing to know what she's thinking.

"Hannah," I prompt.

She sighs. "As much as I hate to say it, it sounds like me. The girls have always told me I'm extremely impulsive when I drink, and I guess because there hasn't been any lingering repercussions, I've never truly believed them. I know I like to push boundaries when I'm sober, so I guess this is just a natural progression of that."

"So, you're not mad?" I ask.

She shakes her head. "Mad for what? That we both let alcohol drive us to get married? No. I was when we first woke up and you told me. It was a lot to take in. I never thought it was something that would happen." She pauses, mulling over her words. "If I look at it now, I can't say it's the worst thing that's happened to me. I've enjoyed the last three months. I've realized a few things that I don't think I could have without it."

There's so much between her words, and I want to ask her, but she beats me to it. "While we're admitting things, I should probably tell you that when this first started, I tried to *How to Lose a Guy in 10*

Days you." She looks at me through her lashes, and it all hits me and I can't help but laugh.

"I see it now," I say, and she blushes. "I knew something about that movie felt familiar."

She looks at me wide-eyed. "You've watched the movie?"

I guess I'm just spilling a ton of secrets to her tonight. "Yeah. I've watched a few of your movies. I've also read some of your books. I wanted to experience some of the things that bring you joy."

She opens her mouth before closing it. She tips her head back and releases a slow breath.

I want to take the attention off me and circle back to her comments about the last three months, but as I open my mouth, our server arrives with our food. He places the plates in front of us before walking away.

Hannah seems to have moved on when she asks, "I know Caleb didn't want a big bachelor party, so what are you guys doing?"

I cut into my steak, taking out some of my frustration at not being able to get more answers. "Poker and beers," I say.

She nods, and the conversation moves on to small talk. I'm not sure if I should be happy that after everything we can slip into simple conversation, or disappointed that we aren't going back to our previous conversation.

When we finish eating, I pay the bill and we leave the restaurant. A cool breeze sweeps through the streets, and Hannah wraps her arms around my right arm and holds herself close to me. I relish the feeling. The breeze comes again right as we reach the car and causes the scent of her perfume to fill my nose. I want to spend the rest of my life smelling that sweet, floral scent on her.

CHAPTER 32

Hannah

Tonight's date with Grayson was one of the best I've ever been on, although every date with him has been that way, so I shouldn't be surprised. Even after the heavy conversation surrounding our wedding night and how it came to be, we were able to effortlessly slip into easy conversation. I like that we can talk about mindless things and enjoy each other's company.

He revealed secrets tonight that had me falling for him more. As if that's even possible. Grayson may not have said the words, I love you, but he's showing just how much he cares for me with his actions. Knowing he wants to experience the things that bring me joy is more than I could ever ask for. Grayson is so different from the way I've viewed him for the last two years, and I'm glad I got to see this side of him over the last three months.

I told myself I would take full advantage of the days I have left with Grayson, and I kept that in mind when I got dressed for tonight. I'm now excited to get home and show him what I put on for him under my dress.

When we walk into the apartment, Grayson loosens his tie and I watch every movement of his fingers as they pull at the material. How they move so skillfully, undoing the top few buttons and exposing a few inches of his bare chest. I want to climb him like a fucking tree. He takes off his jacket and hangs it over the back of a chair before he meticulously undoes the buttons of his sleeves and rolls them up. His muscles flex and the veins bulge, and I'm practically a puddle at his feet.

He catches me watching and smirks. "Having fun, Spitfire?"

I swallow, hoping to fix my dry throat. "Yeah," I practically pant.

He stalks towards me, only stopping when his chest brushes against mine. He leans down, his breath dusting over my ear as he exhales. "I'm glad."

I inhale deeply, his scent completely taking over me. I manage to shake my head and remember I had plans for tonight. I bring my hand to his stomach, and he takes in a sharp breath the second my fingers touch him. They dance up his torso as I rise on my tiptoes.

"I have something to show you," I whisper in his ear before stepping away.

His eyes are molten lava as he looks at me. It's my turn to smirk.

I turn around and make my way towards the bedroom, checking over my shoulder halfway there to ensure he's following me.

When we're in the bedroom, I have him take a seat in the chair in the corner. Facing him, I reach behind me for the zipper of my dress, slowly pulling it down, allowing the sound of the teeth coming apart to fill the room. Grayson's chest rises faster as his breathing quickens. I'm holding my breath, knowing tonight is going to be one to remember.

When the zipper's all the way down, I slowly push my dress off my left shoulder, allowing it to drop halfway down my arm and giving him a nice view of the red strap of my bra. I repeat the process with the other shoulder, this time letting the dress fall to the floor.

I feel so powerful standing in front of Grayson in nothing but the red lace demi-bra I picked out in Willow Valley, and the matching panties and garter belt set. Grayson grips his erection through his slacks, and I tisk.

"Now, Grayson, if you want to touch me tonight, you're going to have to listen to me. Rule number one, no touching me or yourself without my consent."

He removes his hand and nods. I purposefully walk towards him, stopping when I'm right in front of him, and bend over, placing my hands on the arms of the chair. His eyes dip to my breasts before returning to my eyes.

"Be a good boy and use your words. Tell me you understand, and I'll reward you." I grin.

"I understand," he says, and it's like he's injected power straight into my veins.

"Good. I bought this just for you while we were in Willow Valley. I thought of you every time I tried on something new and lacey."

"Fuck," he groans, he eyes trailing over every inch of my body.

"I take it you like," I say, leaning forward and brushing my lips along his jaw.

"Very much."

"I'm glad. Now help me take off my bra."

He reaches behind me, and his hands quickly find the clasps, undoing them. My bra falls forward and down my arms, until it's lying in his lap and around my wrists. I stand and drop the bra on the floor beside him. I slowly remove my garter belt and panties, leaving them with my bra before turning around and moving to the bed, positioning myself so Grayson has a perfect view of me.

"You enjoyed watching me last time, didn't you?" I ask, as I reach into the nightstand drawer.

"Yes," he groans, probably knowing exactly what I'm going to do.

Grabbing what I'm looking for, I plant my heels on the bed and spread my legs, giving Grayson a good look at just how wet I am. He groans as I turn the vibrator on. It's the same one I used that day in the field, and I know he notices, because a whispered, "Fucking hell," escapes him. I trail it over my breasts, recreating that moment. Everything I did that day. Every movement, but this time, I say his name louder. I want him to hear his name on my lips as I come. I want him to know he's who I'm thinking of.

I'm panting after my orgasm tears through me. When I've come down enough that I know I'll be able to walk, I push off the bed and approach him.

"Open," I say, and his jaw drops immediately.

I place the vibrator on his bottom lip. "Clean this off like a good boy, and I'll let you eat dessert again."

He holds eye contact as he cleans every last drop of my cum off the toy. When it's clean, I grab his hand and pull him from the chair and lead him to the bed. I climb on and drop the toy at my side.

"Strip," I command.

He does as he's told but takes his sweet fucking time exposing each inch of skin as he slowly undoes the buttons of his shirt. When his hands reach for his belt, I put a foot out, stopping his movements.

"I've been patient, but don't test me. Now, take them off nice and fast or you'll be punished."

I watch the wheels turn in his head as he decides if he wants me to punish him. I see the moment he decides to do as he's told, and his pants and boxer briefs are on the floor in seconds. My foot returns to the bed, and he drops to the floor. As he leans forward, I close my legs, and he looks up at me. I stare, waiting for him to ask.

"Spitfire, can I eat you pretty pussy now?'

My legs drop to the side in response, and he grins. He leans forward, and his tongue works through me leisurely. He repeats the movement, like he's savouring me. It reminds me of when you have the last portion of your favourite food and you take your time with it, not wanting it to be gone.

I buck my hips, and he hums against me. I'm hovering on the edge. I need to come. When he goes to tease his tongue on my clit, I grip his hair and hold on tightly. He gets the hint and sucks my clit into his mouth, sending me flying. I come, his name on my lips as my muscles spasm. He stands, grinning between my now-limp legs that hang off the edge of the bed. I shuffle back and give him a *come here* motion with my finger, and he follows me.

"I want you to fuck me so good I'm feeling you for days," I say.

He reaches into the nightstand and grabs a condom, holding eye contact as he rips it open and rolls it down his hard cock. He positions a pillow under my ass before he runs the head of his cock through my wetness and teases my clit. He repeats the motion before slowly sliding the head inside me. I moan as I stretch around him. He's meticulously slow, making me take him inch by inch.

Going slow is as hard on him as it is on me. It's all over his face as he clenches his jaw. When he's all the way in, he falls forward, his head in the crook of my neck as he breathes harshly.

"You're mine," he growls, and I clench around him. Those words are more true than he knows.

"Grayson. Move," I moan.

He nips at my shoulder as he pulls out to the tip and then slams back in. My back arches off the bed as my hands find his back. I scratch at his back as he fucks me slow and hard. I feel every inch of him. He's destroying me from the inside out, and I'm loving every moment of it.

He pushes back up and lifts my hips even higher off the bed, and I scream as he slams into me again. He hits that spot with such precision I'm already about to come again. I roll my nipples between my fingers, trying to bring myself to the edge even faster. I want to come. I want to squeeze his cock until he's coming, my name on his lips.

His thumb finds my clit, and a single swipe of it sends me crashing over the edge. As the orgasm begins to subside, he applies more pressure to my clit before his hand leaves and comes down in a slap, and I'm falling over the edge again. He lets me recover before sending me over the edge again.

Leaning forward, he whispers, "You're so pretty when you come with my name on your lips."

My body is so spent, I can't even smile at him. He lifts my right leg to my chest, and I swear I'm going to die. I've never come this many times with a guy.

"One more, Spitfire. I know you've got one more," he grunts.

When his eyes meet mine, it only takes two more thrusts before I'm scratching at his back as my vision fades and I call his name. This orgasm isn't just mind-blowing, it's soul-shattering. I'm giving him a piece of me in this moment, and I'm not sure I ever want it back.

He comes with me, my name on his lips as he empties himself into the condom. We stare at each other as we work to catch our breath. He rolls off me, heading into the en-suite, and I take in the scratch marks I left on his back. I feel a sense of pride leaving my mark on him so that anyone who sees them knows he's spoken for. He returns with a warm washcloth and helps clean me up before he tosses it to the corner and climbs into bed. I shuffle off and head into the washroom. I do my business before staring at myself in the mirror.

It takes everything in me to not burst into tears. After tonight, I only have four days left in this ninety-day agreement, and I'm so torn. I don't want it to end, but there's something missing that I can't put a finger on. It's that one thing that will have me throwing caution to the wind and telling him I've fallen head over heels in love with him. I just don't know that I'll get that before it's too late.

CHAPTER 33

Hannah

Leaving Grayson Friday morning is hard. We spent Wednesday and Thursday wrapped in each other, only leaving the bed to eat and replenish our energy before falling back together. I'm not sure which of us was more insatiable. This morning, he watched me dress before making me a cup of coffee and kissing me on the cheek before I left. No matter what I do, my thoughts continue to return to him, even when I'm surrounded by the girls.

"Earth to Hannah," Zoey says as she waves a hand in front of my face.

"Hmmmm?" I say.

"You're day dreaming, and you walked in a little funny." She grins. "You and Grayson had some fun last night."

She's not wrong, just missing the forty-eight hours before that, too.

"You're not telling us something," Liz says, ever the observer.

I sigh.

"She's fallen in love with him," Bailey says, and my gaze moves to her. She's looking at me with a soft, knowing smile.

Hearing someone else say those words out loud has it hitting so much harder. Knowing I'm still missing something in the relationship has tears gathering behind my eyes, because I also know I won't ever find a love like this again. It's one of those ones that buries itself into your soul and when you lose it, it takes a piece of you with it.

I blink a few times and plaster on a smile. "Today is about you, Bailey. You're getting married tomorrow. So let's focus on that," I say.

She shakes her head. "You're my friend, Hannah, and seeing you find love will always be important."

Ughhh, this girl. As if I wasn't already feeling enough.

Lily, Bailey's best friend, walks in the door at that moment. "I've got several bottles of champagne, homemade chocolate chip cookies, and chocolate," she says while carrying a big box. She sees all of us and places the box down. "What's wrong?" she asks, worry filling her voice.

Bailey stands and gives Lily a hug and says, "Nothing, just Hannah falling in love with her husband."

I collapse back on the couch. "Can we please move on?" I huff.

Everyone shakes their head, and I cross my arms over my chest like a toddler.

Olivia laughs. "Oh, babe, you're just proving Bailey's point."

"I know falling in love can be scary," Bailey says. "But it's so worth it. Don't deprive yourself of it."

Bailey knows what she's talking about. She left an abusive marriage and thought she wouldn't find love again until she met Caleb. I've seen how he dotes on both her and her daughter, Charlie. I know I love Grayson, but we're like a puzzle with one missing piece right in the centre and you can't say it's finished until you find it. It's as though he's holding something back from me and my soul can sense it. I need us to both be in this relationship one hundred percent. I need him to trust me enough to share whatever it is that he's holding back.

"I'm missing something," I admit, and they look at me quizzically. "I don't know what it is. I can't put a finger on it. I just know that even though we enjoy each other's company, he makes my day's better, and the sex is out of this world, there's something missing." I straighten. "But enough about me and my marriage. We're here to celebrate Bailey and Caleb getting married. So let's pour the champagne and head out and get pampered."

The girls, knowing I'm done with this conversation, agree, and we pop the first bottle of the day.

Saturday morning is a rush of excitement as we get ready for the wedding. Caleb stayed at Josh and Liv's last night so we could have the entire house for the girls. They decided to have the wedding at a local park with a gorgeous view and floral area. They wanted to get married somewhere that meant something to them.

Caleb's mom comes over with Charlie after breakfast. With Bailey not having her mom anymore, Lorraine is taking over some of those rolls.

I gasp when Bailey comes out of the bedroom in her wedding dress. It's simple and elegant, very her. It's a white satin dress with a square neckline, and it hugs her body. The way it clings to her is different than anything she would have worn when I first met her, but I've seen her embrace herself since her and Caleb started dating, and I love it for her.

The front of her dress just brushes the floor, and a train flows behind her. Braids pull back the front pieces of her hair into an elegant chignon. Baby's breath is delicately placed into the braids, and her smile makes her glow. She's a vision.

We take a few photos before piling into the cars and making our way to the venue.

The girls all head inside with Bailey, while I take Charlie's hand and lead her to the back of the building. I've taken charge of taking her to her first look with Caleb.

When we turn the corner and she spots him, she calls, "Daddy!"

He spins around, and I hear him gasp as he takes in her pastel-pink dress with a white satin ribbon around her waist. She lets go of my hand and runs towards him as he crouches to catch her. He wipes away a tear as he holds her.

After a few minutes, he puts her down and kisses her cheek before she comes back to me and I lead her inside so we can start the ceremony.

The ceremony is beautiful. Caleb starts crying the second he sees Bailey standing at the end of the aisle. He's usually such a strong and stoic man, so it's not often people see that side of him. Grayson is Caleb's best man. His eyes never leave me as we stand opposite each other. To think we did this eighty-nine days ago.

Everyone filters into the reception hall after, and Caleb and Bailey have their first dance. I couldn't be happier for them as I sit and watch. When the song ends and the MC invites others to join them, Grayson stands and offers a hand to me.

"Would my wife do me the honour of a dance?"

I smile and take his hand, and he leads us to the dance floor. My arms wrap around his neck as his wrap around my waist, his hands resting above my ass, and we sway together.

"You're stunning," he whispers with such reverence.

"You don't look so bad yourself," I whisper back.

As the song ends and transitions into another, we don't separate. We sway back and forth as we stare into each other's eyes. The thought of all this ending tomorrow has my heart breaking. A single tear rolls down my cheek; I can't help it. Grayson reaches up and cups my face as his thumb brushes it away and his forehead leans against mine.

"I'll never say that I regret this," he whispers.

I look up at him through my lashes, trying to hold back my tears as I grip his wrist. "Same," I barely choke out.

At those words, something in his eyes changes. He leans down and, for the first time in eighty-nine days, kisses me. The world fades away as I take in this moment. The kiss is soft at first. His lips gently brush against mine. When I kiss him back, he takes it to another level. His tongue explores my mouth, and mine meets his. When we finally break apart short of breath, it's like I've found that missing puzzle piece. I was waiting for Grayson to give me the last thing he had been holding back.

The song changes to one more upbeat, and I take his hand and lead him off the dance floor and down a hallway until I find the door to a storage room. They seem like our thing. When we're inside, I close the door and I'm on him again. I take control of this kiss, exploring his mouth the way he explored mine. I'm staking my claim, letting him know he belongs to me in all the same ways I belong to him. I'm showing him I'm not done with us. I never will be.

Grayson fights for control. He pulls the fabric of my dress up my legs until it's hitched at my hips and lifts me by the back of my thighs, and my legs wrap around his waist. He nips at my neck, and I moan his name. I'm feral right now, and I'm not ashamed that I need my husband. I reach a hand between us and start working on his belt.

I release my legs from around his waist and work on his belt as he continues nibbling on my neck. When it's finally undone, I grip him through his boxer briefs.

"Condom," I say, and he pulls his wallet out and hands me one. I open it as he pushes his boxer briefs down. The second he pops free, I'm rolling the condom down his length. I hike up my dress again, and he lifts me. Reaching down, I push my panties to the side and position him at my entrance before sinking down. He kisses me, absorbing my moans of ecstasy.

I ride him like my life depends on it and kiss him as if he's the only air I can breathe. Each kiss is like I'm giving him another piece of my soul, and he hungrily devours them.

I'm close as he trails his lips across my jaw and down my neck. He's whispering to himself I think, but I hear him. "My wife. Mine. My fucking wife."

His possessive words send me over the edge. I bite my hand, trying to conceal the sounds he's pulling from me. He follows me, biting my shoulder as he comes. He helps me down and rights my panties before he fixes himself.

Before we leave, he tucks a stray piece of hair behind my ear and kisses me softly. We pop into the washroom before returning to the reception. I guess now I just need to make sure Grayson is on the same page I am.

Grayson's not in bed when I wake up in the morning. I make my way into his home office, hoping to find him there. When I see he's not, I make my way to his desk, taking in the degrees he has framed on the walls and the few family photos he has in here. I sit in his chair, trying to feel and see what he does when he's in here. There are two stacks of papers lying on the desk. My eyes scan the first page of the stack on the left. In bold writing, it reads:

CONTRACT OF EMPLOYMENT BETWEEN
Thompson Memorial Hospital of 8769 5th Avenue, Toronto,
ON L5J 6K9
AND
Grayson Randall Maxwell of 3005 - 481 Smithe Street,
Vancouver, BC V5L 4N8

My heart drops. I can't read any further. Is Grayson planning on leaving me and moving across the country? I thought we had finally got to a good place and things were going well, but I guess I was wrong. I shouldn't be surprised as I haven't told him that I love him and want this relationship. This marriage. Sitting in his chair as thoughts race through my mind, my eyes catch on the second stack of documents.

DISSOLUTION OF THE MARRIAGE OF GRAYSON RANDALL MAXWELL AND HANNAH MARIE SMITH

A lone tear I didn't realize was there falls down my face, and I wipe at it furiously. I take a deep breath, but all it does is make the tears fall in earnest. I've never cried over a man before, but I've also never fallen in love with anyone the way I have Grayson. He promised that after the ninety days, he'd sign the papers and give me the freedom I wanted. I never thought I'd have this kind of reaction to seeing these papers. I thought I'd be happy or excited. I'd be getting what I've wanted this whole time, but he's worked to show me he's not the douchebag I thought he was. He's just as damaged as me and let it get in the way. I guess I should be happy that he always intended to keep his word, and it just breaks my heart, even more, knowing we missed out on being with each other for so long because of someone else and our own trauma that we needed to deal with. But I'm happy that he did exactly what he set out to do. He showed me that, despite our past, we can work.

Now, it's my turn to show him I'm so head over heels in love with him and I don't want to end our marriage. It might not have happened the way I always envisioned, but he's the man I want to spend the rest of my life with. I'm choosing him as my family. Whether kids are in our future or not. I want him. I'd rather live a life without children of my own and be with him than end up with someone else and a huge family.

Grayson Randall Maxwell is my person. He's become the first person I want to talk to in the morning and the last before I go to bed. I want to share the good and the bad with him.

I know I need to rectify this. Grayson deserves to know he's loved unconditionally and that he's my first choice. My only choice.

I pull my phone out and do a quick internet search and make a few phone calls. I push up from the chair and leave his office resolute in my decision.

CHAPTER 34

Grayson

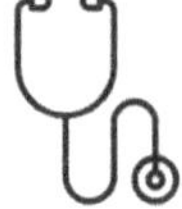

I had to get out of the apartment this morning. I needed time to get my head on straight to be able to talk to Hannah about what we're going to do now that the ninety days are up. I stay out until almost dinner time, trying to grapple with everything. I want her to have the freedom to do whatever she wants. I need whatever happens to be her choice.

Walking into the apartment, I drop my keys on the kitchen counter and see Hannah sitting at the dining table with three stacks of papers.

I smile and say, "Hey."

She smiles back, but it's weak. "We need to talk."

My stomach drops. Those are not words anyone in a relationship wants to hear, and I know now that our ninety days are up, she's likely going to ask for the divorce. I sigh and make my way towards her.

As I get closer to the table, I see that two of the stacks are the divorce papers I had drawn up so that when Hannah asked for them, we could make this as quick and easy as possible, and the employ-ment contract from Thompson Memorial, because I know once those divorce papers are signed, I can't stay here. I need to get as far away from Hannah as possible. I can't be in the same province, let alone the same city as her, and not be able to call her my wife.

She notices my gaze caught on the papers and says, "I found these in your office today."

I grip the back of my neck and take a seat beside her. "I had the divorce papers drawn up for when the ninety days were up."

"And the employment contract?" she asks.

I meet her gaze, needing her to see the truth in my next words. "I can't live in this city and not be able to call you my wife. I can't stand the chance of seeing you at group events and not being able to hold your hand or walk up and kiss you just because I can. I can't watch you date other people while I'm still in love with you. It would be like ripping my heart out of my chest and watching someone take a meat tenderizer to it."

Her eyes remain on me, and I feel her willing more words out of me, and like everything else, her wish is my command.

"Spitfire, you're everything to me. Losing you is not something I want, but I love you enough to prioritize your happiness over my own. I'd rather suffer every day for the rest of my life and know that you're happy than force you into a situation I know you don't want. You indulged me with this agreement. Being able to call you my wife has been the best thing in my life. Letting you go will be hard, but I'll do anything for you."

She wipes at the tears falling down her cheeks before she reaches to the third stack of documents that I have no idea what they are and hands me one.

Termination of Lease
2305-1564 Hornby Street, Vancouver, BC V5L 9K7

She hands me another sheet. This one is yellow and flimsy. I see it's a temporary driver's licence, but I don't get why she's giving it to me. I raise an eyebrow.

"Read the name," she says.

Last Name: Maxwell
First Name: Hannah Middle Name: Marie

My jaw drops. I don't know how I'm supposed to process this

information. I continue reading over the sheet trying to wrap my head around this.

Address: 3005 - 481 Smithe Street, Vancouver, BC V5L 4N8

I look back at Hannah as she wipes another tear away. She stands and pulls her shirt over her head, tossing it to the floor.

"Hannah," I breathe out. "As much as I love seeing you naked for me, I think we should talk."

She turns slightly and shows me a section of her skin now covered in plastic wrap over top of what appears to be a tattoo. She takes a step closer, and that's when I notice it. She has our wedding date tattooed just below her left breast.

My eyes widen as I find hers, and she moves to straddle my lap. She runs her fingers through my hair before she grips my chin tightly, making sure my gaze doesn't leave hers.

"I'm keeping you, Grayson Maxwell." She sniffles. "I'm choosing you. Today, tomorrow, forever. I'm choosing you, Grayson. Those divorce papers will never see my signature. Unless you tell me that's what you want, I will never sign them."

I swallow harshly before I ask, "What about kids?"

She stares at me so intently that I feel it in every part of my soul. I know with all that I am what she's going to say next will be the complete truth.

"All that matters is that I get you. If you never want biological kids, we can talk about adoption. If you never want kids at all, then we don't need to have kids. I want you. I want to spend the rest of my life, until I'm grey and old, with you."

I tip my head back and take deep breaths as tears gather behind my eyes. I'm not one to cry, but to hear Hannah choose me even if I choose to never have children is more than I could ask for.

I cup her face, running my thumbs over her cheeks. "Are you sure?" I whisper.

She nods. "I've never been more sure of any decision I've ever made. Grayson, you're it for me. You own me, body, mind, and soul. Kids are not a need for me. If it's something we both decide on down the line, then great, but right now, I'm content being the fun aunt and being your wife."

I lean in and kiss my wife. I savour her taste as my tongue sweeps into her mouth. Her little moan feeds me, and the kiss becomes more needy. I can't get enough of her. I pick her up and take her to our bedroom, dropping her on the bed. As I reach behind my head and pull off my shirt, she scrambles to take her clothes off as quickly as possible. It's like a race to see who can get naked the fastest. I win.

I climb onto the bed beside her and lie on my back. "Ride me, Spitfire."

She hurriedly moves to her knees and grabs a condom from the nightstand, rolling it down my cock. She straddles me, and I grip her hips as she positions me at her entrance and slowly sinks down. She stretches around me like she was made for me. My gorgeous Spitfire takes me so fucking well.

She tosses her head back as she works to take every inch I have to give her. I can't have that, though; I need her to look at me. I reach up and grip her throat, pulling her head towards me. She follows without hesitation. I encourage her to fall forward, and she does. When her lips are close enough, I kiss her. I've spent the last three months not giving her that last piece of me, knowing if I did, it would destroy me when she left. Not anymore. I'm going to spend the rest of my life kissing her whenever I can.

She rides me like the needy girl she is, taking everything she needs from me. Her nails scrape across my chest, and I relish the feel of them, knowing in the morning I'm going to have physical proof of how needy she is.

I help her grind her clit against my pelvic bone, and when I feel her begin to tighten around me, I suck a nipple into my mouth, running my teeth over it in the way I know she likes. All the sensations together send her over the edge. I follow right behind her.

I'll never get over hearing her call my name as she comes. It's the best thing I've ever heard. Well, second best to what she whispers after she collapses on my chest.

"I love you, Grayson."

I tuck her hair behind her ear and whisper back, "I love you more."

She grins at me, and I know in this moment that we may not have started in the traditional way. Hell, she didn't even want to stay in this marriage, but I know we'll go the distance. We've seen everything the other has to offer. The good, the bad, the painful, and we're deciding our love can withstand it all. I'll grow old with Hannah Maxwell, and I wouldn't have it any other way.

CHAPTER 35

Matt

One Month Later

Sitting in Caleb and Bailey's backyard after dinner, I'm content. I'm surrounded by friends and family, and I know when I leave here, I can text Megan and she'll come to my place. I'm happy my friends and sister have found the people they want to share the rest of their lives with. I want that one day, but right now, I'm enjoying the lack of responsibility and fun. I have plenty of time before I need to settle down.

Liv hands me Cate before she heads into the house. I have a soft spot for my niece. I can spoil her rotten and then send her home to her parents. I can't wait until I can feed her tons of sugar and then send her home. I love my sister and will always protect her, but she's my baby sister and it's my brotherly duty to bug her and get under her skin.

Zoey comes and sits beside me, dancing her fingers in front of Cate's face while she makes silly noises. Cate giggles, and a smile spreads across Zoey's face. She's so good with her. I know she loves being Aunty Zoey and hanging out with Cate whenever she can.

"You want kids?" I ask her.

Her eyes flick to me, her smile faltering for a second before she plasters it back on and returns her attention to Cate. "Eventually."

I nod, not wanting to pry more. Zoey and I've grown closer over the last year, but not close enough that I can push the topic.

Cate starts to fuss in my arms, and I adjust her to bounce her a little, but it doesn't work. Zoey reaches out and takes her from me, standing and walking as she bounces her. Cate calms down almost immediately. I stand behind her and make faces at Cate, and she giggles. The sound warms my heart.

As I stand here with Zoey and Cate, I'm beginning to wonder if maybe I should start thinking about settling down sooner than later and actually putting some effort into dating instead of hook-ups.

Liv comes back and takes her daughter back.

"Zo, your date with the new teacher is all set for next week. I texted you his number so you guys can coordinate the rest," Liv says.

A pang of jealousy hits me, but I brush it off. I shouldn't be jealous that Liv is helping Zoey find someone. When Cate smiles at me from Liv's arms, I set my resolve to stop fucking around and settle down.

Epilogue

GRAYSON

Eight months later

As we get ready to leave to head to my parents, anxiety fills me. I can only hope everything goes how I want it to, but I can never know. I've spent the last nine months attending my therapy appointments and working through my trauma. It took me a while to open up to the therapist, because I wasn't used to talking to anyone about it, but I eventually got to a point where I was able to talk about aspects of it. I'm still struggling with accepting that I didn't fail Rebecca, and some days are worse than others, but having Hannah at my side has made it infinitely better. She's able to read me like an open book and knows exactly what I need on the bad days. Rebecca was right about the difference it makes having someone in your corner on the bad days. It makes them not as bad and makes the good ones so much better.

These last nine months with her have been the best of my life. I've got to see Hannah be truly carefree. Watching her with Cate and Charlie is still hard, but I'm working on it. Hannah has done nothing but show me she meant it when she said she wanted me even if kids aren't in the picture. Not once has she brought up the topic, letting me lead the way in that particular aspect of our lives. I'm not sure where I stand right now on having kids or not but knowing Hannah will be with me no matter what has made me feel like the luckiest man on this Earth.

I stand in the kitchen as I watch Hannah skip towards me, fully dressed and ready to leave. She's always full of energy and excitement when we leave for Willow Valley. She loves getting away from the city and seeing my family. Her and Chloe have become the best of friends and she always has a girls day with Chloe, Brinley, Aspen, and Lennon while we're there. The last time we were in town Rebecca even joined them. I think that was healing for both of them.

I hold out her coffee, and as she reaches for it, I grab her wrist with my free hand and pull her close, kissing her. I never give up an opportunity to have my lips on hers.

"You're gorgeous, Mrs. Maxwell," I whisper against her lips, and she smiles. She loves hearing me call her that almost as much as I love saying it.

"Well, you're quite handsome yourself, Dr. Maxwell."

I grin and place another quick kiss on her lips before handing her the coffee cup. She takes it and inhales the scent deeply before taking a sip. I will never get over the sight of her every morning in this kitchen with me.

"You ready?" I ask when she finishes her cup.

She nods, and I grab our bags before we head to car.

HANNAH:

Today's drive to Willow Valley is different from our first one. During this drive, much like the one's we've made since Randy's hospitalization, I know that in six hours I'm going to see my family. The last nine months have been amazing. I've gotten to see Grayson open up more, and I think his regular therapy appointments are a big reason. He's been going weekly, either in person or teleconference, depending on his work schedule. He's talked to his parents and Chloe about how his sessions have helped him, and I know they're happy for him.

Samantha has left Vancouver Memorial. It was only about a month after she caught us in the storage closet that we were told she had found another job and would be leaving. Everyone else has been great about our marriage. I'm finally working more day shifts, and I think Grayson's more grateful for it than I am. He hates the night shift, but he was working them with me so we could spend more time together. That little revelation didn't come out until I finally was back on days. The relief he showed when I told him my schedule change had him fessing up.

Grayson's hand rests on my thigh as we drive. Excitement fills me as we pass the sign that says:

Welcome to Willow Valley

Grayson takes us straight to his parents' house. When we get there, we have dinner and a bonfire, following Maxwell tradition, before calling it a night.

In the morning, I make my way downstairs and hear familiar voices. When I get into the kitchen, I see Matt, Zoey, Liz, Josh, Liv, Cate, Charlie, Caleb, Bailey, and their one-month-old son Simon all sitting around the kitchen table. Chloe is smiling at me from across the room.

Grayson walks up to me and hands me a cup of coffee, whispering, "Happy anniversary," before kissing me.

"Happy anniversary," I whisper back, still confused as to why all of our friends are here in Willow Valley.

He takes my hand and calls, "We'll be right back," as he takes me to the back deck.

Grayson settles in a chair and pulls me onto his lap. His thumb runs lazily up and down my thigh and it relaxes me.

"I know that our wedding a year ago wasn't exactly what you had planned for yourself," he says, and I turn to him more.

"Grayson—" I start.

He shakes his head. "No, Spitfire, it's okay. It wasn't exactly what either of us had planned." He tucks a piece of my hair behind my ear. "I don't regret it. I will never say that I regret it, because we're here, together, happy. But I thought that today, for our anniversary, if you'll let me, I'd like to marry you again. I want to renew our vows with our friends and family in one of the places that brought us to where we are." He wipes my tears and kisses me lightly.

"Of course, I'll marry you again. I'll marry you every year, if that's what you want," I say.

When I finish my coffee, he pulls a velvet box out of his pocket. "I was hoping that maybe you'd wear this today."

I look at the box wide-eyed. I take it from him, running my fingers over the soft velvet.

"Open it," he urges.

I flip open the lid and gasp as I take in the beautiful necklace. It's a gold necklace connected by three stones in the middle, an amethyst on the left, an emerald in the centre, and a blue topaz on the right.

Grayson takes it from the box and undoes the clasp as I hold my hair up for him to secure it on my neck. He delicately runs his fingers over the gems as he explains, "The amethyst is for me, the emerald is for our wedding, and the topaz is for you. Forever connected with gold."

I kiss him. The thought behind the gift meaning so much.

When we break the kiss, I whisper, "Let's get married."

He grins.

"Let's get married."

I climb off his lap, and we head back inside to our friends and family. The girls help me get ready and tell me my dad is already here in town and will be here to walk me down the aisle for the ceremony. My mother won't be here, and I'm glad for it. I don't need her negativity today. My life has felt so much lighter and less stressful since cutting her out. I don't feel on edge waiting for one of her calls or texts where she sets out expectations for me.

After hair and makeup is done, Liz pulls out a dress bag, and I cry when I pull down the zipper. It's the dress I've always dreamed of wearing on my wedding day. It's white with a sweetheart neckline and tulle off-the-shoulder straps. The bodice is form-fitting, and the bottom is full of tulle, with a delicate lace overlay that covers the entire dress.

"Grayson found your wedding binder," Liz says.

I put that together years ago, and as I got older, I hid it in a box, not wanting it to sit there taunting me that I hadn't found that soul-changing love I wanted so badly. Grayson finding it and getting this dress is all my dreams come true.

I step into the dress, and Liz does the zipper for me. I stand in front of the mirror, taking in how well it fits. Not just me, but my dream. I smile so wide my cheeks hurt. Today, I get to marry my husband again. A man who has shown me over and over that he knows me, he cares for and loves me, that he supports me.

I turn around to face the girls, and they're smiling back at me.

"You ready?" Bailey asks, and I nod.

We head downstairs, and my dad is waiting at the base of the stairs. When he turns to look at me, I see the tears that start and I tip my head back to stop my own.

"Look at my beautiful daughter," he says when I stop in front of him.

"Thank you, Dad."

He kisses my cheek and offers me his arm before leading me to the back door. The girls line up, and music drifts in as they open the door. It's one of the songs from my wedding binder. The girls make their way down to the yard, and when Dad and I stop in the doorway, I can't stop my tears. Grayson has transformed his parents' backyard into my dream wedding. An arch with my favourite flowers, lilies, is behind Grayson as he waits for me. Red and pink rose petals line either side of the aisle where white chairs are set up. Beside each aisle chair is a mason jar with lit candles on top of beach rocks.

When Dad and I reach the top of the aisle, Grayson wipes at his own tears, and it helps to know this is hitting him as much as it is me. Dad shakes Grayson's hand when we meet him and passes him my hand. Dad heads to his seat and Caleb, who's officiating our renewal, starts.

"Welcome, everyone. I've never been a man of many words. I'm not too sure why Grayson chose me for this, but I'm going to do my best. We are here to celebrate Grayson and Hannah's love for one another. They have chosen to spend their lives together and declare their love in front of you, their family and friends. Today, they renew the promise they made to each other one year ago. Grayson, do you have vows?"

He nods.

"Hannah, we did this all backwards. Normally, you date, fall in love, and then get married. I fell in love with you three years ago. Getting drunk with you in Vegas was the best thing I've ever done, because I got to marry you. I know it wasn't what you wanted, but I knew that any time with you would be worth it. To have you love me even a fraction of the way I love you is my greatest blessing. You've accepted every part of me. My past, my present, and my future. Everything I am, and everything I have, belongs to you. I love you more today than I did yesterday, and I will continue to find new ways to love you for the rest of our lives."

I let out a breath and squeeze my eyes shut, pushing past the emotion so I can say my vows.

"Hannah," Caleb says.

"Grayson. When we first met, I was completely enamoured by you. Life had other plans for us and pulled us apart. Finding my way back to you has been the best thing to ever happen to me. You've stood by me during painful decisions, showing me love and compassion along the way. You have been my strength in times of need and a safe place to land when I've needed it. You care for me in all the ways I need and make me feel seen. It was after my mother's party that it hit me how much I love you. Having you near me gave me strength to do something I should've done long ago. And after, you were the safe space I needed. More and more every day, you own me body, mind, and soul. I promise to love you today and until forever, for the rest of our lives."

"You may kiss the bride," Caleb says, and Grayson dips me as his lips find mine and he kisses me in a soul-consuming way.

When we're back to standing, we make our way back up the aisle and head inside. Grayson and I take twenty minutes to ourselves inside before joining everyone outside. There are tables scattered around the yard and buffet tables along the edge. We make our way through everyone, thanking everyone for coming. Music plays from large speakers, and people take off their shoes, enjoying themselves as they dance in the grass. "Boot Scootin' Boogie" comes on, and I drag Grayson out to the dance floor, laughing as I try to dance in my wedding dress.

The night is a blast. We're surrounded by friends and family, laughing and dancing into the night. I'm standing on the edge, watching everyone, when Grayson's arms wrap around my waist. I lean into him.

He kisses my neck, and I hum in contentment.

"I love you," I say, as he nips my ear.

"I love you more," he whispers back. "I have something for you."

He releases me a bit before his hand comes back in front of me holding an envelope.

I look at him over my shoulder. "What is this?"

He grins. "Just open it, Spitfire."

I open the envelope slowly, trying to see if I can get any hints, but I can't. I pull out a folder and open it. Sitting inside are two plane tickets out of Vancouver to Paris. My jaw drops, and tears fill my eyes. My trip. I didn't think I could love this man any more than I already do, but he's making my dreams come true and so much more.

I turn and face him, placing my hands on either side of his face. "I love you, Grayson Randall Maxwell." I go up on tiptoes and kiss him as his arms wrap around my waist and hold me close to him.

He rests his forehead against mine and whispers, "I'll spend the rest of my life doing everything I can to make you happy, Hannah Marie Maxwell."

I grin, loving the sound of my full name like that.

I turn back around and face our party. As we stand here in each other's arms, watching everyone who came to celebrate our love dance and laugh together, I'm happier than I ever thought I'd be.

THE END

Want more of Grayson and Hannah? You can now in this bonus epilogue https://BookHip.com/SJWMHWT
Want to read Josh and Liv's story? You can now in *Always Been You* http://mybook.to/dlalwaysbeenyou
Missed Josh and Liv's bonus epilogue? Check it out here: https://BookHip.com/VQARQQX
Want to read Caleb and Bailey's story? You can now in *Saving You* http://mybook.to/dlsavingyou
Missed Caleb and Bailey's bonus epilogue? Check it out here: https://BookHip.com/PJNKDBG
Can't wait for Matt's story? You can pre-order *Taming You* now https://mybook.to/dltamingyou

Dicktionary

Acknowledgements

I have enjoyed writing Grayson and Hannah's story so much. The more I revisit their story, the more I fall in love with them.

Chelsey, I'm not sure this story would be what it is without you. You were there in my corner during every moment of self-doubt and every stressful thing I faced. I am forever grateful to have you as one of my closest friends and that you agreed to alpha read Grayson and Hannah for me. I can't wait to work on more stories with you and all the other amazing things in store for us.

Sydney, my ultimate hype girl! You are an amazing and wonderful person, and I'm so glad I got to have you on my beta team. I feel like I keep spilling so many secrets and plans in your DM's that you'd be able to manage to wrangle my social security number out of me. All jokes aside, thank you for being there and listening to all my ideas always being in my corner. I'm so glad to have met you through this journey and can't wait to squeeze you in person!

To my best friends who have been with me from the beginning, cheering me on and being the best support system a girl could ask for. I love you guys.

My husband who has put up with my mood swings when I've been stressed about everything when it comes to publishing these last three months. Thank you for your support and love even when I was snippy and let the stress get to me. I love you.

Ellie, I don't have enough words to describe how grateful I am to call you a friend and how proud I am of your accomplishments. You've been there to listen to me rant, but have also given such great advice. I can't wait to meet you in person and hug you! I'm counting down the days.

Alyssa, if only we lived closer. We would totally have those drunken craft nights. Thank you for your support and listening ear. I'm so glad that we found each other, and I get to call you my friend.

Andrea, my amazing editor. You have helped my writing improve and have been so extremely helpful. I'm so grateful for your communication and monthly check-ins. I'm so excited to continue working with you and that we get to meet in person! Thank you for all you've done with *Keeping You* and for me.

Kim. I cried when I saw this cover. With *Always Been You* and *Saving You*, I was seeing a cover for a second time and I loved those, but with this one, it was all new and you knocked it out of the park. I can't wait to see what you do with the rest of this series, and I have so many exciting plans for us.

To my beta readers. You were a godsend. Thank you for diving into such an early version of *Keeping You* and helping make this story be the best it could be. I can't wait to share the next story with you.

Lastly, to my readers, without you, I wouldn't be here. This story means so much to me, and I hope you love Grayson and Hannah as much as I do. I look forward to sharing more stories with you.

About the Author

Living in the Vancouver area of British Columbia with her husband, Alex enjoys spending her free time reading, watching Hockey (go Canucks), watching Disney movies and crime TV shows, and spending time outdoors. She started writing in 2023 when her first story just wouldn't leave her mind. From there, the ideas of a series formed and she's never looked back.

She enjoys talking to other authors and romance lovers. Her TBR is never-ending, but that doesn't stop her from adding at least one new book every day. Alex looks forward to experiencing more in the indie author community and can't wait to share her books with the world.

Connect With Me:

https://www.instagram.com/authoralextaylor/
https://www.threads.net/@authoralextaylor
https://www.tiktok.com/@authoralextaylor
https://www.facebook.com/profile.php?id=61552508379128
www.authoralextaylor.com
alex@authoralextaylor.com

DESTINED LOVE SERIES

Always Been You

Saving You

Keeping You

Taming You - Coming March 20, 2025